THE FIRST MOVE

Even though I should have listened to Augie when he told me that Alejandra needed special handling, I didn't. Instead, on the first day of school I stuck a note into her social studies book. This wasn't a kissing kind of strategy to show her how cute I am, it was because my voice is changing so fast I couldn't count on it not to crack when I told her I loved her. And who wants a boyfriend who sounds like he needs a tune-up?

> DEAR ALLIE: I'M CONSIDERING A RELATION-
> SHIP WITH YOU. AND BY THE WAY, FORGET
> THAT MRS. FITZPATRICK CALLS ME ANTHONY.
> YOU CAN CALL ME T.C.   —T.C.

After phys ed there was a vanilla envelope on my desk with purple writing on it that looked like it came from the principal's office—and I don't usually get called in *there* until at least November.

> Dear Anthony:
>
> I appreciate your recent interest, but I'm not accepting applications at this time. Your letter will be kept in our files and someone will get back to you if there is an opening.
>
> Thank you for thinking of me.
>
> Respectfully,
> Alejandra Perez
>
> P.S. It's not "Allie." It's "Alé."

OTHER BOOKS YOU MAY ENJOY

My Most Excellent Year

A NOVEL OF LOVE, MARY POPPINS, & FENWAY PARK

STEVE KLUGER

speak

An Imprint of Penguin Group (USA) Inc.

SPEAK
Published by the Penguin Group
Penguin Group (USA) Inc., 345 Hudson Street, New York, New York 10014, U.S.A.
Penguin Group (Canada), 90 Eglinton Avenue East, Suite 700, Toronto, Ontario, Canada M4P 2Y3
(a division of Pearson Penguin Canada Inc.)
Penguin Books Ltd, 80 Strand, London WC2R 0RL, England
Penguin Ireland, 25 St Stephen's Green, Dublin 2, Ireland (a division of Penguin Books Ltd)
Penguin Group (Australia), 250 Camberwell Road, Camberwell, Victoria 3124, Australia
(a division of Pearson Australia Group Pty Ltd)
Penguin Books India Pvt Ltd, 11 Community Centre, Panchsheel Park, New Delhi - 110 017, India
Penguin Group (NZ), 67 Apollo Drive, Rosedale, North Shore 0632, New Zealand
(a division of Pearson New Zealand Ltd)
Penguin Books (South Africa) (Pty) Ltd, 24 Sturdee Avenue, Rosebank,
Johannesburg 2196, South Africa

Registered Offices: Penguin Books Ltd, 80 Strand, London WC2R 0RL, England

First published in the United States of America by Dial Books,
a member of Penguin Group (USA) Inc.
Published by Speak, an imprint of Penguin Group (USA) Inc., 2009

3 5 7 9 10 8 6 4

THE LIBRARY OF CONGRESS HAS CATALOGED THE DIAL BOOKS EDITION AS FOLLOWS:
Kluger, Steve.
My most excellent year: a novel of love, Mary Poppins & Fenway Park / by Steve Kluger.
p. cm.
Summary: Three teenagers in Boston narrate their experiences of a year of
new friendships, first loves, and coming into their own.
ISBN: 978-0-8037-3227-8 (hc)
[1. Interpersonal relations—Fiction. 2. Friendship—Fiction. 3. Homosexuality—Fiction.
4. Boston (Ma.)—Fiction. 5. Humorous stories.] I. Title.
PZ7.K6877My 2008
[Fic]—dc22
2007026651

Speak ISBN 978-0-14-241343-2

Printed in the United States of America

For my nephews and nieces, Bridgette, Emily, Audrey, Elisa, Noah, Paloma, Logan, Evan, and Robbie—the nine kids who own my heart

—and for Julie Andrews, who gave them all the sound of music

My Most Excellent Year

Juniors

(but not for long)

English Assignment
T.C. Keller, 11th Grade
Ms. LaFontaine's Class

MY MOST EXCELLENT YEAR
Part 1: My Family

[Note to Ms. LaFontaine: I didn't mean to give you a hard time about the title of this assignment, but "My Totally Excellent Year" would have been like so 1995, we'd have been laughed out of Brookline if anybody found out. Especially if these things are going to be attached to our college apps. So in the future, you might want to check with me ahead of time about this kind of stuff. —T.C.]

Since you'd never guess it from looking at me, nobody can tell that words like *because, fart, there,* and *banana* come out sounding like "becazz," "faht," "they-a," and "bananer" when I say them out loud. I got this from Pop, who's even worse than I am. One time we took the train down to New York so he could show me where Ebbets Field and the Polo Grounds used to be, and while we were ordering pizza in Brooklyn and back-and-forthing about who you'd rather have batting cleanup behind you—Pistol Pete Reiser or Charlie Banks—the waitress asked us what country we were from. (Like they've got room to talk in Brooklyn.)

A lot of the snoots on Beacon Hill like to tell you that their ancestors came over with the Pilgrims, but this didn't happen to us Kellers. We came over with the Red Sox. My grandpa's name was Tris Speaker Keller (after the 1907 outfielder they called "The Grey Eagle"), my dad's name is Theodore Williams Keller (world-famous slugger with 'tude in 1940-something), and I even have an Aunt Babe and an Aunt Ruth. (This was a lucky coincidence. They met thirty-eight years ago at a Bobby Kennedy rally in Rockport and they've been together ever since. Aunt Babe swears they would have fallen in love even if Aunt Ruth's name had been Sheba, but I'm not so sure.) Pop couldn't decide whether to call me Rico Petrocelli or Freddy Lynn, but Uncle Yaz had twins that year and beat him to it. That's how I wound up Anthony Conigliaro Keller (another snarly batting champ who got zapped in the face with a fastball in 1967, which somehow turned him into a hero). And the only one who's allowed to call me Tony C is my dad, because I'm the only one who gets to call him Teddy Ballgame. To everybody else I'm just T.C. Except to my brother Augie, who calls me Tick.

I should probably explain the brother thing, except I don't really remember how it happened. We were in first grade, the Red Sox were in fourth place, and I had a brand-new hole in my heart from losing my mother. But even though Augie and I had never talked to each other before, he was the only one who knew what to say and how to say it. (Everybody else thought they could get away with blowing smoke up my ass about Guardian Angels and Eternal Paradise, like my mother had gone on a Princess Cruise.) Pretty soon we were taking make-believe trips to the planet Twylo and losing our thumbs to alien walnuts, and that's when I knew for sure that I wouldn't be sad forever. Well, anybody who can pull off something like that for you isn't just a best friend—that's brother territory. So Augie told his mom and dad that they had a new son, and I told Pop the same thing. Screw biology.

Mama died when I was six. She was the one who taught me to believe in magic, but not by reading me books like *The Silver Sorceress of Oz* or Brothers Grimm—she proved it instead. Right after my third birthday, we went to Derry, New Hampshire, for her cousin's wedding, and before we left they gave me a purple balloon that said "Congratulations Bobby and Penny" on it. (Mama's half of the family all has normal names.) Well, when you're three, you just know that a purple balloon is pretty much the biggest thing that's ever going to happen to you—especially when you let go of it on the way back to Brookline and it flies out the window of your Subaru. My mother finally got me to stop crying by promising that my purple balloon was flying all over Boston looking for me, and that if I watched the sky long enough, it'd see me and come home. So Pop and I stood in the backyard looking straight up for two hours, waiting for it to zero in for a landing. But no snap. Then all of a sudden from inside the house I heard Mama calling out, "T.C.!

Come quick! Look who's here!" And damn if my purple balloon wasn't bobbing up and down against the ceiling of our front porch. (I was ten before I figured out that she drove all the way back to Derry, New Hampshire, just to get me another one.)

So except for my brother Augie, who lives in the Kennedy half of Brookline, it's just me and Teddy Ballgame and our eight-year-old spaniel named Nehi. Usually Pop wakes me up at 6:00 every morning and we put on our sweats. Then we bike over to B.U. and run along the Charles River up to the Lowell tower and back—and on the way home, I give him a sixty-second head start, which he says is never enough because I always catch up to him at Dunster House. (Not that it really matters, since Nehi beats both of us back to our bikes anyway.) Boston University is Pop's old hangout. He played football and baseball there, and he still looks enough like Joe Montana that once in a while people ask him for Joe's autograph (usually around Super Bowl weekend). So he gives it to them. My dad's easy. Even if he's never heard of Stevie Nicks, Justin Timberlake, or Avi Vinocur.

That was my life until ninth grade, my most excellent year. And then I got drop-kicked by a six-year-old kid and the girl of my dreams.

Augie

English Assignment
Augie Hwong, 11th Grade
Ms. LaFontaine's Class

MY MOST EXCELLENT YEAR
Part 1: My Family

Even though my mother is an FOB (fresh off the boat) who snuck out of Chekiang Province with Grandma and Grandpa Der two steps ahead of the Secret Police, she doesn't run around the house like those chopsticky people in *Flower Drum Song* singing "ching-a-ling-a-ling" with her finger in the air. She already knew how to speak English before they sailed into San Francisco Bay, and somehow she wound up launching every one of her civil rights crusades in the theatre column she wrote for the *Boston Globe*—even when she was reviewing *Peter Pan*. Now she covers symphonies, social events, and local celebrities. It's safer for everybody that way. But Mom's the one who taught me all about original cast albums and black-and-white movies while I was still learning how to crawl. (Do *you* know who sang opposite John Raitt in *The Pajama Game*? Have *you* ever heard of Reta Shaw? Didn't think so.)

My father and I are both ABCs (American-born Chinese), but that's where the resemblance ends. He once played Bruce Lee in a college production of *Dragon,* and I once played Ethel Merman in a living room musicale for Grandma Lily. Dad graduated from Notre Dame without a chip on his shoulder and opened an independent bookstore on Harvard Street called The Word Shop, which is one of the most popular hangouts in Brookline. For grown-ups it's the coffee bar, the chocolate chip lattés, and the lemon honey cakes. For kids it's the polished wood walls, the polished wood shelves, and the polished wood floors. You can skateboard from Naked Travel Destinations to Socratic Theory in under five seconds. My brother Tick is aiming for 4½. Suddenly, so is every other sixteen-year-old in our zip code.

Even in first grade everybody wanted to be Tick. If he invented a word like *gink,* it was part of every kid's vocabulary by the end of recess. When he wore his Red Sox T-shirt backwards because he felt like it, all the other boys started wearing their T-shirts backwards too because they felt like it. (Which, by the way, is the only fashion statement my brother ever learned to make.) But he always acted like he wasn't even aware of it. *I* was. As a professional sideline watcher with plenty of time on my hands, I never missed a thing. In fact, the only day I ever remember being spoken to up until then was when some gink asked me if slanted eyes hurt.

All of that changed after Tick's mom died. He was out of school for two weeks, and when he came back none of the other guys knew what to say to him. Partly because "sorry, dude" seemed kind of ginky for the occasion, and partly because—thinking like six-year-olds—they were afraid to get too close on account of what if a dead mother was catching? But I didn't have to worry about social graces, seeing as I'd never had a chance to speak to him anyway.

"What are those?"

"Huh?" I was sitting on a low brick wall underneath a couple of spruce trees and eating a sandwich, guaranteed to be by myself as usual. That day's menu featured roast beef on rye with something scary peeking out from under the crust. Mom always insisted on adding bok choy, chin-chiang, tat soi, shunkyo, or just about anything else that belonged in a lawn mower. For some reason mustard was out of the question.

"They look funny," said Tick. "Like the long fingers that aliens have."

"Uh—sprouts," I stammered. "Want some?"

"Trade."

So for a week I took charge of his tuna fish and ham while he had to figure out what to do with the mei qing choi. (One afternoon we decided to plant some of it and see what would happen. Nothing grew, but all of the grass died.) He never ever said anything about his mom, and I learned pretty quick that this was the Forbidden Zone—but he told me about the twenty-foot model of Fenway Park that he and his dad were building in the basement and about why he thought the rings around Saturn were made out of marbles and about his Carlton Fisk rookie card and about having two aunts who were married to each other. I didn't realize it just yet, but my future had abruptly made a left turn. After a couple of days all the other kids were talking to me. More important, I was talking to *them*.

Meanwhile, Tick and I were so busy making plans, I didn't even notice. Who had the time? On any day in particular, we were pirates, aliens, cops, dino hunters, and brothers. But it was "brothers" that turned out to be a lot tougher than it looked. Once we'd thought about it, we figured out that brothers tell each other all of their secrets, buy each other cool birthday presents that nobody else would think of, yell at each other and not mean it, and always believe each other no matter how dumb it sounds. (Brothers also share the same bedroom, but we'd fixed that problem with sleepovers—because you just can't play Galaxy Fighters on the ceiling with colored flashlights unless it's dark.) So going by the rules, we already *were* brothers. The only thing we didn't have was the same parents to call Mom, Dad, or Pop.

"Why can't we call them that anyway?" Well, we tried it just to see what would happen, and our families got used to it so quick that nobody remembers who's genetic anymore. Whenever Pop takes us out to the Union Oyster House for dinner, he always introduces us as his kids—and when we went to Daytona Beach over Easter with Mom and Dad, the hotel rooms were reserved for "Mr. and Mrs. Hwong and sons." Of course, once in a while people look at us funny and you know they're trying to figure out how both of us can be brothers when only one of us is Asian, but we just tell them that we have different fathers. (Hey, it's *true*, isn't it?) And nobody ever had to ask twice.

Then Tick decided it was time to add one more member to our family when he fell in love for the first time. Up until then, the girls he generally went after were quiet, timid, pliable, and all over him—but his new target was headstrong, opinionated, intelligent, an admitted pain in the ass, and she couldn't stand the sight of him. Most people don't like challenges. Tick collects them.

INSTANT MESSENGER

TCKeller: DEFCON 3! DEFCON 3! Did you see the new girl in the third row??

AugieHwong: That's Alejandra. Her father was the ambassador to Mexico, so this one has substance. The Kissing Bandit routine isn't going to work. (Like it ever did anyway.)

My brother had most of the answers—and if he didn't, he usually knew where to look for them.

But by ninth grade we *all* needed a little help.

Alejandra

English Assignment
Alejandra Perez, 11th Grade
Ms. LaFontaine's Class

MY MOST EXCELLENT YEAR
Part 1: My Family

My brother Carlos is the ideal ambassador's son. He knows how to bow, he can make small talk with foreign diplomats in six different languages, he never passes gas, and he'll be Secretary General of the United Nations before he turns twenty-five. That is, assuming his little sister can learn how to keep her mouth shut.

"Alejandra, say hello to the Prime Minister of Denmark."

"Why?"

I don't mean to suggest that I disliked the Prime Minister of Denmark, or any of his policies for that matter. I was five. I would have answered with the same "Why?" had I been told "Abuela is taking you to see the elephants," "It isn't polite to talk about Tía Maria's mustache," and "Don't flush until you wipe." You really couldn't take me *any*where.

But thanks to my best friend Clint (a Secret Service agent who managed to carry an assault weapon and understand children at the same time), I learned early on that I could always find a welcome at the Georgetown Public Library. Every Saturday morning, Clint walked me through the cavernous reading room to the much cozier children's corner, which we weren't allowed to leave until I had at least three books under my arm. One of them turned out to be *The Bracelet* by Yoshiko Uchida. That was a mistake. A *big* mistake. In it I met a little girl named Emi, who lived on the West Coast in 1942. For some reason, all of the kids who were partly Japanese and partly American had to leave their homes and go into prison camps with barbed wire and guns, and that meant that Emi had to say good-bye to her best friend Laurie. So Laurie gave her a friendship bracelet to make sure they'd remember each other until Emi could come home again. I got as far as the part where Emi lost the bracelet at camp and was afraid it meant that Laurie was going to forget about her before I burst into tears and had to be calmed down by Mamita's maid and three of Papa's most devoted chargés d'affaires. *Who makes up a story like that for a child??* It was only at dinnertime that Consistently Correct Carlos admitted that the Japanese American internment was, in fact, one of the less fortunate chapters in our history, and that there really might have been an Emi after all. I was furious. And that was before anybody had told me about the Freedom Riders.

Naturally there were bound to be a few conflicts with Papa,

Mamita, and Forever Flawless Carlos. The family business depended on tact and diplomacy, and meanwhile they were raising a ten-year-old activist who could find a social issue in a box of Kleenex. After I'd told the Korean ambassador that I had little use for either half of military Korea but at least the south knew how to say "May I?" before they shot you, I was persona non grata all along Embassy Row. And since I'd obviously become a disappointment to every one of my relatives, I compensated the only way I knew how: straight A's, Honors English, Honors Math, and first prize in two national creative writing competitions. I decided that if I *had* to join the diplomatic corps sooner or later, at least I'd have the academic credentials for it—and all I'd need to learn in the meantime was how to stop talking. But two things happened back to back that turned my plans inside out.

The first was an accident. I'd been sent home from school with the flu, and Clint was so determined to cheer me up that he went DVD-shopping to find an extra-special movie that might take my mind off the fact that I was never going to eat again. What resulted was a copy of *Damn Yankees*, which was either a lucky choice or a deliberate move by Clint to start a civil war in my own family. Until I recovered enough to return to class, I was glued to the television screen watching Gwen Verdon dance a tango and a mambo again and again until I could match her step for step. And except for the vomiting, I'd completely forgotten that I was supposed to be sick.

Less than a month after that, Papa had business at the United Nations, so we found ourselves in New York at the Broadhurst Theatre for a performance of a musical called *Fosse*—where, for two and a half hours, the most beautiful men and women imaginable used their bodies to create sheer magic. By the time the curtain had come down, my eyes were wet and I was absolutely certain I knew what I wanted to do with the rest of my life. I also knew that I'd need to be re-born to different parents first. (Proof: Papa thought the show was "mildly diverting," Mamita wished that the boys had worn more clothing, and Utterly Unassailable Carlos—eighteen at the time—missed the whole thing when he ran into the only Argentine vice consul on West Forty-fourth Street and spent both acts in the lobby, chatting him up about tin and copper deposits outside of Buenos Aires.) Faced with the prospect of bringing shame to my very visible family, I was convinced that I could keep myself from even *thinking* of becoming a dancer just as long as Papa never retired as ambassador to Mexico—something that certainly wasn't going to happen in *my* lifetime.

So naturally Papa retired as ambassador to Mexico when I was fourteen because Harvard University's history department made him an offer he couldn't refuse. We sold the houses in Mexico City and Washington, D.C., emancipated all of the serfs, and moved into one of the loveliest homes in Brookline, Massachusetts. The rest of that summer was taken up with visiting the museums, walking the Freedom Trail, learning how to ride the T, and trying to figure out what these people saw in the Boston Red Sox. (I discovered no rational clue. Perhaps it's viral.)

I didn't realize what Papa and Mamita had done to me until right after Labor Day, when I found myself sitting in the third row of a ninth-grade public school classroom filled with thirty-five chattering kids I'd never seen before in my life, but who all seemed to have known each other from the womb. And just *kids*. No nannies, no bodyguards, no heads of state, no dinners with Chelsea Clinton or Tobey Maguire, and no one who wouldn't think you were a stuck-up pain in the ass if you mentioned either one of them. I was terrified. There was one boy in particular who always wore blue and white sneakers, easy-fit jeans, and gray T-shirts (half of them unraveling so badly he could have played The Mummy). He spoke with such an unseemly Boston accent that you were lucky to catch every fourth word, he tried to be cool by pretending he didn't know how cool he was, and his bangs looked like brown flax woven on a loom.

His name was Anthony and I detested him. I even told him so— and assumed he believed me.

I didn't know it then, but my clock was running out fast for a lot of things. Especially since my much-loved Gwen Verdon had recently passed away, and there was nobody in the wings to replace her.

Yet.

Freshmen

INSTRUCTIONS: While we're studying Anne Frank, try to remember that a diary isn't just a book with blank pages. It's a place where you can put down all of the thoughts and feelings that nobody else knows you have. Anne Frank called hers "Dear Kitty." So think carefully before you give your own diary a name.

Dear Mama,

Pop and Nehi and I go to visit you all the time with flowers, but there's a lot of things we don't have time to tell you while we're sitting on the ground. These are some of them.

1.   I'm getting a B+ in everything except for the A in algebra,

which is the way I like it to square out. Pop always says you should never pretend to be something you're not, and I don't want to be a know-it-all gink who thinks he's better than anybody else. Besides, Pop got a B+ in everything except for an A in algebra too.

2.   Right after you left, me and Pop started building a model of Fenway Park in the basement. And you know how Pop is when he gets started on projects like these. One time we had an assignment at school on the solar system and all I had to draw over the weekend was Jupiter. But when Pop found out about it he made me a planetarium from an old crate, a motor, and nine cut-up bicycle spokes with different-sized rubber balls on the ends of them that we painted to look like planets. They spun around a yellow lightbulb sun and had all of the constellations in the sky behind them except for Ursa Minor because we ran out of stars. Lori Mahoney is my adviser, and she was a little pissed off that we got carried away, but not as pissed off as the time our homework just said to list the ten biggest cities in the state. It took two people to carry the map Pop built down the hallway.

So the only reason the model of Fenway Park is twelve feet long is because there wasn't any more room in the basement than that. It took us two years to finish, but it has the Citgo sign behind it and all 33,871 seats inside. Pop said, "Tony C, where are we going to find the right color green for the walls?" and I said, "Maybe we could puke on them," and he said, "You have your mother's sense of humor." Then when it was all done, we opened our old scorecards to find our ticket stubs and we painted each of the seats that we ever sat in. Bluish green for the ones that just me and Pop had, sparkly silver for the ones we bought when you were with us too, and gold for the two that you and Pop were sitting in when you first met each other.

3.   When they decided that they weren't going to tear down the ballpark after all, Pop and I had to give up our "Save Fenway Park" website and our hotline and our T-shirts. We used to stand at different corners on Yawkey Way and Kenmore Square, hand out flyers to people, get them to sign petitions, and make them call all of the Red Sox phone numbers so many times that nobody could get through to buy tickets. Pop always says, "Tony C, the best thing Mama ever taught me was how to be a pain in the ass. That's how I got my own company instead of just being somebody else's carpenter." Mama, it worked this time too. I mean, they stopped talking about tearing down Fenway Park, didn't they?

4.   But we missed being troublemakers, so Pop told me I could be in charge of the next crusade. So I picked Buck Weaver. He was one of the eight Black Sox who got banned from baseball for cheating in the 1919 World Series—except that he didn't do it. The other seven guys asked him if he would throw games with them, but he called them hosers and said "Count me out." And they busted him anyway for not squealing on his team. What's up with *that*? But that's all going to change once I get 20,000 signatures on my "Free Buck Weaver" website.

5.   I wish you'd known Augie while you were still here—but come to think of it, if you were still here I wouldn't have needed him so much. We play soccer together in the fall, we're both forwards, and the other team hates it when we get the ball because they know it's already over. We pass it back and forth to each other so many times that they get mixed up, and all of a sudden the ball is in the

net. We never practice who's going to make the kick—we just know when it's the right time.

I'm five weeks older than Augie is but he's a lot smarter than I am, except that he doesn't know he's gay yet. I don't see how he couldn't. I guess he figures that because he loves women like Audrey Hepburn and Judi Dench so much, he's automatically going to wind up with one. (Shh. What he really loves is their clothes.) But Augie is the best at everything he does and I'm betting that once he puts 2+2 together, he'll have a steady boyfriend before I even get this new girl Alejandra to *think* about kissing me. Of course, once in a while he gets called things like "fag," and since we're brothers, sometimes I do too. But the kids who say it usually aren't around for very long. Besides, I found out that when girls think you might be gay, you turn into a chick magnet on the spot. It's like they can't help themselves—even the ones who tried to smack your face off in fifth grade when you hit on them. So I go with the flow. I'm easy that way.

6.   Remember how you told Pop that if he didn't get married again you would kick his ass? Because I think he finally got the hint. Last month, he wrote an ad for the Internet and I got to help. "49 y/o SWM, 6'2", athletic, with irresistible son who owns a Carlton Fisk rookie card, seeks intelligent, romantic woman for long walks, long talks, and candlelit moments." Even though the candlelight part made me and Augie gag, he started getting answers right away. The first girl he went out with was a blond grad student who didn't tell us until she got there that her diploma was for witchcraft. So Nehi and I stayed awake until Pop got home, and while he was brushing his teeth I asked him things like "When she spilled her water, did she melt?" and "Was your waiter a scarecrow?" and "Did she land on

the roof and throw fireballs?" Pop sprayed me with a can of Right Guard and I stunk for three days.

7. Even though I'm almost fifteen, I'm getting tall fast. You probably wouldn't even recognize me anymore. But I still remember what your voice sounds like.

Love,

Your son,

T.C.

BASEBALL ENCYCLOPEDIA
(revised by me and Pop)

807   Player Register

		G	AB	H	2B	3B	HR	R	BA	G by POS

Bucky Fucking Dent

BR TR 5'9" 170

DENT, RUSSELL EARL (Dream Smasher, Overpaid Cheeseball)
B. Nov. 25, 1951, Savannah, Ga.

Year	Team	G	AB	H	2B	3B	HR	R	BA	G by POS
1973	PHI N	40	117	29	2	0	0	17	.248	SS-36, 2B-3, 3B-1
1974		154	496	136	15	3	5	55	.274	SS-154
1975		157	602	159	29	4	3	52	.264	SS-157
1976		158	562	138	18	4	2	44	.246	SS-158
1977	NY A	158	477	118	18	4	8	54	.247	SS-157
1978		123	379	92	11	1	*5	40	.243	SS-123

*—No. 5 was a cheap shot. And everybody knows it.

Dear Mama,

Pop says he knew you were already falling in love with him after the first two hours because you held on to his arm when Bucky F. Dent hit the home run. But I remember when you would tuck me in and tell me the same story, you always said it was the other way around and that Pop kept sending you snapdragons so you would call him back. I used to think that somebody was making up their half of it until I started to fall in love. Then I found out how complicated it really is.

Even though I should have listened to Augie when he told me that Alejandra needed special handling, I didn't. Instead, on the first day of school I stuck a note into her social studies book. This wasn't a kissing kind of strategy to show her how cute I am, it was because my voice is changing so fast I couldn't count on it not to crack when I told her I loved her. And who wants a boyfriend who sounds like he needs a tune-up?

DEAR ALLIE: I'M CONSIDERING A RELATION-
SHIP WITH YOU. AND BY THE WAY, FORGET
THAT MRS. FITZPATRICK CALLS ME
ANTHONY. YOU CAN CALL ME T.C. —T.C.

After phys ed there was a vanilla envelope on my desk with purple writing on it that looked like it came from the principal's office— and I don't usually get called in *there* until at least November.

Dear Anthony:

I appreciate your recent interest, but I'm not accepting applications at this time. Your letter will be kept in our files and someone will get back to you if there is an opening.

Thank you for thinking of me.

Respectfully,
Alejandra Perez

P.S. It's not "Allie." It's "Alé."

She calls Mrs. Norwood "ma'am," she turns in her quiz papers first, she didn't laugh when Stu Merliss farted in the middle of factoring x^2-y^2, and her father knows the Queen of England. Big zow. Any poser can say that. But when Mrs. Fitzpatrick introduced her to the class and asked her who the most famous person she ever met was, she didn't say the Prince of Wales, she said Hilary Duff. By lunchtime, all the other girls were afraid of her and the boys were conferencing on their cell phones in study hall to figure out who was going to make the first move. Andy Wexler won. It was too late for me to come up with a new game plan and even my Benedict Arnold of a brother wasn't going to be any help. Why? BECAUSE HE WAS THE ONE SHE WAS HAVING LUNCH WITH!!

INSTANT MESSENGER

AugieHwong: Between homeroom and algebra I grew another armpit hair. That makes 9. Do you still only have 6?

TCKeller: Like I would have told the *Boston Globe* first?

AugieHwong: Don't worry. I'm trying to slide you into the conversation. Meanwhile, there's something else you should know. Andy Wexler asked me to work on his soccer moves with him after he makes his play for Alé. Are you still speaking to me?

TCKeller: No. Not now. Not ever.

But it was the picture of you and Robert F. Kennedy at the rally in 1967 that *really* got me into hot water. Pop hung it on the wall next to my bed when I was seven, and because I liked the way RFK's eyes squinted while he was smiling at you, I read an old kids' book called *Meet Senator Kennedy*. Now I know everything there is to know about him, from the Freedom Riders to his blue ties. That's why I signed up for the Young Democrats Club at school, and Alé joining right before me didn't hurt either. So when she picked President JFK as the most important American who ever lived, Pop said it meant we had something in common. He also said she might need to know who was the brains in that family and who wasn't. But he left it up to me to choose my own arguments.

RFK	JFK
Stuck it to Mississippi and integrated the colleges there.	Hid under the desk so nobody would snap at his ass by mistake.
Told his brother not to fall for a war in Vietnam.	Told his wife to decorate the White House.
Figured out a navy blockade of Cuba instead of an invasion so that we wouldn't give Russia an excuse to toast us with missiles.	Played with Marilyn Monroe's underwear.

Yeah. That was like a really good idea. Alé called me an empty-headed buffalo and walked to science class with Andy Wexler.

Mama, I wish you could have stayed with us long enough to teach me about girls. Pop is clueless.

I love you,

T.C.

NAME: T.C. Keller   **CLASS:** Mrs. Fitzpatrick

ALGEBRA QUIZ

QUESTION: Factor x^2-y^2
ANSWER: x^2-y^2 = (x+y) (x-y)
However, I have some questions too. What do I need this in my life for? Am I going to get a job in an XY factory? Am I going to go to work at Ben & Jerry's selling XY ice cream cones? No. My dad and I are going to build houses and offices buildings, but out of bricks and glass, not out of X and Y. Right?

T.C.: Please see me after 6th period about this.—Lori

Dear Mama,

Up until this year, I could always turn a B- into a B or a C into a C+ just by throwing the enemy off the scent. **(QUESTION: What is the significance of December 1? ANSWER:** 1955. Rosa Parks said no when they told her to stand up in the bus. Then civil rights happened. In 1949 the Sox got Al Papai from the Browns. He once tripped over the chalk line on his way off the field. We'd have been better off with Rosa Parks.) And they'd always fall for it. At the bottom it would say things like "T.C., a little more history and a little less Red Sox, please" or "T.C., thanks for the travelogue," and the grade at the top was usually five points higher than it should have been. But not this time. **"T.C.: Please see me after 6th period about this."** Not even from my teacher, but from my adviser. Notice how she couldn't have said "See me at lunch" or given me a hint about how deep a hole I was in. No. That isn't the way it works. You have to suffer first. Like I don't have enough things on my mind.

<u>English notes</u>: Puck blew a few sparks in his hard drive and zapped the wrong guy by mistake. Alé's hair is long and black and falls down across her back like it doesn't even care.

<u>History notes</u>: We fought the British again in the War of 1812. Nobody knows why. Maybe a battle during the Revolution got rained out and this was their makeup game. I need Alé to wear the light yellow dress with the red and pink flowers on it again. It makes her skin look like an oil painting.

<u>Science notes</u>: The telegraph got invented. Alé sneezed. So I sneezed back. She didn't even look over her shoulder, even though she *had* to know it was me. Alexander Graham Bell discovered the telephone. His first words to Mr. Watson on the other end were **"T.C.: Please see me after 6th period about this."** Then it was the end of 6th period.

The way to Lori's office is down a green hall with lockers on both sides. Not even posters of Halloween Week or anything else that has color in it. No. Just green. *Dark* green. It's a long hall anyway, but it was even longer today.

INSTANT MESSENGER

TCKeller: If I don't come back alive, cut me out in little stars and I will make the face of heaven so fine that all the world will fall in love with night and pay no attention to the garish sun.

AugieHwong: Olivia DeHavilland said it better in *Gone With the Wind.* "Take care of my Ashley, Scarlett." Less is more, Tick.

Lori was already standing in the doorway with that kind of a smile on her face that people always have when they're going to ruin a kid's life.

"T.C.?" she began. *Translation: Any last words?* If she was anybody else, I might have noticed her light brown hair and the way the bottom half of her dress swishes just the right way when she walks. But I didn't. Instead, I came up with a sudden-death play before it was too late.

"Um—boys' room," I said while I was bending over so it'd look real. "Be right back." Then I ran for it.

I didn't really have to go, but it was the only chance I had. Once the lav door closed all the way behind me, I hid in a stall and flipped open my cell phone. When Pop's at work, the only calls he takes are mine.

"Tony C?"

"Why do I need algebra in my life?"

"It teaches you how to solve problems and weigh variables and factor out the crap. But you didn't hear that from *me.*"

"Got it in the back pocket. Peace out, dude."

After that I put my cell phone away and peed for good luck. I was untouchable.

STUDENT/ADVISER CONFERENCE
Lori Mahoney/Anthony C. Keller

LORI: How much is $(x+y)^2$?

T.C.: $x^2+2xy+y^2$.

LORI: You got that one wrong on the algebra quiz.

T.C.   It was October 2. The anniversary of the day my parents met each other and Bucky F. Dent hit the home run. My mind was thinking about that instead.

LORI: *Je suis, tu es, vous* what?

T.C.:   *Êtes.*

LORI: You got that wrong on the French quiz.

T.C.:   Probably a brain fart.

LORI: T.C., you're an A student with a B+ average. Why?

T.C.:   I'm a B+ kind of kid?

LORI: I need a better answer than that.

T.C.:   Everybody knows that only posers get A's. And I'm not a poser. I'm a chip off the old block.

LORI: Maybe. But you still don't understand why you need algebra.

T.C.:   Sure I do. It teaches me how to solve problems. And weigh variables. And factor out the crap.

LORI: How do you know that?!

T.C.:   Doesn't everybody?

A long time ago I never thought I was going to like school the way you said I would. Because after you left, I didn't even know how to get kids to talk to me anymore. I remember being in first grade and doing weird things like wearing my shirts backwards or drawing Saturn on my arms just to see if anybody would ask me how come. But nobody ever did. Some of the guys instead wore their shirts backwards too like they were making fun of me, so I pretended I didn't notice and waited to cry until I got home. I told Pop it was because I was still sad.

When we were seven and pretending we were knights, Augie killed a dragon to save my life. But if you were still here he wouldn't have had to.

I love you,
T.C.

Laurents School
Brookline, Massachusetts

VIA E-MAIL

Dear Ted:

Please. You've got to stop bailing Anthony out of a leaky skiff. "It teaches me how to weigh variables." Did he call you on his cell or are you hot-wired directly into his head?

While we're here, I need to warn you that their first out-of-class projects are going to be assigned in three weeks. They're studying the history of the nation's capital and they'll be asked to build models of their favorite landmarks. Let's not have a replay of fourth grade. A 200-foot Washington Monument that lights up in eighteen different colors won't be greeted with a sense of humor.

Know what? I'm in charge of 91 kids, and you're the biggest discipline problem I've got.

Lori

KELLER CONSTRUCTION
BOSTON · GLOUCESTER · WALTHAM

ELECTRONIC TRANSMISSION

Dear Lori:

First of all, how do you know he doesn't have a crush on you? Maybe the B+ thing is a way to guarantee that you'll call him into your office at least once a month for a one-on-one. When you think about it, it's a pretty provocative ruse for a kid.

Second of all, Tony C did all of the work on the planetarium and the map. I just helped out with the odd jobs like hammering, nailing, building motors, and painting. Period.

Third of all, if you'd finally agree to go out with me, I wouldn't have to subvert the entire school system just to get you to send me notes. Like father, like son. And I'm only half kidding. This is the first time since Nikki died that I've found someone who might actually be able to coax me back onto the field of play. So you'd better think about it unless you want a life-sized replica of the Iwo Jima statue (in bronze).

Ted

P.S. Besides, we've had one date already. So it's out there.

LAURENTS SCHOOL
BROOKLINE, MASSACHUSETTS

VIA E-MAIL

Dear Ted:

What's out there?? That wasn't a date, it was a chance encounter at Starbucks. And I paid for both Fraps.

Anthony doesn't have a crush on me and you know it. He idolizes his father, who—improbably—earned a B.A. from B.U. with a B+. But that was 1974. It's 2003. "A" is the new "B+."

I'm not going out with you because I'm your son's adviser. But if I weren't, I might. Unless you were serious about the statue. Then you'd be out of luck.

—The Field of Play

KELLER CONSTRUCTION
BOSTON · GLOUCESTER · WALTHAM

ELECTRONIC TRANSMISSION

Dear F.O.P.:

Don't worry about Tony C. He knows how to go for the
gold when it's time. So does his dad.

TK

Augie

www.augiehwong.com

THE FABULOUS WORLD
OF AUGIE HWONG

| click | Was Barbara Stanwyck really a man? |

| click | Ten reasons to come back as Angela Lansbury |

| click | Proof that Eve Arden and Kay Thompson were the same person |

| click | Augie the Jock: soccer, swimming, and track photos; worth a fortune on eBay after my first Olympics |

| click | BULLETIN: AUGIE HWONG SIGNED TO DIRECT FRESHMAN TALENT SHOW! TONY AWARD SHOO-IN! |

DIVA OF THE WEEK

Liza Minnelli

("Ring them bells, honey.")

Diary
Augie Hwong, 9th Grade
Mrs. Norwood's Class

Dear Liza with a Z,

I can't believe you married David Gest and didn't check with me first. All he wanted was your money and to find out if your mother sang "Over the Rainbow" when she put you to bed so he could tell his tacky friends about it. Trust me. David Gest is a gink. But you can still call me after the divorce if you need to borrow my shoulder. I'd never say "I told you so" to anybody except Nicole Kidman.

Incidentally, I know I have a big mouth—but why the hell did they pick *me* to direct the talent show?

INSTANT MESSENGER

AugieHwong: I'm having an anxiety attack.

TCKeller: Is it a new one? 'Cause I'm working on my diary.

> **AugieHwong:** Tick, it's happening too quick, that's what scares me. How did I get to be an A-list director already?? Where's all the torture you're supposed to go through before you click? And the hard knocks? And the setbacks you're supposed to learn from? I haven't suffered enough yet.

> **TCKeller:** Dude, it's just a talent show!

My brother is enjoying this too much. He's been waiting for the axe to drop ever since I found out that third grade wasn't ready for my impression of Bette Davis in the Holy Grail of movies, *All About Eve* ("Why, Max—you sly puss!"). He also grew two more pit hairs during homeroom, so he's finally broken ten, and now he thinks he's bulletproof. That's the last time I let him make more kicks than me in soccer so that people won't guess who *really* rocks.

Okay. Maybe I'll cave in after all. I don't like making people beg. But I told Mrs. Fitzpatrick I'd only sign a contract if she agreed to my terms.

1. There's just one prima donna in an Augie Hwong show, and that's Augie Hwong. Everyone else is expendable.

2. A curtain made of gold tinsel, a silver disco ball, and my entire cast dressed in sequins. Blue for the boys, pink for the girls.

3. A pit band of exactly nine musicians. I'm not paying overtime for more than that.

4. A celebrity M.C.—either Melissa Etheridge, k.d. lang, or Coretta Scott King.

Liza, if you think George Abbott gave you a hard time in *Flora, The Red Menace*, that's because you never worked with *me* before. I'm ruthless. The only act I'm pre-approving without a tryout is Tick and John Siniff and Andy Wexler and Grid Tarbell in a staged version of "Casey at the Bat," which probably sounds like playing favorites with my brother. But let's face it, sweetheart—when Judy let you sing with her at the Palladium, you weren't exactly ready for the Big Time either.

I'm holding auditions after school all of next week. You can come if you want, but there might be no point. I get the opening spot and I'm singing "Maybe This Time." It's a cruel, cruel business.

Love,
Augie with an A

Alé,

I need you to co-produce my show with me. Even Florenz Ziegfeld couldn't do it all by himself. I can also use you as property mistress, wardrobe mistress, and stage manager. What do you think?

—*Augie*

Augie,

I think you ought to read about the Triangle Shirtwaist fire in 1911. This is what happens when you employ slave labor. They jump out of windows to get away from the smoke. The answer is no.

I stopped by The Word Shop yesterday to see if they had any nonfiction on oppressed Filipino salmon packers in Alaska. How much is your father paying Phyllis to run the store? Because she knows more about books than the Library of Congress does. I asked her why *Huckleberry Finn* wasn't on the Classic Literature shelf and she said, "Alejandra, no black man says 'dem de d'wyne de goan' unless he's coming out of a coma—*that's* why." If your family is exploiting a minority, there will be pickets.

—*Alé*

Alé,

My family *is* an exploited minority. Our ancestors built the Union Pacific Railroad for twenty cents a day. If it was a good day.

Dad made Phyllis a partner in the store ten years ago and our insurance even paid for her mother's cataracts. So she doesn't need pickets.

What if I make you a producer all by yourself?

—*Augie*

Augie,

Maybe. But with top billing and a retirement plan.
And as long as this isn't just another one of your
excuses to get me to run into Anthony. "I'm considering a relationship with you." Was I supposed to
faint over that? Besides, he couldn't possibly want
to go there. I say awful things to him and whenever
I see him coming my way I grab that boy with the
curly hair and walk him to our next class.   —Alé

Alé,

That's Andy Wexler. We've been bonding during
soccer practice. We both like Swiss Miss and chocolate
chip cookies, and he calls me Spidey because he
says I'm lithe enough to swing from the Prudential
Tower even without red tights and a mask. Have
you ever met anyone who could use "lithe" in a
sentence before? I'm teaching him how to improve
his kick, and he's going to be a shell of his former
self when he finds out you're just using him to make
my brother jealous.

Can we schedule our first production meeting
for tomorrow after school?   —Augie

Augie,

Not tomorrow. We're having Bill and Hillary over

for dinner. Do you want to come? Carlos is bringing a date and Mamita hates odd numbers at her table.

Anyone with a cute quotient as high as Anthony's deserves to suffer. Things come too easily to those people already. And no girl will ever break Andy Wexler's heart. Trust me.

I can squeeze in a production conference on Saturday. Meet me outside of the Lycée Francais at 1:00 after my French lessons. (There's no use telling Papa that I'm already taking French at school because as far as he's concerned, if it doesn't cost him money it can't be worth much.)   —*Alé*

Alé,

Don't tell that to anyone else. People will think you're a stuck-up snob.   —*Augie*

Augie,

I *am* a stuck-up snob.   —*Alé*

Dear Liza,

I thought she was kidding. I thought she was making it up. I almost didn't wear my suit because of it. Hillary Clinton spooned Hollandaise onto my asparagus! With her own hands! Alé's beginning to scare me.

Mrs. Fitzpatrick got back to me with a counter-offer.

1. No sequins, no tinsel, no disco ball.

2. A pit band of Mr. Disharoon on the piano. Period.

3. Two-hour rehearsals, not eight. And only three times a week.

4. No prima donnas, *including* Augie Hwong.

5. Our adviser Lori Mahoney as celebrity M.C. Melissa Etheridge and k.d. lang weren't available, and Coretta Scott King costs $40,000.

There was a time when I would have had an artistic meltdown, but when you've had a former First Lady practically feeding you, you learn how to rise above it all.

Love,
Augie

The Globe

FROM THE DESK OF   *LISA WEI HWONG*

Honey—

I tried to make you something special from *The Irish Cookbook*, but it backfired halfway through. So I invented sweet-and-sour mackerel. It's on the top shelf in the fridge. If it still looks like it's alive, Dad's only allowed to take you to the Brookline Café or Huskies for dinner. They pay their people sixty cents an hour more than they have to.

Home late tonight, so kisses for bedtime. I have to review *My Fair Lady* downtown. Wish I could send the mackerel instead.

> I love you,
> Mom

The Globe

THEATRE

MY FAIR LADY RETURNS TO BOSTON

BY LISA WEI HWONG

. . . and at this point in Act I, we're forced down to the lowest rung of the social ladder, where the economically less fortunate are given their own anthem in "With a Little Bit of Luck"—a song designed to show us how much fun it is to be poor, in much the same manner that Stepin Fetchit proved for all time that African Americans were the toasts of the town as long as they tripped over their own feet and said things like, "Mah, mah, mah, dis sho' is a crazy bunch of folks." And if Henry Higgins is not the most reprehensible character ever written for the stage, that's only because somewhere, somehow, someone is composing a musical biography of Ronald Reagan.

Dear Liza,

Your mother liked to sing and take pills, my mother likes to write and start riots. The day after her review came out, they had to shut down Tremont Street because the protesters in front of the theatre were blocking traffic. The State House even had to close early. I'm surrounded by rabble-rousers. If I ever introduce her to Alé, Boston is finished. Especially if it turns out that we have Filipino salmon packers living here. Besides, I have bigger fish to fry.

Tick talked about his mom. I know that doesn't sound like the kinds of Oscar-winning headlines you're used to, but you're wrong. He hasn't done that in six years. The last clue I ever had about her was the lost purple balloon that she promised was going to come back to him if he watched the sky long enough. He told me that story at the beach when we were eight, and nothing else until this afternoon. And it wasn't even a special occasion. Has he been keeping it locked up all this time? Or did he only just remember it?

It happened at 4:11. We usually eat Sno-Kones on the overpass above Mass Pike after school and discuss the things we can't tell anybody else—but Tick's gotten so into this diary thing and trying to have some dead guy named Buck Weaver allowed back into baseball, and I've been so busy helping Andy Wexler with soccer, today was our first Mass Pike summit in almost a week.

Nehi sat between us with his head in Tick's lap and his eyes on Tick's Sno-Kone (he must have been in a root beer kind of mood), while we went through one of our usual quizzes.

"Best hot dog."

"McCoy Stadium in Pawtucket. Best thunderstorm."

"The one in Newburyport on spring vacation. Best worm."

"Under the rock at Castle Island. Best Christmas Eve."

"When I was three and a half." This kind of threw me. Usually we always agree that it was the Christmas when we were seven. We stayed at my house the night before, and after we were asleep Pop brought in this life-sized mechanical Santa Claus whose arm went up and down like he was waving. He and Dad set it up by the fireplace and turned off all of the lights except for the Christmas tree. Then they woke up me and Tick and carried us to the doorway of the living room to say hello to Santa. Well, when you're seven years old and you're three-quarters asleep and your head is on your father's shoulder, you'll pretty much believe anything you see—even without the special effects. But this was the real deal. Santa Claus waved to us and we waved back. And we could never make anybody believe that it had really happened.

So when Tick switched Christmases on me, I knew something major was about to happen. While he stared hard across Mass Pike at the lights behind Fenway Park, he told me about how his mom had surprised them on December 24 with a sleigh and a horse and a driver. And how—after dinner—they rode through Bowdoin Street with the snow coming down all around them and the people on the sidewalks shopping at the last minute to buy presents for relatives they didn't like or ginky friends they weren't crazy about either, and with the colored lights blinking in all of the windows and "Silver Bells" piping out of the speakers in front of Faneuil Hall. The picture that the driver took of them shows Pop and Tick's mom with their heads leaning in together and Tick in between them with a "this is going to last forever, right?" grin across his face. (Kids are so clueless.) Pop still has the picture framed in their living room and they even used it for their holiday cards two years in a row. "Happy 1993. Love, Nikki, Ted, and Anthony" and "Happy 1994 from T.C. Keller and his two best friends." But there wasn't any Happy 1995. And I never knew the story behind the picture until today. No wonder.

After he finished telling me, his eyes stayed glued to the highway underneath us like he was memorizing it. By then there were only two rules in my mind: (a) don't cry, and (b) don't let him stay sad. So I said the first thing I could think of to break the silence.

"Best Christmas present." Tick looked up suddenly and there was the usual Tick smile again.

"Blue Rollerblades," he said. "Best blizzard."

"The one that started while we were watching *Peter Pan*. You even clapped for Tinker Bell, you gink."

"Oh. Like you didn't."

Adolescence isn't just about growing hair, it's about growing up. I hope I'm ready for it.

Love,

Augie

INSTANT MESSENGER

AugieHwong: Alé, I had a great idea. I see a finale in front of a curtain with stars on it. Everybody in the show gets to be in it. If we have time on Saturday, I'll need you to help me block it out.

AlePerez: What song?

AugieHwong: Something that made me think of you. From *West Side Story.* "America."

AlePerez: Thanks, but my castanets are in the laundry. (Did you ever hear of ethnic stereotyping?) I assume you want me to stand in for Anita.

AugieHwong: No, *I'm* Anita. I want you to play Bernardo.

SORRY! USER ALEPEREZ HAS LOGGED OFF

Dear Liza,

I don't know why Andy Wexler thinks he needs help. He kicks a soccer ball better than David Beckham does. A couple of times during workouts this afternoon I could swear he fell on his ass on purpose. This is what happens when you're a famous director. Everybody wants a piece of you, even if they have to fake a reason. What price glory?

Tick was working on his diary again, so after practice Andy and I went to Dad's store and took over a booth in the café for two hours of hot chocolate and all the cookies we could sneak. What a remarkable guy he is. All 5-feet-5 of him. He started off by apologizing for calling me a gink in second grade (I got the last grape Jell-O in the cafeteria line so he was stuck with orange), but he said I was the one who raised his consciousness by making him figure out that Asians have feelings too (!). If he hadn't been so serious about it, with his forehead crinkled and his eyes looking so sad, I'd have dumped my hot chocolate all over his curly light brown hair. Instead, all I wanted to do was hug him and tell him it was okay—because if he really thinks that "gink" is the worst kind of name-calling that a Chinese American kid has to hear all his life, his consciousness never needed raising in the first place.

Other things:

- His father is a pilot for American Airlines, and on 9/11 he'd just taken off from Logan Airport for San Francisco when the World Trade Center was hit. For two hours nobody knew which planes had done it and his family didn't even know if he was alive. I tried to put myself in his shoes while he was remembering, but I just couldn't go there. What if it had been Dad or Pop??

- He loves football and the Pats the same way that Tick loves baseball and the Sox. So there's another whole language I'm going to have to learn. First and ten. Hang time. Flower Bowl.

- He wasn't crazy about doing "Casey at the Bat" in the talent show, but he changed his mind when he found out I'd be directing him. My reputation precedes me.

- He has a great smile—but I mean a great smile. It's like getting a present you didn't expect. When he flashes one of those things you know he means every word he's saying.

- Neither one of us could figure out why we didn't become

friends until now. It was always just "Hey"/"Hey" in the hallway and "See ya"/"See ya" after scrimmages.

Before we left the store, Phyllis let him have *Day By Day in New England Patriots History* as long as he promised to keep it their secret.

"I don't do this for everybody," she warned him, hiding it in a bag. Which is actually bullshit. She does it for every one of my friends when she meets them for the first time. And since it looked like we were on a roll there, I handed her the new Audrey Hepburn bio and tried to get away with the same thing. But all she did was slap my fingers and say, "Augie, do *not* make me put on my heels." (Slipping one over on Phyllis is like tossing a pair of dice and waiting for a seven. You get lucky maybe one out of fourteen tries.)

"Holy crap, Spidey!" blurted Andy, pointing to page eighteen while we were crossing Harvard Street. "There's even a Jim Cheyunski autograph in here!"

"Holy crap, Andy!" I blurted back. "Who the heck is Jim Cheyunski??" Andy groaned and put an arm around my shoulder when we hopped the curb.

"Boy, have we got a lot of work to do on you."

We sat on a bench in Emerson Garden until we ran out of talk. By then it was getting dark and I *really* wanted to ask him to come over for dinner, but I couldn't figure out how. So after a couple of more seconds of looking at each other, it was back to "See ya"/"See ya" again. Then we went home in opposite directions.

I thought about him a lot last night. He's the kind of friend I can see getting into capers with, like Butch and Sundance. Scratch that.

Like Thelma and Louise. He'll be wearing mauve and beige at the same time, the fashion police'll be closing in behind us in squad cars, and just before we take off down the highway he'll turn to me with his brown hair and blue eyes and shoot me one of those grins that could easily last me the rest of my

SCREEEEECH.

Oh, no.

Oh, please God, no.

"*Zing! went the strings of my heart.*"

Too late. When he calls me Spidey I turn into grape Jell-O. His favorite kind.

I'm doomed.

Love,

Augie

The Word Shop
BROOKLINE'S FAVORITE BOOKSTORE

E-Memo From the Desk of

Craig Hwong

Heya, Teddy.

This comes under the heading "Father-to-Father Communication: Insecurity," so keep it under your hat because I have my kung fu image to maintain.

Augie's almost fifteen and about three steps away from Adolescent Hell—but he still hasn't told us he's gay yet. He couldn't possibly think it would make any difference to us. Wei and I have been encouraging him to be himself ever since he memorized *Annie Get Your Gun* at the age of two and told his grandma Lily, "Got no diamond, got no pearl, still I think I'm a lucky girl." I mean, it's not like we needed a road map.

Should I bring it up to him or leave it alone? He's at the age where kids discover puppy love, and I've always looked forward to commiserating with him about *my* first crush. (Her name was Wendy and she smelled like aluminum foil. Remind me to tell you the whole story when Wei and the kids are in another state.)

Craig

KELLER CONSTRUCTION
BOSTON · GLOUCESTER · WALTHAM

ELECTRONIC TRANSMISSION

Craig, Augie's afraid of nothing. He taught Tony C how to be dauntless when they were six, and that's the only thing that got him back on his feet after he lost his mother.

He's not hiding anything from you or Wei. Two possibilities: (a) he doesn't know it himself yet or (b) he's straight. Think about it for a minute. Just because you were a t'ai chi champ when you were ten didn't automatically mean you were going to like girls. It's a whole separate deal that works the same way in reverse. I mean, there must be *some* straight guys who know the lines from *All About Eve*.

By the way, I finally got Lori to admit that if she weren't my son's adviser, she'd consider going out with me. I think I'm winning.

Ted

P.S. And you're going to have to explain how a human being can smell like aluminum foil. You can't just say something like that and then leave it hanging out there in the Universe.

The Word Shop
BROOKLINE'S FAVORITE BOOKSTORE

E-Memo From the Desk of
Craig Hwong

Ted:

This week my son thinks he's the Supremes. *All* of them. So we can scratch "straight" off the list. At least I hope we can. As a gay kid he'll be a natural leader. Put him in a macho bullshit environment and he's going to have a hard time. I don't want that to happen. (Let's also not forget Wei's immortal words to him nine minutes after he was born, when she first stared into those big brown eyes: "Oh, honey. Promise me you'll grow up to like boys. Because I don't want any other woman in your life except me.")

Girls smell like aluminum foil when they're sixteen, sweating, and dancing with you only because a camp counselor told them they have to. It's a scent they put out when they despise the fact that you're alive. (By the way, we need to schedule a guys' night at Mulligan's before you screw up anything with Lori. You've been out of practice way too long not to need some brush-up work.)

We're thinking about taking the kids skiing between Christmas and New Year's. You game?

Outta here. I've got to pick up Diana Ross at soccer practice.

Craig

Alejandra

Diary
Alejandra Perez, 9th Grade
Mrs. Norwood's Class

Dear Jacqueline,

Of all the Kennedy men you could have had, I think you picked the right one. Teddy was too cute to trust, and Bratty Bobby must have gotten on your nerves from day one, the way he was always chasing after Jack like a dog that's looking for a rear end to sniff—and it doesn't matter whose. Actually, you'd probably have done best with Joe Jr. if he hadn't gotten himself killed in the war. He was handsome, and he may even have had some morals.

But at least you were given a choice. After one month of public school, these are my only options:

BARRY   Brown nose; cuts out newspaper clippings for current events even on days when we don't have current events

ANDY   Gay (doesn't know it)

JONATHAN   Says "would of" instead of "would have"

STU   Thinks farting is a riot

DRAKE   Gay (doesn't know it)

GRAYSON   Rumored to have eaten a salamander on a dare; won 35¢

DONALD   Hasn't met Mr. Hygiene yet and doesn't appear to want to

TYLER   Gay (knows it, in denial, reads *Hustler*)

I left Anthony off the list because he was never in the running. Even for a boy, he's reckless, over-confident, and obvious. In the middle of an already disquieting "pop quiz," I just *know* he's going to clear his throat, sneeze, or cough—all to get me to turn around and look at him. (As if I would ever look at him.) Then he "just happened" to join the Young Democrats Club when he found out I'd been accepted, though all he does for sixty minutes is search for opportunities to challenge me on the subject of your parasitic brother-in-law, intentionally forgetting that it was President Kennedy who saved us from nuclear extinction in 1962. All Bobby did was whine. Am I right?

He also follows me around after school on days when he's not playing baseball with some of the neighborhood children in Amory Park (second base, prone to make errors on infield hits, not a bad swing but not exactly all-star either, and I can't help it if Amory Park is on my way home). So I copied a page from the Cambridge Dictionary of American English and left it on his desk.

> **stalker**, *noun*, someone who pursues another person, usually intending harm

Two hours later, he left me a page of his own.

> **bodyguard**, *noun*, a person or group of persons, usually armed, responsible for the safety of another

"Usually armed." His only weapons are a Red Sox keychain and an insidious persistence that would have made your professionally irritating brother-in-law look like a novice.

NAME: Alejandra Perez   **CLASS:** Ms. Reed

HISTORY QUIZ

QUESTION: Define the purpose of the Bill of Rights.

ANSWER: The Bill of Rights is a piece of paper that says we're all entitled to the same freedoms, unless (to use one of many examples) your grandparents are Japanese. In that case, the Bill of Rights guarantees you the freedom to be locked up in a "Relocation Center" like Manzanar until the rest of the country decides it doesn't detest you anymore. Then they sweep it under the rug so that the next generation doesn't even know what Manzanar *is*.

From: TCKeller@earthworks.net
To: AlePerez@earthworks.net

We need to call a truce for about 10 minutes.

From: AlePerez@earthworks.net
To: TCKeller@earthworks.net

How did you get my e-mail address?

From: TCKeller@earthworks.net
To: AlePerez@earthworks.net

I have my sources. Alé, I'm really worried about Augie. He was walking into walls all day, he hasn't IM'd me since last night, and Mom says he's been sitting in his room watching the end of *Funny Girl* for 3 hours.

From: AlePerez@earthworks.net
To: TCKeller@earthworks.net

Oh, *that's* not good.

From: TCKeller@earthworks.net
To: AlePerez@earthworks.net

Why? What happens at the end of *Funny Girl*?

From: AlePerez@earthworks.net
To: TCKeller@earthworks.net

She sings "My Man" and cries. I hope he hasn't fallen in love with Omar Sharif.

From: TCKeller@earthworks.net
To: AlePerez@earthworks.net

By the way, just because Ms. Reed read your quiz answers to the whole class doesn't mean you were right. Manzanar had over 30 baseball teams. Some of them were made up in camp like the Gophers and the Pioneers and the Señors, and some of them were already teams in their real lives before they got sent away (like the San Fernando Aces), so they kept on playing the way they always did, even with the guards and guns. Their field was on Block 25 near the fire break.

What generation doesn't know what Manzanar is?

From: AlePerez@earthworks.net
To: TCKeller@earthworks.net

Who told you that?

From: TCKeller@earthworks.net
To: AlePerez@earthworks.net

Baseball Behind Barbed Wire. Years ago. If you gave me a chance, you'd find out that I'm more than just messy hair and dirty sneakers.

From: AlePerez@earthworks.net
To: TCKeller@earthworks.net

Is the truce over?

From: TCKeller@earthworks.net
To: AlePerez@earthworks.net

Yeah. You can hate me again.

I don't see why he can't take a hint. Surely he'd be happier with one of the other girls in our class. Kathy Fine, for instance. Although she hasn't stopped talking since Labor Day, she seems to have a genuine flair for attracting boys. I'm certain she'd appreciate how Anthony blushes so vulnerably when his voice cracks and how his hair overlaps the neck of his cotton sweatshirt in a way that makes you wonder which is softer. Why does he think *I* would care?

Fondly,

Alejandra

LYCÉE FRANCAIS

STUDENT: Perez, Alejandra

VOCAL RANGE: Mezzo soprano

Course Schedule

Dance, Modern	Saturday, 10:00–11:00 a.m.
Dance, Jazz	Saturday, 11:00 a.m.–12:00 noon
Voice	Saturday, 12:00 noon–1:00 p.m.

UNITED STATES SECRET SERVICE
WASHINGTON, D.C.

CLINT LOCKHART
AGENT

Hey, Princess.

No, I don't think you'll start an international incident if
your father finds out what you're really studying at your
Bastille there. Kids are allowed to switch their majors
whenever they want. But do *not* lie to him. Tell him that
you love the Lycée and make sure he knows that you're
also pulling straight A's in French. The implication is
that you're pulling straight A's in French *at* the Lycée,
but you never said that. (This is how we've been playing
it in the federal government since 1789, and if Bill
Clinton hadn't gotten careless we'd still be batting a
thousand.)

xoxo,
Clint

Dear Jacqueline,

I'm not cut out for Covert Operations. Were you? I leave the house on Saturday mornings with a French book in my hand, a craving for all things Gallic written across my face—and tights, a leotard, and a towel hidden in a $750 Gucci backpack that I wouldn't be caught dead wearing otherwise. (There's a darling little retro bag made out of brown and tan canvas that's on sale for $12.99 at the Downtown Crossing Gap—but when I suggested it to Papa, he acted as though I'd just asked him if I could walk to school naked.) By the time I reach the Lycée, I feel like an advertisement for a youth reformatory. There was a police car parked in front of the building this morning, and until I realized it belonged to the crossing guard, I was all ready to turn myself in. I don't do guilt well.

But oh, my God, what difference could it possibly make when you're standing in front of a mirror and barre with eleven other kids and Benny Goodman coming through the speakers, and you don't even recognize yourself anymore?

"Pivot turn, Alejandra. Good!" I'm no longer an ambassador's quarrelsome child, I'm not my brother's obnoxious little sister, and I'm not ninth grade's most famous prig. I'm the first girl in the second row in the third scene in the fourth number in fifth position at ten o'clock on the nose. Nothing less. I can't imagine anything half so intoxicating, especially when Mrs. Salabes shows us a four-part combination—including an arabesque—and I'm the only one who gets it right. The first time!! Did you ever take modern dance at Miss Porter's? Did you know that your body can say more with eight bars of music than you could possibly write in a fifteen-page essay?? I don't need Gwen Verdon or Chita Rivera after all. I'd settle for being a chorus gypsy the rest of my life.

(I'm not quite as optimistic about my voice. So far all they've done is take me up and down the scales to see how far they can push it, which I really don't think is a good idea. Whenever we slide above high C, I get a little nervous. There was an E that technically should have broken a window on the other side of the room. I hope they know what they're doing.)

By the time I met Augie on the sidewalk after class, I'd changed back into the Other Alejandra, but I still had to explain why I was out of breath and sweaty. So I told him we'd spent an hour learning French aerobics. One day he'll forgive me. He and his brother are too close to keep secrets from each other. Including mine.

ALEJANDRA PEREZ
AND AUGIE HWONG
present
THE FRESHMAN FOLLIES 2003
CONCEIVED AND DIRECTED BY
AUGIE HWONG

PRODUCTION MEETING
Participants: Alé and Augie
Location: The Word Shop Café and Bakery
Conference Room: Rear Booth

ALÉ: I *knew* you'd never let me have solo billing above the title!

AUGIE: You're in Times Roman bold. I'm not.

ALÉ: And what's with the "conceived by"?? Talent shows are older than the ice caps!

AUGIE: Maybe. But whose concept was it to stage the whole thing like *A Chorus Line*? I see rotating columns and Mylar mirrors and—

ALÉ: Augie, our budget is $100. We can just afford posters.

AUGIE: Can they have a gold top hat with glitter on it?

ALÉ: They can have a gold top hat with glitter on it.

AUGIE: Okay. Then we'll tell *Variety* that we're going in a different direction. That way I won't lose face when they wonder what happened to "conceived by."

I've never met anybody like Augie Hwong in my life. By 11:30 in the morning on my first day of school, I'd been written off by an entire classroom as a nose-in-the-air name-dropper who had no place on the ninth grade A-list. Then Augie grabbed my arm in the cafeteria line and insisted that it would ruin his adolescence if I didn't have lunch with him. At first I thought he was mocking me (that's the way it usually starts), but he was quite serious. It turned out that he had an entire roster of celebrity names that he needed to run through in the event I knew any of them personally—and over an inedible dessert of cling peaches, we finally discovered common ground. Who else but Augie would light up to learn that Judi Dench wears pantsuits to opening night parties? Who else would *care*? Which is probably why I surprised myself by revealing a few things that I'd never told another breathing soul before. Me, of all people.

"Whenever my father went overseas, I always thought it was because I'd done something shameful again."

"Ouch. Did you really piss off Korea?"

"Yes. I was awful."

"No. You were Elizabeth Taylor in *Giant*."

He's truly extraordinary.

He's also twice as pretty as I could ever hope to be. It isn't just the exquisitely shaped almond eyes or the hazel sunburst that hides behind them until he smiles; it's the way his entire face absorbs life whenever you say something that delights him. One thing is certain: The boy who gets to kiss him for the first time is never going to be the same again.

But Anthony was right (a sorry yet inevitable conclusion). Augie was only operating at 75 percent this afternoon. He gave in too quickly on the Mylar mirrors, he only had one cup of cocoa instead of his usual two-plus-half-of-mine, he said, "No, thank you," when Phyllis offered to slip him an advance copy of the Thelma Ritter biography, and he misquoted Bette Davis in *All About Eve*. Something was *definitely* on his mind.

"Are you all right?" I asked, interrupting him in the middle of yet another defensive argument.

"I'm fine," he insisted.

"Hey," said a third voice. We both looked up at the same time. It was that curly-haired boy Andy Wexler—the one who needs help with his soccer kick.

"Hey," mumbled Augie, inexplicably staring down at the tabletop. *Is he blushing?!*

"How goes it?"

"'Kay. You?"

"'Kay. See ya."

"See ya." Augie watched intently while Andy moved over to the counter and sat down on one of the stools—glancing back over his shoulder as he did it and nearly landing on the floor.

ALÉ PEREZ NOTES ON PRODUCTION MEETING

Posters will have glittery gold top hats on them.

The overture will consist of two verses of "Everything's Coming Up Roses," provided that Mr. Disharoon has the sheet music. Otherwise there won't be an overture. And we're not using cymbals on the opening chord, no matter *how* good it sounds on the album.

Auditions will be held on Tuesday and Wednesday from 3:30 to 5:00.

Augie is falling in love with Andy Wexler.

Andy Wexler is falling in love with Augie.

Augie doesn't know that Andy is gay.

Andy doesn't know that Augie is gay. (Hello?)

I'm glad I'm a girl.

From: AlePerez@earthworks.net
To: TCKeller@earthworks.net

Stop worrying. Augie has a crush on Andy Wexler, so he's operating on six levels of panic at the same time.

\---

From: TCKeller@earthworks.net
To: AlePerez@earthworks.net

I should get him to watch *Casablanca* again. He'll handle this a lot better as Ingrid Bergman. He always does.

Why did he tell you and not *me*??

From: AlePerez@earthworks.net
To: TCKeller@earthworks.net

Relax, big brother. He told me nothing. Romance is a universally unspoken language understood by every living organism on this planet except heterosexual men. So I'm not surprised that you didn't pick up on it.

From: TCKeller@earthworks.net
To: AlePerez@earthworks.net

Then how come you like me?

From: AlePerez@earthworks.net
To: TCKeller@earthworks.net

I don't.

From:　TCKeller@earthworks.net
To:　　AlePerez@earthworks.net

You e-mailed me first.

From:　AlePerez@earthworks.net
To:　　TCKeller@earthworks.net

It won't happen again.

United States Secret Service
Washington, D.C.

Clint Lockhart
Agent

Princess, Augie isn't your only friend, he's your *first* friend. The CIA calls guys like him keepers because they have the kind of 20/20 intuition that could read somebody's character through a concrete retaining wall. Everybody else needs a few markers along the way. Including you. So try these for starters:

1. Don't talk about the kiss from Brad Pitt or the bracelet Princess Di gave you or anything else that belongs in *People* magazine. Bite the bullet and pretend you're just a kid. (Oh, wait. You *are!*)

2. Every couple of days, ask someone sitting next to you to explain a quiz question that you didn't understand. And if you *did* understand it, shut up and act like you didn't. You'll be surprised how fast the word spreads: "She's human!"

3. At least once a week, try to make a mistake. And on the off-chance you discover that the world hasn't exploded, make another one.

You rock, girl. But you need to give everybody else a chance to find that out.

xoxo,
Clint

Dear Jacqueline,

Lee Meyerhoff is the most popular girl in the ninth grade. She wears her hair in an early Beatles cut (almost always a fatal mistake, but somehow she makes it work), her face is so Becky Thatcher wholesome that she really ought to draw freckles on her nose to complete the picture, her I.Q. is somewhere around the temperature of water when it begins to boil (in degrees Fahrenheit), and her parents have a swimming pool in their backyard. Naturally, the boys can't take their eyes off of her and the girls have booked all of her available sleepovers three months in advance.

She also sits next to me for seven hours a day, so she seemed the likeliest prospect for trying out what was destined to become the least credible experiment of my life—and which hatched itself spontaneously as we were passing our English tests to the front of the room.

"Lee?" I mumbled under my breath, leaning in to her through an improvised mask of pure panic. *Why is my voice shaking??* To say she was startled is a matter of understatement; she later told me she never suspected for a minute that I even knew her name.

"I didn't understand question four," I lied, looking for all the world as if I were about to cry. "Why couldn't Hermia love Demetrius?" Lee glanced around the room furtively, then propped up her notebook in front of her so that Mrs. Norwood wouldn't notice that we were having an illegal conversation behind it.

"Because she fell for Lysander first," she whispered back, "who sounds like he had better legs anyway." Oh, wrong, wrong, wrong. Hermia couldn't love Demetrius because he was a vain and shallow schmuck who needed a codependent neurotic like Helena to make him feel like he had balls—though he certainly wasn't going to be much of a support system when she wound up in AA because of him. But I didn't tell that to Lee. Instead, I clapped a fraudulent hand over my mouth and blurted, "Boy, did I screw *that* one up." As I was soon to discover, one of the most annoyingly natural things about Lee is that she loves being a big sister—so of course she was now in her element.

"Don't worry about it," she assured me confidently, wrinkling her freckle-free nose like she was flipping off both Shakespeare *and* the entire seventeenth century. "It was only worth five points anyway."

"Lee and Alejandra," barked Mrs. Norwood from the front of the room as she slid our papers into a manila folder. "If it's not something you can share with the rest of the class, button it up." Lee grinned sheepishly and seemed to take it in stride, but now I really *was* ready to cry. *A reprimand?? ME??* My face turned scarlet and I heard not one more word for the rest of the lesson. Eight years of perfect behavior down the drain because of that idiot Demetrius. What were my parents going to say?

"Alejandra forgot that she was a lady."

"<u>Again</u>?"

However, my shame lasted only another fifteen minutes—or roughly until I discovered between third and fourth periods that being publicly busted with Lee Meyerhoff is apparently the gateway to the Social Register.

"Alé, where do you get your hair cut?" asked Renee Panitz in front of the mirror in the girls' room.

"Alé, settle an argument," begged Soupy Pondfield, almost closing her locker door on Beth Birnbaum. "Doesn't J Lo look like she's had liposuction?"

"Love that shirt, girl," observed Quita Tapper as she snapped an approving finger in my general direction.

Jacqueline, you were the most admired woman in the world. Please tell me that it's not always so complicated.

INSTANT MESSENGER

AlePerez: Lee, I've run out of ways to delete my conscience from my hard drive. I didn't really need help with question four. I've had Hermia's number since I was 11.

LeeMeyerhoff: Duh. And Demetrius had the morals of a cotton rat. But that isn't what you wanted to hear. Same thing happened to me in third grade. Nobody wanted to talk to the rich kid either. It also didn't help that I was the only one in class that Mrs. Strawn liked.

AlePerez: Who's Mrs. Strawn?

LeeMeyerhoff: Former math teacher and Bride of Satan. Since she left right before the sinkhole opened up on Longwood, we think it was her husband's way of calling her home. It gets lonely ruling Hell by yourself.

Anyway, the cold shoulder thing lasted until I deliberately misspelled "fluctuate" in front of the whole room and then burst into tears. It was a masterful performance. After that, I had sleepovers coming out of my ears.

AlePerez: It's not my fault that I met Ben Affleck!

LeeMeyerhoff: Nobody said it was. It's not my fault that I have a pool in the backyard either.

AlePerez: So what does it take to be prom queen around here—all F's???

LeeMeyerhoff: Look, Jane Austen wrote the playbook on how girls are supposed to behave. But she's been dead for 186 years, so we need to update her. And if Judy, Beth, Soupy, and the rest aren't ready to follow us, then we can do it by ourselves, can't we? I mean, we may not be as fabulous as Augie Hwong, but we're not far behind.

AlePerez: Right. We also know what works with boys and what doesn't. No flirting. Let them come to *us*.

LeeMeyerhoff: Except when the boy in question has an ass like Anthony Keller does.

AlePerez: Lee, I'm SO not ready to go there yet.

Over today's indigestible cafeteria lunch of corn fritters doled out by an understandably dour Mrs. Dowdy, we continued our examination of boys from every conceivable angle and so lost track of time that we were yelled at by Mrs. Carsiotis for being late to geography class. Big deal.

Fondly,
Alejandra

AUDITIONS
FRESHMAN FOLLIES

Members of Actors' Equity and those with agents will be seen first. All others, please take a number.

—A. Hwong, Director

HIGH POINT: "Casey at the Bat." (And who ever would have suspected it?) Gridley Tarbell plays Casey, Andy Wexler and John Siniff act out the other parts, and Anthony narrates. They don't know it yet, but Lee gave them their first ad quote: "Utterly charming."

MOST EFFECTIVE MOMENT: "A straggling few got up to go in deep despair"—which Anthony pronounces "despay-ah." For some reason he reminded me of Gary Cooper in *Sergeant York*, and I have no earthly idea why. Lee says it's because I recognize a certain honest nobility in both performances. No, I don't. Do I?

MOST ENTERTAINING COMEDY ROUTINE: Watching Augie and Andy not watching each other.

MOST OBVIOUS QUESTION: Why do guys insist on wearing those odious jeans with the rear ends hanging down around their ankles? Do they really think it's hot? Lee is grateful that Anthony, Gridley, and Andrew wear the regular kind. "See what I mean?" she whispered, staring shamelessly across nine rows of seats. "T.C.'s had a cute butt ever since third grade. It'd be a waste to hide it."

MOST UNEXPECTED SURPRISES: Ricky Offitt on alto sax, Ruthie Andress on piano, Robin Potts in taps, and Bruce Daniels doing stand-up. (You can always count on the quietest kids to be the funniest. Brucie hasn't said two words all year, yet halfway through his riff on having to go to the bathroom in the middle of a history test, Lee and I dissolved into clinical hysteria. Especially when he crossed his legs so he wouldn't pee until he could remember what year the Battle of Saratoga was fought.)

LOW POINT: Stu Merliss on electric guitar singing his own composition: "I Feel Like a Dick." Augie rejected him on the basis of the title. Stu claimed censorship. Lee suggested "I Feel Like a Dork" instead. All agreed. Now we're stuck with Stu Merliss on electric guitar.

But most important, Augie seemed back to normal again. Or at least as normal as you can be when you're Augie, when your life has turned upside down practically overnight, and when you're not confident enough to share the news with anyone else yet—not even the people who love you most.

"We'll work out the running order as we go along," he informed his eager young cast as we sat in a circle onstage. "But I'll start the ball rolling myself with 'Maybe This Time,' we'll use Tick and the kids to close the first act with 'Casey,' Brucie can bring up the second act curtain with his monologue, and all we need is a kick-ass finish. So let's keep our eyes open, people. I want one more number with the kind of razzle-dazzle that'll send us to Broadway and West Forty-fourth Street."

Augie's going to be fine. And it doesn't take much brainpower to figure out who's steering him in the right direction.

INSTANT MESSENGER

AugieHwong: If you had to choose between Humphrey Bogart and Paul Henreid, who would you pick?

AlePerez: Bogart, you idiot. Henreid was a pompous narcissist who deserved a wet dishrag like Helena.

Anthony must have gotten him to watch *Casablanca* again. And he *is* handling this better as Ingrid Bergman.

T.C.

FREE BUCK WEAVER!
www.freebuckweaver.com

Total Hits: 724,013

GEORGE DAVIS WEAVER (also called The Ginger Kid) played for the Chicago White Sox for all 9 years of his major league career, and most people thought he was one of the greatest shortstops who ever lived. But nobody even remembers him anymore. Why? Because 3 weeks before the World Series in 1919, a bunch of gamblers talked 7 of the guys into throwing the games. They even asked Weaver if he wanted in on the scam too, but all Weaver said to them was, "Piss off, you cheeseballs" and played his guts out. It wasn't good enough to beat the fix, though. The White Sox lost to the Cincinnati Reds anyway, even though they might have had the best team anybody ever saw. But the Reds didn't really win either. The crooks did.

When the beans were spilled a year later and everybody found out about it, Buck was banned from baseball forever, right along with the 7 ginks who started it all. But not for throwing games. He was banned for not ratting on his team. What's wrong with this picture? My father says that you can always be proud of yourself for listening to your heart. Buck Weaver listened to his heart too, but all he got was punished for it. And just because he's dead doesn't mean it's not unfair anymore. Buck Weaver deserves to be un-banned.

Please click on the "Sign Petition" button. When we hit 20,000 names, we'll send them to the Commissioner of Baseball and make him do something about it.

Thank you.

T.C. Keller

T.C.:
I'm with you, dude. Weaver got screwed.

Dear Mr. Keller,

I'm 16 and I don't know anything about baseball, but my brother made me watch *Eight Men Out*. John Cusack was so cute as Buck Weaver that I'm signing your petition anyway.

Hey Freak.

How did you ever get 18,731 people to sign your stupid petition? Buck Weaver was a jerk. Those guys were a disgrace. They should've run the whole team out of town on a rail. Go Reds!

Dear T.C.:

I'm a features editor at *SportsAmerica* magazine, and I'd like to find out whether your father would allow us to interview you for one of our upcoming issues. For eighty-two years, popular opinion has held that Buck Weaver was handed a raw deal, but this is the first grassroots movement that actually appears to be growing.

Please contact me at your convenience.

Colleen Wilson
SportsAmerica

Dear Mama,

(One of our vocabulary words this week really gave me a hard time, so I'm supposed to practice using it in a sentence. See if you can guess which one it is.)

Whenever something really kick-ass happens to me that I didn't expect, Pop always says "There's your mom pulling strings for you again," so I figure you already know about the lady from *SportsAmerica* since it was probably your idea. She called last night to ask me Buck Weaver questions, and Pop got on the other phone to fill in anything I might forget. I quoted Buck's stats in the World Series that proved he wasn't playing crooked and why he deserved civil rights, and Pop mentioned the bedtime stories you made up for me about Rosa Parks and Dr. King. By then I was pretty sure we could trust her with our secret plan to organize a protest rally in front of the Hall of Fame, but Pop interrupted me before I could finish. (After we hung up, he explained what "off the record" means.) So when you see Buck Weaver, please let him know that he's making news again. *On* the record. Because if we can't get him put back into baseball, at least a lot of people are going to want to know why, which is just as valuable. You once said that a friend is somebody who believes in you no matter what, and Buck is going to find out that he has a lot of friends. Even if that's all he gets out of it.

Mrs. Norwood gave us our first project assignments of the year. She wants us to build a model of our favorite monument in Washington. I couldn't decide between the Capitol, the Lincoln Memorial, or the White House, so Pop said we'd make a scale diorama of the whole L'Enfant Plan—which is the Mall and the Ellipse together, with all of the federal buildings around them and the Washington Monument in the middle. The Hobby Shop on Thayer Street has white plastic replicas of all the marble landmarks, but we're going to have to make the weird ones like the National Archives and the Smithsonian out of balsa wood. All of the buildings are going to light up in different colors and there'll even be real water in the reflecting pool and real Astroturf on the Mall. Lori told Pop that it can't be as high as the planetarium was, but she never said anything about how wide—so we're thinking five feet by fifteen feet. Pop says it's a shame we have to end it at the Potomac River because he promised her the Iwo Jima statue too, and that's in Arlington. I'm glad he's checking with her first this time. She acted kind of funny about the eight-foot map of Massachusetts.

But there's definitely something spurious going on here that I'm not supposed to be able to figure out. Back in the old days (like last month), it would have gone right over my head—but ever since Cupid shot me in the butt, nothing gets by me anymore. This morning in the middle of our jog, me and Pop were sitting on the grass across the Charles River from Lowell House (from our favorite spot we can see the street corner where you let him kiss you for the first time). That's where we usually discuss the women in our lives and tell each other what we're doing wrong.

"Alé hates me."

"Alé can't stop thinking about you. Nobody tries that hard to drive a guy nuts unless she's already fallen for him. Monica hates *me*."

"But you were asking for it," I repeated for the hundredth time. "She told you she was vegetarian. You shouldn't have ordered salmon."

"I apologized for that, didn't I?"

"Uh-huh. And then you laughed when she told you that fish have feelings too."

"Who knew she was *serious*?"

"*I* did! And I wasn't even *there*!" Nehi raised his head from my lap and barked, which either means he saw a squirrel or else he agreed with what I'd just said. Then Pop squirted me with his water bottle. He always does that when I win.

Pop's Internet dating hasn't been going so hot. Marina was a pretty lawyer, but she had mean eyes. Natalie was a twenty-six-year-old graphic artist who thought the moon was a planet. On top of that, she was young enough to be Pop's daughter. The dumb one. Then there was Gina. She was forty-one and blond and a personal trainer. She also had two you-know-whats that were bigger than basketballs. Pop thought they were real and I didn't. Two reasons: (1) She wore T-shirts all the time to make sure you could see them. If she'd had them her whole life she'd be used to them by now and wouldn't have to show them off. That meant they were new. And (2) They were *too* big. Whenever she stood up, I was afraid she was going to tip over.

So this morning by the river we went over his newest list, and that's when I first noticed something I should have seen before. These were the girls he talked about:

Kimberley

Lori

Jodi

Lori

Katharine

Melodie

Lori

Tara

It made me remember the last student/adviser conference I had
with Lori and the things *she* talked about:

> French verbs
> Pop
> Applying myself
> Pop
> The time you took me to see *Aladdin* and promised
> me a magic carpet for my birthday
> Why Carlton Fisk has nothing to do with the Bill of
> Rights (she's wrong)
> Pop
> The steppes of Russia and a B+ in geography
> Pop

Pop scored three Loris and Lori scored four Pops.

And now a lot of other things are starting to make sense too. For
instance, on our way home from Family Nights at school, Pop is
usually so preoccupied that we sometimes wind up in places like
Lechmere or Quincy before he realizes he made a wrong turn ten
miles ago. Meanwhile Lori wears sexy dresses for the next two days
like she's under some kind of a spell, and she doesn't go back to
pants until it wears off. (I *knew* there had to be a reason.) Mama,
how come adults are so dense? Augie's a third their age and he
already figured out he's in love with Andy Wexler, even if he won't
tell anybody yet. Does getting old mean getting stupid too?

I think you'd like Lori, though. She started at Laurents the year
after you left us, and when she found out I didn't have a mother

anymore, she'd take me on special adventures after school, like buying floppy disks for the computer room or napkins for the faculty lounge or *Ivanhoe* for the out-of-luck kids who had to read it. So she kind of feels like family already. But she and Pop are going to need help getting their act together, so maybe you could pull some strings for them too. Meanwhile I'll start working the fix from this end. Doesn't it feel like we're a team again?

I love you,

T.C.

P.S. It was "spurious."

STUDENT/ADVISER CONFERENCE
Lori Mahoney/Anthony C. Keller

LORI: A+ on an English test? You're slipping.

T.C.:   That was a mistake. I should have gotten the gerund question wrong. My mind was on other things.

LORI: Such as?

T.C.:   Alé not looking at me again and Pop's new girlfriend.

LORI: Oh. I didn't know he was seeing anybody.

T.C.:   He only sort of is. Her name is Hannah. She's not as pretty as Alé is but she's in the same ballpark. And she's a social worker. Pop likes her because she likes kids.

LORI: Ah. That's a good sign.

T.C.:   Wait 'til you see our diorama. We already finished a third of the Mall. We're keeping it short like you told us, so it's only seventy-five square feet.

LORI: Did he ask her out again?

T.C.:   Who?

LORI: Hannah.

T.C.:   Don't remember. But I think so.

LORI: *Seventy-five square feet?!?!*

Dear Mama,

After "Casey at the Bat" rehearsals, Andy Wexler asked me to go to The Word Shop Café with him for lemon loaf cake and cappuccinos made out of hot chocolate so that we could practice some more. "I'm not very good at this yet" were the words he used to throw me off the scent—but Andy had a whole other agenda that he really needs to work into conversations a little more casually so that it doesn't stick out like a swollen thumb that just got hammered with a snow shovel. I said, " 'The outlook wasn't brilliant for the Mudville nine that day,' " and Andy answered with, "How did you and Augie get to be brothers?" I said, " 'The score stood four to two with just one inning more to play,' " and Andy said, "Was Augie always so funny even when he was six?" I said, " 'And so when Cooney died at first and Barrows did the same,'" and Andy said, "Augie wears the coolest shirts. Where does he get them?" See what I mean?

But that was only the first inning, because right after " 'But Flynn let drive a single to the wonderment of all' "/"Augie doesn't have a girlfriend, does he?" who walked in but Alejandra and Funny Cool-Shirted Augie. They were there for a production meeting and it would have been weird not to move over and let them sit with us, so we did. But all that happened after that was different combinations of hardly-talking people who were afraid to look at each other. What we really needed was for Puck to sprinkle some of his magic dust on each one of us, even though he probably would have screwed it up again so that I fell in love with Andy while Augie and Alé were getting married. Like my life isn't fire-wired enough already.

If I thought that Alé could at least tolerate me, I might have a shot. But I talked Lee Meyerhoff into showing me the minutes of last week's Young Democrats Club meeting at school, and it didn't exactly score points for my confidence. Like when I said that the National Recovery Act was the only one of FDR's programs that didn't work and Alé said that the National Recovery Act was the only one of FDR's programs that *did* work and that the rest could have been used for landfill. I could be wrong, but I'm pretty sure she's yanking my chain on purpose. *Everyone* knows that the National Recovery Act was bogus from the start, especially me and Alé. Does she really hate me that much??

I've got a plan. And Alé won't even know what hit her. . . .

I love you,

T.C.

The Word Shop
BROOKLINE'S FAVORITE BOOKSTORE

E-Memo From the Desk of
Phyllis Bryant

Anthony Keller, if either one of your fathers knew I was doing this, my big ass would be hung out to dry. So do *not* think it's going to happen a second time. Reread your Constitution. This is illegal.

In the last three weeks she's bought *Profiles in Courage, The Speeches of John F. Kennedy, JFK: The Man and the Myth, The Kennedy Wit,* and—off the topic—*America's Concentration Camps: The World War II Internment of Japanese Americans.* That girl is too damned smart for her own good. Whatever happened to Nancy Drew?

You'd best end up marrying this one. I don't intend to do jail time for anything less.

—Phyllis

From: TCKeller@earthworks.net
To: augie@augiehwong.com

Reminder. You're my brother and we can count on each other no matter what. So when I have a crisis and only you can help, you'll always say yes. Have I got that in the back pocket?

From: augie@augiehwong.com
To: TCKeller@earthworks.net

I hate it when you pull rank like that because I can't handle much more today. Robin Potts broke her ankle and they won't let us put taps on her cast so we're minus our next-to-closing act, I still can't find a splashy production number to bring the curtain down with, and for some reason Dad keeps trying to talk to me about this girl he had the hots for at camp who smelled like Reynolds Wrap. This is SO way too much information.

From: TCKeller@earthworks.net
To: augie@augiehwong.com

I need Robin's spot in the talent show.

From: augie@augiehwong.com
To: TCKeller@earthworks.net

You *what*?! What about "Casey"?! Tick, I swear

to God, if you leave me holding the bag the way Fanny Brice left Flo Ziegfeld in Baltimore—

From: TCKeller@earthworks.net
To: augie@augiehwong.com

Dude, who pissed in your Cheerios?? I'll still be in "Casey," but I want to do John F. Kennedy's inaugural address too. This is life or death. Trust me.

From: augie@augiehwong.com
To: TCKeller@earthworks.net

[DRAMATIC PAUSE.] You're joking, right?

From: TCKeller@earthworks.net
To: augie@augiehwong.com

Okay, so it won't be a commercial success. But at least it'll be an artistic one. And it's got to be our secret.

From: augie@augiehwong.com
To: TCKeller@earthworks.net

Who would I want to *tell*??

Dear Mama,

Anybody who ever thought that Augie was just a lot of hot air really needs to see him in action. He sketched out a backdrop for the show that has a golden sunburst in the middle and stars and sparkles coming out of it (Pop built it for him), he climbed a ladder and aimed all of the lights in different directions and combinations of colors so that each act is lit with its own mood, he figured out the tempos for all of the music and now Mr. Disharoon is afraid to disagree with him (he'd be wrong anyway even if he did), and he designed the programs and posters by himself. All for a hundred dollars.

The kids love him and I can understand why. He's a natural. When he says something like, "Brucie, you can make that funnier if you say it faster" or "Don't rush it, Ricky, we've got plenty of time," he says it in a way that doesn't hurt anybody's feelings but just makes them want to do better instead. I always knew that Augie could push the edge of any envelope whenever he wanted to—but even so, I've never been more proud of him in my life.

Actually, *I'm* the one who's in over my head here. President Kennedy must have really gotten off on the sound of his own voice because once he started talking, he never stopped. And didn't anybody ever tell him about run-on sentences before? Or were those allowed in 1961?

> Let the word go forth from this time and place, to friend and foe alike, that the torch has been passed to a new generation of Americans—born in this century, tempered by war, disciplined by a hard

and bitter peace, proud of our ancient heritage—
and unwilling to witness or permit the slow undoing
of those human rights to which this Nation has
always been committed, and to which we are committed today at home and around the world.

Eighty words and only one period!!

Pop says it's not enough just to memorize the speech, because
anybody can do that. "Tony C, people need to think it's really JFK
on that stage, even if he's shorter than they remember." So first we're
going to Filene's to find a dark blue suit with pinstripes and a light
blue shirt and a red and blue tie (which Pop calls "the standard-issue
JFK uniform"). After that we'll watch the inauguration DVD and
practice. Practice taking a breath where he took a breath, practice
moving my hands the same way he moved his hands, practice
punching the key words exactly like he punched them. Pop says to
count my blessings that Alé didn't idolize Gorbachev instead.

I hit my first home run of the fall today, and I'm pretty sure you
had something to do with it. We play at Amory Park after school
and it's just the kids from the neighborhood divided in two teams
(Grid's Grenades and T.C.'s Titans), but we still draw a pretty big
crowd. My own cheering section is usually Pop (as soon as he gets
off work), Phyllis or Dad (depending on which one of them is
working the register at the bookstore that day), Augie (always),
and Lee Meyerhoff. Lee doesn't care about baseball all that much,
but she shows up anyway just to give me a hard time and to stare
at my ass. She's been doing that since we were eight, even after
it stopped making me nervous (which was originally her whole

point, though only girls would understand why). Lee is also one of my most trusted operatives. Ever since she and Alé started hanging out together, I've been cornering her for debriefings in coatrooms, library stacks, and once in the computer closet.

"Did you tell her I have a cute butt?"

"I pointed her in that direction. She'll figure out the rest for herself."

"Please don't let her know that I used to be your boyfriend. That could create complications."

"How? It was in third grade and it only lasted two and a half hours. She'd get over it."

Today Pop showed up at the top of the fourth and found Dad in the bleachers—sitting with Andy and Augie and trying to make a conversation happen between them like he was a rehab counselor. (Andy is our backup third baseman, so he doesn't always get to start. Which is actually a good thing this season, because whenever he sees Augie in the stands, he starts getting hit by softballs from not paying attention to what he's doing.)

But this afternoon I played like a bush leaguer with a broken leg. Eighth inning, I was still hitless, and there were two out with two men on when I came to the plate for my last at-bat. While Grid Tarbell and Kip Tracey held a mound conference to figure out what to pitch to me, I noticed a little boy sitting by himself behind the third-base line and studying every move I made like I was under a microscope: He watched me adjust my helmet, he watched me take a practice chop, and he watched me knock the mud off my cleats (okay, there really wasn't any mud, but it looks *so* cool when you do that). He was maybe five or six years old, his hair was cut short with a little piece sticking up in front, and he—

"Yo! Keller!"

"Sorry." By then, Kip was back behind the plate with his mask on and Tarbell was winding up like he meant business, so I had to snap out of it fast. But just before Grid let go of the ball, I glanced over at the kid one more time and saw him shaking his head no. I swung.

"Steee-rike one!" *What kind of a gink ARE you, Keller? Even Grandma Lily wouldn't have fallen for a meatball like that!* Pop and Dad cheered me on anyway, so I shrugged as if I'd done it on purpose, then cocked my bat and leaned over the plate like I expected Tarbell's second pitch to be an early dinner. (Pop calls this "an intimidation tactic." So far nobody's been intimidated.) But I couldn't help looking over at the kid first—who was still wearing the same frown and wrinkled forehead and who was shaking his head again. I swung.

"Steee-rike two!" *Dude, this SO isn't the way to get to the Hall of Fame. Not unless you want to hitchhike there.* Well, by now I was a little weirded out. It almost seemed like he was trying to help me. That's when I started wondering if it was really you looking over my shoulder, the way Pop always says you do. So when he shook his head *again*, I watched the third pitch go by without doing anything about it.

"BALL ONE!" *It's just a coincidence! He's not Harry Potter, dude. Get a grip!* I got a grip, all right. Just before pitch number four, the kid and I locked eyes like we were finally in synch, and he nodded his head yes. This time I swung the bat with every muscle I had, and the next thing I saw was the ball clearing left field—just the way Carlton Fisk's did in 1975. And while I was circling the bases and listening to the cheers and watching Dad and Augie and Pop and Andy high-five each other in the stands, there were only two questions on my mind. "How?" and "Who is he?" But when I crossed the plate to score, he was gone.

Was that you, Mama? Or did I imagine the whole thing?

I love you,

T.C.

LAURENTS SCHOOL
BROOKLINE, MASSACHUSETTS

VIA E-MAIL

Dear Ted:

I heard a rumor that the school is going to have to purchase an additional seventy-five square feet of floor space in order to accommodate your latest construction project. Are you insane?! I *know* I made myself clear. I recognized my customarily strident threats. I also saved a hard copy of my e-mail warning you about the consequences. Call it plaintiff's Exhibit A.

How does Hannah put up with you?

Lori

KELLER CONSTRUCTION
BOSTON · GLOUCESTER · WALTHAM

ELECTRONIC TRANSMISSION

Dear Lori:

Assuming there was even a shred of truth to such a spurious rumor (and there isn't—I had to shave twelve inches off the board just to get it through the front door, so it's only seventy square feet), you might want to reserve judgment until you see the finished product. Tony C is downstairs right now playing with the Vietnam Wall and gluing the houses of Congress together (hey, it's about time *some*body did it). Besides, if you really didn't want us to turn in an entire city, all you had to do was have a hamburger with me and you'd have gotten a six-inch Jefferson Memorial instead (without any cherry blossoms either). In hindsight, can't you see how easy that would have been? The defense rests.

By the way—who the hell is Hannah?

Ted

P.S. Did you like the "spurious"? It's my son's vocabulary word this week and it's contagious.

Laurents School
Brookline, Massachusetts

VIA E-MAIL

Dear Ted:

Hannah is the social worker you're dating. Isn't she?

Lori

KELLER CONSTRUCTION
BOSTON · GLOUCESTER · WALTHAM

ELECTRONIC TRANSMISSION

Dear Lori:

No, I think you've been ambushed. But you've got to admire Tony C's style.

We can probably sort all of this out tomorrow night at Legal Sea Foods on State Street (that great street). I'll even meet you there so it doesn't look like a date.

Ted

Augie

Natalie Wood

("I'm a pretty girl, Mama.")

Dear Nat,

Do you remember what happened in between takes on *Inside Daisy Clover* while you were shooting the circus scene? You and R.J. were already divorced, but as you were going back to your dressing room, you saw him standing on a ladder near the set and you realized he'd come over from the soundstage where he was making *Harper* just to watch you work. You didn't say much to each other except "Hi" and "That was great" and "You look good" and "So do you"— but the next thing the headlines knew, you were getting married all over again. It was those couple of words on the ladder that did it.

Even though Andy and I can hardly even look at each other anymore—let alone talk in person—our cell phones and IMs are a whole other story. We've had about 100 ladder conversations of our own, and they keep getting more and more unbearable. Especially when he calls me things like Spidey and Wonderboy and (sigh) Sleepyhead. I've got a Broadway-bound talent show on my hands and I just don't have the time for the mess my life has turned into. In fact:

- I know now that Emma Thompson will not be bearing my child.

- School shower rooms are evil. I can never figure out what to do with my eyes. I mean, they've got to look *somewhere*. AND DOES EVERYBODY HAVE TO BE NAKED?? Thank God Andy's always at least five nozzles away. I'm not cut out for routinely scheduled vascular incidents. (And this doesn't even include the *other* targets suddenly registering on my scope: Kyle. Aaron. Derek. Bobby. Jay-Jay. Zack. Doug. *Holy shit! When did Micah get cute?!*)

- "Mom? Dad? I'm gay." Oh, please. That is like *SO* pedestrian. What happened to my sense of style?! Maybe I'll throw a coming-out party. With a grand entrance down a staircase. "Fasten your seat belts, it's going to be a bumpy night." No. Engraved coming-out announcements.

- I can't stop thinking about him. Andy while I'm brushing my teeth, Andy while I'm pouring Rice Chex, Andy while I'm trying to remember what a pluperfect subjunctive is, Andy while I'm lying in bed at 11:30 at night with my eyes wide open and wondering if sleep deprivation ever killed anybody.

- These are supposed to be the best years of my life. What's *that* all about?

INSTANT MESSENGER

AugieHwong: This is a crisis. I need you to be a supportive brother for a minute.

TCKeller: Oh. Like I'm usually the other kind.

AugieHwong: What would you say if I told you I think I like boys? I mean LIKE boys. I mean the way you like Alé.

TCKeller: "Duh"?

AugieHwong: That's it??

TCKeller: Depends. Who's the boy?

AugieHwong: Andy Wexler.

TCKeller: The jury's out. I need to see how he treats you first. Hey, listen. Even if I don't win a Tommy Award for Best Supporting Actor, this inaugural address may be the most bitchin' thing I've ever done in my life—including the back-to-back home runs in fourth grade. Pop says I'm only ten steps away from the White House already. Just promise me that when I kick the bucket, you won't let them put anything on my epitaph except "Here lies T.C. Keller. Tempered by a hard and bitter peace."

AugieHwong: I promise. And it's "Tony Award," not Tommy. Does everybody else know?

TCKeller: About my epitaph?

AugieHwong: About me being gay, you gink-head hoser-face!

TCKeller: Not everybody. There's a night watchman at a Dunkin' Donuts just outside of Detroit. He doesn't know yet.

Dear Nat,

A year after Tick and I decided to be brothers and our parents realized we weren't kidding, they knew that the sleepover routine was going to get old fast if we kept having to remember to bring things like our pajamas and clean socks and comic books and sleeping bags whenever one of us spent the night. So we both began moving in piece by piece—starting with the comic books. That was six years ago, and now Tick has his own bed in my room, his own dresser and desk and DSL port, his own toothbrush in the bathroom, his own half of our closet, and his own bulletin board for his Red Sox scorecards and the picture of his mom that he just put up last week. Meanwhile, I have all of the same things on *his* side of town, except for my Suzanne Pleshette production stills in place of the Red Sox junk. Whenever I stay over, Nehi sleeps on my bed and not Tick's. He knows who the real diva is.

Our room at Pop's is definitely the cooler of the two. The green-shingled house is almost a hundred years old and plunked halfway down a hill in the middle of a narrow little neighborhood street. There's no front yard and only a couple of feet of grass in the back, but inside it's a whole other century. We've got sliding doors and secret panels, a stone fireplace and wooden beams, and a living room that's big enough for either thirty people or a half-finished diorama of Washington, D.C. But the best part is the original servants' quarters on the top floor, especially after Pop turned two of them into one big hideout for me and Tick. (Since it's the same size as my room at home, Tick and I figure that they must have been really little servants.)

Once Mom and Dad and Pop discovered they'd each inherited an extra eight-year-old without expecting it, they came up with one set of ground rules for both of us, no matter which house we were sleeping at.

"We're sunk," groaned Tick. "Whose idea was it to let them talk to each other?"

"Don't look at *me!*"

The only difference between their two empires is that Mom and Dad gave us thirty minutes after lights out for Galaxy Fighters on the ceiling or View-Master slide shows on the wall, and Pop let us have forty-five before he told us to knock it off and go to sleep. These days, I don't know what we'd do without the extra fifteen minutes.

•   •   •

Tonight's Topics

1. The time Tick's mother sat with him on the Plum Island beach at night and told him to pick out his favorite star so they could name it "Anthony."

2. Going to China with Dad someday to see where my great-grandpa was born and wondering if they have Slurpees there yet.

3. An invisible boy who Tick says he's seen twice at Amory Park and who tells him what pitches to swing on. Either my brother has an overactive imagination or else he needs Ritalin.

4. Why Route 128 is also I-95 South and I-93 North. And how.

5. A hard and bitter peace.

6. Claudette Colbert's childhood. (Tick's usually in the bathroom during this one. Some people have no interest in broadening their horizons.)

7. Plots for getting Pop and Lori together. As in really together. (Has Tick thought far enough ahead to figure out that his adviser would be his stepmother? Or should I let him be surprised?)

8. Where the hell I'm going to find a closing act for the talent show since we're almost out of time and Phyllis didn't go for the idea of stepping in with Sophie Tucker's "Red Hot Mama."

9. Why Rhode Island accents are annoying.

But there's one new addition. Ever since fifth grade, I've been a little worried about what would happen if my brother and I grew up and discovered that we liked the same girl. Would we fight over her? Would we stop speaking to each other? Forever?! But now that somebody's calling me Wonderboy, I'm pretty confident that girls will never be a problem for us as long as we live.

"Are you asleep yet?" I whispered, living on the wild side by pushing the edge of our forty-five minute envelope. From the other half of the dark bedroom, Tick yawned.

"I'm thinking about Alé's eyes when she's trying to be mad at me," he sighed dreamily. Well, since nobody ever upstages me and gets away with it, I stared up at my own part of the peaked ceiling and sighed right back.

"*I'm* thinking about Andy's nose when it wrinkles."

"*I'm* thinking about Alé's hair."

"*I'm* thinking about Andy's smile."

"Alé's sparkle."

"Andy's butt."

"Too much information, dude."

Maybe I was wrong. This is more fun than I thought.

Love,

Aug

The Globe

FROM THE DESK OF   *LISA WEI HWONG*

Honey—

This morning you left your socks in the refrigerator
and put sugar in your orange juice instead of on the
Rice Chex. If Dad and I aren't supposed to notice
the stars in your eyes yet, you need to do a better job
of hiding them.

Home early tonight. Somebody decided to revive
Carousel. (Remember how I warned you about that
one when you were eight?) This won't take long.

> I love you,
> Mom

The Globe

THEATRE

"WHAT'S THE USE OF WOND'RING?"
A NEW *CAROUSEL* AT MERRIMACK
BY LISA WEI HWONG

Nice songs to beat your wife to. Attend at your own risk.

---

www.augiehwong.com
PRIVATE CHAT

AndyWexler: Spidey, I saw your mom on *Boston Today*. How cool is that? Especially when they called her "the Lizzie Borden of drama critics." Does she like *anything?*

AugieHwong: Yeah, she loves *Guys and Dolls*. But she says that's because there's so much wrong with it, you just have to know when to surrender.

AndyWexler: Hey, were you feeling okay today? I was worried. I'm usually the one who falls on my ass, not you.

AugieHwong: I don't kick well in the mud. I always slip.

AndyWexler: There wasn't any mud. It hasn't rained in two weeks. Face it—Spidey's getting old.

AugieHwong: Sorry I kept landing on you. Were you really worried?

AndyWexler: Well, yeah. How were we going to beat Rockport High if our Spider-Man wasn't 100%? How was Brookline going to survive without him?

AugieHwong: Do you want to come over to my house for dinner? You don't have to.

AndyWexler: I'm there. When?

AugieHwong: How about the night after the talent show? I'll be back to normal by then.

AndyWexler: Spidey, don't *ever* get back to normal. Then you'd be just like everybody else.

AugieHwong: Gotta go. My brother is shooting spitballs at my neck. It's the only reason he saves his Slurpee straws.

AndyWexler: Sleep well, Wonderboy.

AugieHwong: U 2.

Dear Nat,

I changed my opening number in the Follies from "Maybe This Time" to Daisy Clover's "You're Gonna Hear From Me." You're lucky the show goes up during one of my Natalie Wood obsessions.

Tech rehearsals went as well as the *Titanic* did. Ricky Offitt accidentally bit the reed off his saxophone in the middle of "In the Mood" and wound up with splinters in his tongue. Tick won't let anybody find out about his secret JFK monologue until the night we go on (our cover story is that he's doing the "Friends, Romans, and countrymen" speech from *Julius Caesar*, which is about as believable as William Shakespeare playing center for the Celtics), so he made up for it by forgetting three verses of "Casey at the Bat." In today's version, Casey came up to the plate with nobody on base, which defeats the whole purpose since who gives a shit whether Mudville loses 4–2 or 4–3? And Stu Merliss thought it would be really funny if he farted on every downbeat. It so wasn't. In the meantime, Alé timed the whole thing to make sure that we came in under an hour, but with all of the screwups we ran longer than the Italian Renaissance. I'm getting out of this business before it eats me alive. No money in my budget for sequins, no crowd-pleaser to bring down the curtain with, AND WHO NEEDED TO SEE ANDY WEXLER IN BASEBALL PANTS A SIZE TOO SMALL??

"Do you want to come over to my house for dinner? You don't have to."

"I'm there. When?"

Oh, God, my heart hurts.

COMPUTER CLASS IS NOT FOR PERSONAL E-MAIL, AND INSTANT MESSAGING IS FORBIDDEN

Subject: URGENT!!!
From: TCKeller@earthworks.net
To: augie@augiehwong.com

1. Lee Meyerhoff just peeked over Andy Wexler's shoulder, and before he could scroll up or turn off his monitor, she pretended not to see "Augie Spidey Augie Spidey Augie Spidey" written in 11 different fonts. You're winning, dude. Now if only I could get Alé to do that (even though the whole Spidey thing is getting a little barfy).

2. Lee says you should NOT meet Alejandra at 1:00 in front of the Lycée tomorrow for the production meeting. Instead show up at 11:30, walk the halls like you belong there, and keep your eyes and ears open. She also says you should try to find the room where they're holding the class in Jazz Dance, because you'll probably find

your closing act inside. "Somebody needs to be dragged out of her shell, whether she likes it or not." Whatever that means. You're lucky you like boys. Girls are so over-complicated.

3. Lee says if either one of us ever tells anybody that she's spying for us, we'll never get out of high school alive. Her reputation is at stake and we're expendable. No matter how cute she thinks we are.

4. Get rid of this e-mail now!

Dear Nat,

I got to the Lycée at 11:30 like my coded instructions told me to, but I still didn't know what I was supposed to be looking for. "Keep your eyes and ears open." Great. I'm having an anxiety attack and Lee Meyerhoff thinks she's Yoda. "Use the Force, Luke." To play it safe I brought my French book along, so that any time a teacher passed me in the hall, I'd lower my head and flip through the pages so they'd think I was looking for "*ou est le bureau de poste*," "*je m'appelle Barbra*," or preferably eighteen conjugations of "I love you, Andy." The Lycée actually surprised me—it looks just like any other school. I was expecting little Eiffel Towers and Arcs de Triomphe on the walls and souflettes in the cafeteria. *"Augie Spidey Augie Spidey Augie Spidey." Okay, I'll admit it's an encouraging sign, but there could be other more normal reasons for it. Maybe he was practicing his typing and that was the first thing that came to mind. I mean, it makes sense. No, it doesn't make sense. Wait. What if he was figuring out how to cut and paste, and those happened to be the first two words he picked to paste? If Lee had kept watching he'd probably have added Jim Cheyunski and Chewbacca. Who am I kidding? He loves me. Now what do I do?* The only thing that snapped me out of my panic was that somebody was playing the *Chorus Line* CD at the end of the hall, and they'd picked the Prince Charming of all showstoppers—"The Music and the Mirror"—to listen to first. So I stuck my head back in my book and *"comment allez-voused"* my way in that direction, figuring I'd hang out and listen until my eyes and ears found what they were supposed to find. Which would have been a plan if I hadn't peeked through the window in the classroom door and suddenly realized that what I *really* needed to learn was how to say "holy shit" in French.

Alé.

Alé in tights and a leotard, belting out the number while a dozen other kids sat around her and watched. *You mean it's not the CD??* No, it was an old lady on a piano, but Alé made her sound like a sixteen-piece orchestra. And that was just the appetizer—because after the last verse was over, she hitch-kicked to her left, lunged into the dance, and turned into Donna McKechnie right in front of my eyes and ears. I've watched the DVD a hundred times from when Donna did the number on TV, and Alé must have seen it too— except that her legs have a photographic memory and mine don't. She didn't miss a step. Not one. *Why hasn't she told me she could do these things? She's more fabulous than I am!* Then she happened to twirl in my direction—and stopped dead in her tracks mid-pirouette when she saw me staring through the window with my jaw hanging open onto French linoleum. Busted!

INSTANT MESSENGER

AugieHwong: If you don't call me back, I'm coming over there and breaking in through one of your stained glass windows. I may be too short for that gesture, but I'm doing it anyway.

AlePerez: The answer is no. I said I'd help you produce and I did. I crunched the numbers, I distributed the posters, I okayed the programs, and I didn't vomit on Stu Merliss. That's all we agreed to.

AugieHwong: Yeah, and that was also before I found out you were Roxie Hart and Velma Kelly combined. You're closing the show with "The Music and the Mirror," so get used to it. I can't believe you've been holding out on me when I've spilled so much of my own blood for art.

AlePerez: Get over yourself. My parents don't know about my secret life and they're not going to. Maybe in another fifty years. And what were you doing there an hour and a half early anyway??

AugieHwong: Look, if I can come out, you can too. And they don't even need to find out about it. Tell them you have a sleepover with one of the girls that night. I'll call them myself and use my Celeste Holm voice. It never fails.

AlePerez: Hello? When did you come out?

AugieHwong: Oh. I forgot to tell you. I'm gay and I love Andy. It's a secret even from Andy. Nobody knows except Tick (although Lee Meyerhoff may be catching on), so please keep it that way until I'm ready to face the media. NOW will you do "The Music and the Mirror"?

No, of course she won't do "The Music and the Mirror." Her mom and dad won't let her because it might upset the Prince of Greenland. Like there's actually a need for Greenland. You can get ice at 7-Eleven.

I'm dressing her in Donna McKechnie Red with a slit down the right thigh, and one way or another I'm getting her mirrors. Screw the budget. What difference will it make when we're fielding nineteen curtain calls? And since she obviously won't cooperate with any degree of professionalism, it's going to have to be done the cheap and tacky way. Like accidentally taking the programs to Kinko's tonight instead of Monday. It's for her own good anyway.

"Alé, I'm sorry. Somehow they got their hands on the copy two days early. How did that happen? Please unlock the computer closet. It's very warm in here and I can't get out."

Watch. I'll probably have to drag her to the Tony Awards too.

Love,

Je m'appelle Augie

The Word Shop
Brookline's Favorite Bookstore

E-Memo From the Desk of
Craig Hwong

Hey, Teddy.

Augie invited Andy Wexler over for dinner next Wednesday. You ought to be hearing about it on CNN any minute. He pulled out Wei's good silverware and embroidered tablecloth four days early and left them sitting on the dining room credenza "so we'll be ready when the time comes." This was in between producing a talent show, rehearsing his song, and executing seven laps of the 500-meter bureau-to-laundry dash to make sure the shirt and pants he'd chosen to wear for My Dinner With Andy were already ironed and didn't have any "dings or loose threads on them."

I still wish he'd talk to us about it, but maybe that's not really necessary after all. I mean, it's so *Meet the Parents* obvious that he thinks he's bringing home a prospective son-in-law for us, what's left to discuss? But why are they so shy around each other? Online, they're practically married. Proof? Last night my kid fell asleep on his keyboard. Again.

Thanksgiving's in less than a month. Wei's bringing
Dan-Dan noodles along with the string bean casserole,
and Phyllis'll only have two of her kids with her this
year—Darius has to stay at Cornell for the holiday.
Figure on us for around 1:00.

Craig

KELLER CONSTRUCTION
BOSTON · GLOUCESTER · WALTHAM

ELECTRONIC TRANSMISSION

Craig—

In case you've forgotten, we were just as shy as our own kids are, even without an Internet. My first date (Charleen Paul, anatomical details classified) lasted four and a half hours and contained eleven syllables. Ten of them were hers. We need to face it—guys are a washout at every facet of romance except for the ability to pop a woody on a dime. But take notes next Wednesday anyway. I'll need to know how to maneuver the obstacle course when Tony C brings Alejandra home for dinner.

By the way, Lori and I had our first date last week. Sort of. She wouldn't agree to go out with me, but she made sure I knew where she was having dinner and grading progress reports so I could bump into her by accident and pull up a spontaneous chair. This is a hell of a lot more work that I remember. How does Augie make it look so easy?

Ted

P.S. Hey, you never did tell me what happened to that chick who smelled like aluminum foil.

The Word Shop
BROOKLINE'S FAVORITE BOOKSTORE

E-Memo From the Desk of
Craig Hwong

Ted:

She grew up to become a handy liner for most toaster-ovens, a convenient means of wrapping leftovers, and an excellent cover for casserole dishes, helping to seal in flavor and freshness.

Craig

FRESHMAN FOLLIES 2003

Tuesday, October 28, 2003

ACT I

"You're Gonna Hear From Me" (*Vocal*) . . . . Augie Hwong

"In the Mood" (*Alto Saxophone Solo*) . . . . Ricky Offitt

"I Feel Like a Dork" (*Bass Guitar and Vocal*) . . . . Stu Merliss

"Heat Wave" (*Vocal*) . . . . Quita Tapper and the Qui-Tettes

"Somewhat Damaged" (*Guitar, Keyboard, Vocals*) . . . .
The Ninja School Dropouts: Kyle Cummings,
Derek Powell, Aaron Bailey

"Casey at the Bat" (*A Play in Verse*). . . . T.C. Keller, Andy Wexler,
Gridley Tarbell, John Siniff

ACT II

Dear Jacqueline,

You might remember that when you and Jack first moved into the White House, you told Tish Baldridge, J. B. West, and anyone else with ears that you had no intention of becoming a public figure. You wouldn't hold press conferences, you wouldn't visit hospitals or charity wards, and you wouldn't take up canasta and make a national spectacle of yourself like Mamie Eisenhower. Absolutely not. You detested the idea of being First Lady.

However, I do seem to recall the photograph of you and de Gaulle taken during the Paris visit in 1961 when you were received like a queen and he was gaping at your Givenchy breasts. And I've watched your televised tour of the White House on Valentine's Day 1962, which I somehow remember as three shots of the East Room and fifty-nine close-ups of Jacqueline Bouvier Kennedy.

Yes, I can see how much you loathed your role as First Lady. But I imagine it probably grew on you before you'd even noticed what had happened.

Augie didn't just run off tonight's program without telling me. He actually had it displayed in the glass case outside the administration office on the same bulletin board where the National Merit Scholarship finalists are posted—guaranteeing that everyone in the building would see it, including visiting dignitaries from neighboring school districts and half the Massachusetts Board of Education. Lee Meyerhoff had to drag me toward the closest exit just so I could cool off to a body temperature of 115.

"You can let go of me, Lee. I'm all right now."

"Then stop hyperventilating!" Our tug-of-war over my left arm lasted only until we turned the corner of the hallway and found my locker pasted over with notes and Post-its. I stopped in my tracks so suddenly that Lee nearly broke her nose when it hit the back of my head.

"What are those?" I asked, alarmed.

"I could be wrong, but they look like notes and Post-its."

"Thanks for your help." Since I had absolutely no idea what they were going to say—except perhaps "Fraud!" or "Get out of town!"—I peeled them off one at a time so we could take turns reading them out loud. And with each successive sentiment, I grew progressively more speechless while Lee grew a little too smug for her own good. *Now I know who told Augie to show up at the Lycée an hour and a half early. Like 120,000 Japanese Americans interned during World War II, I've been shot down by a conspiracy.*

Alé,

Singing *and* dancing? Only J Lo can do both, and look how far *she's* gotten. I'll be there.   —*Renee*

Alé,

Break a leg. I don't know how you can do it. I'd
be so nervous I'd die.   —*Beth*

Alé,

I can't wait to see what you're going to wear. I
hope it's something exotic.   —*Marsha*

Alé,

I'm having a sleepover with three of the kids next
Friday. So far I've only invited Soupy. Let me know
if you can come.   —*Kath*

Alé,

You go, girl.   —*Quita*

So I suppose I can understand how your head might have been
turned by celebrity. Come to think of it, if I'd gone from being a
Washington Times-Herald photographer to having the president of
France drool on me, I might have compromised my morals too—
but at least I would have tried to argue myself out of it first.

First period. I definitely *won't* perform this evening. If there's to
be egg on anyone's face, let it be an omelet on Augie's. This wasn't
my idea.

Second period. Besides, I plan to graduate from Harvard with a
degree in political science and an international post in the diplomatic
corps soon after—which certainly doesn't leave time for anything as

idiotic as prancing half-naked across a gymnasium stage.

Third period. Furthermore, just because I can imitate Donna McKechnie in front of a mirror doesn't mean that I belong in front of an audience. Carlos imitates Ricky Martin in the shower and sounds as if he's being beaten to death by a Puerto Rican street gang.

Fourth period. After I call Mamita with a cover story about a sleepover at Lee's, Lee and I make plans to sneak in to Brookline Village during lunch period and buy a dress for tonight's performance. Something wine red with a slit up the right thigh, though the slit isn't really necessary—Lee's bringing scissors.

Fifth period. I tell Augie that I'm only appearing in the show because I've been pressured into it by my constituency, but that still doesn't mean I'm ever going to speak to him again. Augie pretends to believe me. Anthony doesn't. He stands there with a barely hidden "I *knew* she'd do it" plastered across his face as though it were Clearasil.

Suddenly the thought of Anthony watching me perform tonight makes me very nervous. Why should that matter? He's hardly de Gaulle.

> Fondly,
> Alejandra

INSTANT MESSENGER

AlePerez: I changed my mind. I'm not doing it. Furthermore, you're devious and disloyal, and I'd have to be clinically psychotic to trust you again. Ever.

AugieHwong: You're going to perform "The Music and the Mirror" exactly as written and bring down the house with it. And that, Miss Brice, is the end of this discussion.

United States Secret Service
WASHINGTON, D.C.

Clint Lockhart
Agent

Princess, you're going on tonight—under orders from the United States government. I've been waiting for you to step out of everybody else's shadow since you were six. And I get the first "I told you so."

The Globe

EMAIL FROM   *LISA WEI HWONG*

Dear Alé,

Of *course* you're going to do the show. There's no time between now and curtain to discuss the hundred reasons why, but your father's expectations shouldn't have anything to do with it. Trust me when I tell you that women stopped living under the repressive thumb of a patriarchal autocracy the day Myrna Loy said, "Shut up, Al" to Frederic March in *The Best Years of Our Lives.*

We'll be in the front row.

Wei

Dear Jacqueline,

It looked good on paper, but when I found myself standing in the downstage wing at the top of the show, all I wanted to do was beg Papa and Mamita to move us back to Mexico City, preferably within the half hour. I was so thoroughly paralyzed with flop sweat that an emergency room physician would have thought rigor mortis had set in on Saturday. *Have you lost your sanity entirely?! Who ever said you had talent? And only one run-through with Mr. Disharoon! Dear God, even Chita Rivera knew better than to go on without at least six weeks of rehearsal. And she was Chita Rivera!!* If Lee Meyerhoff hadn't been standing behind me with her hands on my shoulders, I'd have fallen forward like a glass chopstick in a red cotton dress and shattered into a hundred pieces.

Since I watched the first fifty minutes of the show through a scarlet glaze over my eyeballs and a deafening heartbeat in my ears, I vaguely remember only occasional moments of consciousness:

Augie wearing a top hat and tails, carrying a cane and selling "You're Gonna Hear From Me" as though he were a very short Fred Astaire, only much, much cuter.

Stu Merliss grabbing his crotch in the middle of "I Feel Like a Dork," which, compared to his lyrics, was probably his idea of class.

Andy Wexler as "Blake, the much despised"—sliding into first, overshooting the base, and skidding butt-first into the stage left wing. It was the acrobatic highlight of the evening.

Brucie Daniels running six minutes longer than we'd timed him because nobody had counted on the screaming laughter that just wouldn't stop.

Lee's grip on my trembling shoulders growing inexplicably

stronger until I realized that she'd been replaced by Anthony, who began whispering softly into my ear as we moved closer and closer toward the end of the show. "Stop shaking. Augie's been talking about you for forty-eight hours straight without taking a breath. He doesn't even do that for *Madonna*."

Regaining just a shred of confidence—not because I believed what he was saying, but because *he* did.

Watching him calmly walk out onto the stage toward the podium in a dark suit, a conservative tie, and the poise of Mount Rushmore. *Look at that. Not even a tremor. <u>Nothing</u> scares him.* Only then did I vaguely wonder why on earth he was dressed that way in order to recite Marc Antony's monologue.

And that's when I snapped out of it.

Oh, my God, Jacqueline. Nobody was prepared for the Kennedy Inaugural. I don't know how long it took him to learn Jack's moves, his inflections, or the utter conviction of every word he spoke, but when he jabbed the air with a restless right forefinger, the clock instantly turned back forty years. "*We observe today not a victory of party, but a celebration of freedom.*" Then he zeroed in on the "pay any price, bear any burden" passage, and there were actually gasps running through the audience—like an ungrounded electrical current. More than anything else it was the voice. The voice I've laughed at for its overbroad *a*'s and its three-syllable pronunciations of two-syllable words has deepened so gracefully over the last two months, I never noticed how much he's come to sound like your husband. Even *you* would have been fooled. And when he reached the finish, the ovation began while he was still delivering "knowing that here on earth God's work must truly be our own." That's when he turned toward the downstage wing, stared directly into my eyes, and ended on a shrug and a sheepish grin that was pure Anthony.

Oh, if only I could have gone home after he was done. I was already on emotional overload. *He put himself through all of that for you, girl. Get used to it.*

"For our last act, please welcome Alejandra Perez from Mrs. Fitzpatrick's homeroom, who knows that the two most important things in her life are the music and the mirror." GET ME OUT OF HERE!!

I turned to Lee in a blind panic, but without any warning the lights blacked out while Mr. Disharoon played a long drumroll on the piano—and when they came up again, all that was lit was a bank of upstage mirrors that hadn't been there before. *Mirrors. My God, Augie actually got me mirrors!* Maybe they were only the six-foot kind that you can buy at Target for $5.99, but they were mirrors! Ten of them hammered together, side by side, glittering like I doubt they ever did for Donna McKechnie. *Okay, Augie. All is forgiven.* In fact, I was so mesmerized by the dazzling visuals, I completely forgot that I was supposed to be a part of them. Then Lee shoved me out onto the stage bodily and it all came back in a rush—especially after I'd been hit with a spotlight that Augie had insisted on commandeering himself. At that point I stared out into the darkened auditorium at a silent audience that was waiting for me to do something—and that's when I realized I had four choices: I could die, I could scream, I could run, or I could sing. There really didn't seem to be any other alternative.

"Give me . . . somebody . . . to dance for," I began tentatively, wondering whose voice I was hearing. It sounded a little shaky, but since Cassie is nervous anyway when she sings the song in the show, it's *supposed* to come off shaky. (The Perez family knows how to rationalize on its feet, though nobody excels at it the way Carlos does.) Yet it was at that exact moment that I had my first musical comedy epiphany—*such* an Augie thing to do. *What did Ethel Merman say in Gypsy?* "Here she is, boys! Here she is, world! Here's Rose!" And that was all it took. On some level I must have channeled her attitude, because the next five and a half minutes passed in an accelerating blur. *"Play me the music—" Pivot, lunge, hitch kick, you go, girl. "Give me a chance to come through." Anthony watching me from the wings with both of his thumbs in the air. "All I ever needed was the music and the mirror—" A red streak twirling in front of Augie's mirrors. Is that me?? "And the chance to dance—" Center stage again. "For you!"*

Lee told me at the party that when I stumbled into the wings at the end of the number, I was crying. I don't remember that. I don't remember the unending hug from Augie, I certainly don't remember the kiss on the cheek from Anthony, and I have absolutely no recollection of the inexplicable noise coming out of the audience. Lee said it was something called applause. I took her word for it.

Now I know how you must have felt in Paris. I think we both surprised a lot of people—especially ourselves.

Fondly,
Alejandra

LAURENTS SCHOOL
BROOKLINE, MASSACHUSETTS
★ ★ ★ ★ ★ ★ ★

PLEASE JOIN US IN CONGRATULATING
THE WINNERS OF OUR 2003 TALENT SHOW—STARS OF
TOMORROW!

★

FIRST PRIZE
ALEJANDRA PEREZ
★

SECOND PRIZE
ANTHONY KELLER
★

THIRD PRIZE
BRUCE DANIELS
★

BEST DIRECTOR
AUGIE HWONG
★

Dear Jacqueline,

Augie's parents and Anthony's father took us to Bartleby's for our own version of a post-Oscar party, along with Lee—my resident alibi for the evening—and the inevitable Andy Wexler. (Augie "sort of asked" Andy if he wanted to join us, and Andy "sort of said yes.") Bartleby's is smack in the middle of Kenmore Square and it's almost always a safe call for hamburgers, celebrations, and Stevie Nicks—especially on a night like this.

"Say 'Kenmore Square,'" I insisted.

"Kenmaw Sqway-ah," replied Anthony automatically.

"Say 'Nothing could be finer than to be in Carolina.'"

"Nothing could be finah than to be in Caroliner."

"You're doing that on purpose."

"I'm *not*. I sway-ah."

We were out in the middle of the dance floor, and I'm still not entirely sure how we got there. An hour earlier I'd been ready to kiss off my toe shoes for the rest of my life, but shortly after we'd been seated, Anthony looked up awkwardly from a Coca-Cola and blurted, "Um, do you want to dance?"—and there was no way I could have turned him down. It was probably the "um" that did it. Men become vulnerable when they're unsure of themselves, and "vulnerable" is the new "hot." Besides, Alanis Morissette was blaring through the speakers, so I had an entirely different set of reasons for saying yes. Really. I did. (I also pretended not to notice the high five that Anthony and his father exchanged behind my back. They're all such children.) Which is how we wound up shimmying shoulder to shoulder on the parquet floor while I tested the limits of his suddenly legitimate Kennedy accent.

"Just say it!"

"Okay! 'Jackie, I'm out of underway-ah.'"

"You think that's the way they sounded behind closed doors?"

"Oh, right. Like I'm *so* sure she did his laundry." By now, Alanis had given way to k.d. lang, and we were drenched in swirling colored lights. Aqua is a dangerous shade for anyone who doesn't want to get too close to Anthony—it brings out everything it shouldn't: his teal blue eyes, how well he moves his body, how little it takes to make him smile, and how effortlessly he can be charming when he leaves the gray T-shirts and Gap easy fits at home. *Be careful, Alejandra. It's the same old Anthony who all but propositioned you on the first day of school. Don't let the suit and tie fool you. He didn't get us out of the Bay of Pigs mess, he didn't insist on a nuclear test ban, he didn't go after Big Steel, and he most certainly did not promise to put a man on the moon. He's just Anthony.*

Meanwhile, Lee had gotten so fed up watching Augie and Andy staring dejectedly at the D.J. and each other like two sock-hop wallflowers who'd just dropped in from the 1950s, she grabbed them by their respective arms and dragged them out onto the floor with us.

"*Some*body's going to dance with me," she warned them, hiding her game plan behind a frown. Only then did they remember that they had feet. Augie was the better hoofer, but once Andy had loosened up, he got prolific fast. Never give your boyfriend an edge, even when he's not officially your boyfriend yet.

"Dude," insisted Andy, pulling Augie toward him, "show me how you did that." By the third verse, Lee had them boogeying face-to-face and getting used to the fact that they were doing just fine without her—which of course was the whole idea. Only then did she edge over to where Anthony and I were trying out a new lockstep that we'd both seen on *American Idol.*

"Well, *that* only took ten minutes," she mumbled into my ear. "Do you think they realize they're actually dancing with each other?"

"Probably on some primal level," I whispered back. "But don't tell them that." Lee thought about it for a minute before she shrugged in agreement.

Correction. They're not teal blue. They're azure.

Fondly,

Alejandra

INSTANT MESSENGER

AugieHwong: Oh, my God. Three times while we were dancing, our bodies bumped together. Once might have been an accident. Even twice. Not three times. I need to absorb this fast. He'll be over for dinner in 6 hours and 43 minutes.

AlePerez: Anthony actually let me teach him how to say "Alejandra" instead of "Alejandrer." I'm still reeling.

AugieHwong: Is there a rule on who's supposed to say "I love you" first? I know it's probably way too premature, but I want to be ready just in case.

AlePerez: Don't be such a pushover. He

needs to sweat a little. You can't just hand him everything on a silver serving tray like that.

AugieHwong: Look who's talking. Like you didn't fall for Tick's "um" routine.

AlePerez: You know, Anthony wears jackets and ties well. He might want to consider it more often.

AugieHwong: Maybe I'm reading into this whole dinner thing more than I should. What if he's just hungry?

Dear Jacqueline,

I won first prize and fell for a premeditated "um." All in the same evening. I played into his hands as though I were a viola. Whatever happened to my learning curve??

Lee insisted that I accompany her to Amory Park this afternoon, where Haller's Hornets and T.C.'s Titans were evidently battling for the title of Most Appealing Butts. (One glance at the infield proved that the Hornets had no competition, but Lee insisted on keeping a detailed scorecard. She's nothing if not thorough.) I'd begun to wonder if Lee's pathological attachment to boys' backsides deserved a conversation with a counselor, when Anthony's name was announced as the lead-off hitter. As he grabbed hold of a bat and stepped confidently up to the plate, Lee promptly interrupted her own monologue on the Hornet shortstop's crack to lean in conspiratorially and point toward Anthony crouched in the batter's box.

"Does he look as dreamy to you in daylight as he did last night?" she whispered.

"For God's sake, Lee," I retorted impatiently, throwing her off the scent. "Nobody's used the word *dreamy* since 1963!" Yes. He looked as dreamy to me in daylight as he did last night. So what?

That's when I noticed the little blond boy sitting on the ground beside the on-deck circle, who'd been lost in a game of tic-tac-toe he'd been playing in the dirt with a Popsicle stick. But only until he looked up and realized that No. 25 was batting for the Titans. From that moment on, Anthony had his undivided attention. And Anthony knew it too. Before every pitch he glanced back over his shoulder nervously to check on the kid—and he went 4 for 4 while he was at it.

Ordinarily I would have been intrigued. But not today. I'd already been duped by an "um" and I wasn't about to fall for another routine.

Oh, incidentally. Three sixth graders who were present at last night's talent show came up to me between innings and asked for my autograph. I'm glad my fifteen minutes of fame are almost up. I do a lot better in the real world.

> Fondly,
> Alejandra

LAURENTS SCHOOL
BROOKLINE, MASSACHUSETTS

TO: Diana Fitzpatrick, 9th Grade
FROM: William Koutrelakos, Principal
SUBJECT: Frosh/Soph Winter Play

Diana:

Pending approval by the PTA, the Arts Committee has decided on *Kiss Me, Kate* for the frosh/soph winter play. Generally, the tenth graders have first crack at all the parts—but in light of this year's talent show, we'd like to invite Augie Hwong to audition for the supporting role of Bill and likewise ask Alejandra Perez to try out for the role of Lilli Vanessi. Since Lilli is the female lead, we may run into a few political problems with a couple of the tenth-grade parents, but if she performs it as well as she performed in the Follies, nobody's going to complain for long.

Please find out if the kids would be interested. Thanks.

T.C.

Dear Mama,

Augie and Alé got asked to audition for parts in the school play. They're going to be stars but I'm not. I don't care. I didn't really want to be famous anyway. Why didn't they ask me too?? I won second prize! Was it because of the JFK thing? Was it because *Kiss Me, Kate* has something to do with Shakespeare and they were afraid of my *Two Gentlemen of Veroner* accent? What a bunch of cheesers.

The little boy I told you about didn't turn out to be you in disguise after all (even though I still think you had something to do with it). His name is actually Hucky Harper. For three games in a row he sat in the dirt by the on-deck circle and watched me play, and for three games in a row he kept shaking his head yes or no so I'd be able to tell whether to swing or not. It gets kind of weird when you think about it too long. I'm the only guy in Brookline who's hit safely in fourteen at-bats. Even the *real* Tony C never had a record like that. So of course I've gone looking for him after each game to find out how he did it, but he's always gone by then. And since you couldn't see him from Augie's seat in the bleachers because of the green pads on the bottom of the backstop, my brother thought I'd finally popped my top. (To tell you the truth, I wasn't so sure I hadn't either.)

Nehi was the one who proved that I wasn't making up mirages after all. It's not just that he understands most of the things I say, but also that he saw the kid watching me too. So at the beginning of game four of my hitting streak, he hopped off the bleachers where he was playing "Catch the Snicker Snax" with Dad and Pop and trotted over to the dirt by the on-deck circle. At first Hucky looked sort of nervous (even though Hucky's a little bit bigger than a cocker spaniel, he's got smaller teeth), but all Nehi had to do was flop down onto his stomach and put his head in Hucky's lap to prove that he wasn't really a velociraptor in disguise. That made it easy for me to wander down the third-base line while our side was up so I could hang out with my dog. One way or another I was going to find out how the kid knew what pitches I should swing on.

At first I thought Hucky had issues with people in general or with me in particular, because after I plopped down on the ground next to him, I said all of the usual things you say to somebody who you never talked to before.

"Hey."

"What's your name?"

"How old are you?"

"I'm T.C."

"How did you know the second pitch was going to be a fastball over the center of the plate?"

But he never said anything back. He looked up into my face with a kind of half frown as if he'd never seen another talking person in his life, and he tugged on the front of his hair until I thought he was going to pull it out. By then I'd pretty much decided he was flipping me off, until there was a loud bang from Parkman Street where they're putting in a new sidewalk. Nehi and I both yelped at the same time, but Hucky never even noticed—he just yanked on his hair some more and looked like he was wondering why I'd just jumped a foot and a half into the air.

"Hey, are you deaf?" I wondered out loud. Which is probably the dumbest question I ever asked anybody in my life. When all I got back was a different brand of frown, I figured the answer was yes. But that didn't mean I wasn't still up a creek. What do you say to a deaf kid anyway? So I went back to the dugout and watched him play tic-tac-toe in the dirt and not pay attention to anything else until my fourth-inning at-bat—when he looked up long enough to get me to swing on a third-pitch slider that probably landed in Canada (assuming it *ever* came down). Then he went back to tic-tac-toe like all of this was supposed to be normal. By now I needed answers.

For the next three innings I sat next to him near the on-deck circle, drawing pictures in the dirt of things like bats hitting baseballs with big question marks on them, and writing in capital letters "H-O-W?" as if that was supposed to clear up his hearing.

"Do you understand what I'm saying?" I asked for the tenth time.

The look he gave me was the same one I got from Augie when I told him I could never tell the difference between Ethel Merman and Esther Williams.

But at the bottom of the seventh, a lady in a green dress came down from the bleachers and interrupted us before I had a chance to use the sign language I'd seen once on *Gilligan's Island* when a native showed up out of nowhere. (How come visitors never had a problem finding that place, but those seven ginks could never figure out how to get *off* of it?) First she kneeled down in front of him, and then she pushed the tugged-on hair away from his forehead.

"Who's this?" she asked him (meaning me), while she moved her hands and wiggled her fingers at the same time. "A new friend?" (Usually I hate how adults get singy-songy voices when they talk to little kids, but this time I didn't mind. I mean, it's not like Hucky could hear her anyway.) After he shook his head no (NO?!) and did the finger things right back to her, she told me that she was a social worker named Elizabeth Jordan and that she had to take Hucky home to the Boston Institute for the Deaf in the other half of Brookline so he could work on his arithmetic before dinner. She was also the one who filled in some of the blanks that Hucky couldn't answer just with his face and eyes and hands. (1) His whole name is Hucky Evan Harper. (2) He's six. (3) He was born without a father and when his mother found out he couldn't hear, she gave him to the Institute because she didn't know what to do with a deaf son. (4) They put him in three different foster homes that he liked a lot but they were only temporary. (5) Now he lives at the Institute in a big house with other kids, so he's not alone anymore.

I guess I could have asked Mrs. Jordan how Hucky knew what pitches I should swing on, but I didn't want to get him into trouble—or piss him off—if he turned out to be one of those weird little guys who says things like "I see dead people." I have enough on my plate already.

> I love you,
> T.C.

INSTANT MESSENGER

AugieHwong: Andy's family does Thanksgiving a lot earlier than we do, so he says he might stop by on Thursday afternoon and have turkey with us. You think it means anything?

TCKeller: Dude, you can't do this every time you invite him someplace! He's falling for you. Get over it.

AugieHwong: I'm not so sure. Maybe he just wants to hang out with us because he and Dad still have 40 more Patriots games to talk through. Maybe he has weird taste buds and he actually likes Mom's bok choy casserole. Maybe he just wants to see the Fenway Park model that Pop has in the basement. Maybe I'm just the convenient excuse.

TCKeller: How many times did his knee touch yours under the table when he came over for dinner?

AugieHwong: 18. But when we were

alone in my room, he didn't try to kiss me. Instead, he says he's joining the swim team because I'm on it and he's going to audition for the chorus of *Kiss Me, Kate* if I get cast as Bill. That means we'd be together for at least two hours a day in Speedos, tights, or both. Oh, God. I'm being tested.

TCKeller: Aug, if you were 6 and deaf, do you think I could turn out to be your role model?

AugieHwong: Yeah, but only after you learned how to dress better. I got you 4 more Buck Weaver signatures. Is that enough?

TCKeller: No. You owe me 10 for telling Alé about the "um," you lowlife. You set me back 3 weeks with her. Hey, Aunt Babe is taking you and me shopping the day after Thanksgiving for our entry-level Xmas presents. I'm going for the Red Sox DVD. What about you?

AugieHwong: Black contact lenses so I won't have to look at Andy in Speedos or tights.

Dear Mama,

I may not know how to do the sign language thing, but I've definitely figured out how to tell when this deaf kid is cheesed off at me. This afternoon I struck out four times by swinging on what he told me to swing on. And he did it on purpose too. In the army they call it giving false information to the enemy.

It was my own damn fault. Nehi and I got to the park an hour early so I could warm up with Glen Brunswick, who nobody told me threw up during fifth period and had to be sent home. Hucky was already there too, racing around the bases by himself (from third to first, by the way)—but as soon as he saw me, he stopped in his tracks and ran back to the bleachers to sit in the top row with Mrs. Jordan. I don't get it. Do I smell or something?!

I guess that would have been the end of it if there hadn't been a carnival on the south side of the park. Mrs. Jordan had this "great idea" that we should walk the kid to the midway for an ice cream cone. (She may not be deaf, but if she hadn't noticed by then that Hucky had about as much use for me as another spleen, then "dumb" and "blind" were still up for grabs.)

So we made our way across the football-sized field between the bleachers and the red-and-white-striped booths, with me holding Hucky's left hand (Mrs. Jordan's idea, not mine) and Nehi hugging close to his right one. But because he can't hear, nobody was saying anything (not that Hucky would have been shooting off his mouth anyway), and I really didn't see much point in kicking off a bonding experience with Mrs. Jordan. But you know how it gets after a while—when the silence amps up so loud you're afraid you're going to break it by farting? So what kind of a choice did I have??

"Uh—how come he likes to watch me play but other times he runs away from me?" I asked Mrs. Jordan, who had bent down to re-tie Hucky's sneaks.

"Because he's not used to grown-ups who talk to him the way they'd talk to anybody else," she answered back, standing up and steering us toward the midway. "He hasn't figured you out yet." It was the "grown-up" part I couldn't wrap my mind around. I'm not even fifteen. What's the "adult" cutoff for a six-year-old? Nine? Meanwhile, Hucky had turned around to make sure Mrs. Jordan wasn't watching and then he yanked his hand out of mine. Which actually added to my short list of deaf gestures that I know now. Up until then, there was only one kind of Hucky talk I'd learned so far:

Pulling on his hair	"I don't need anybody
and looking in the	to take care of me" and
other direction	"Why are you still here?"

The carnival was like a total bust. He hated the mime, he wouldn't go anywhere near the petting zoo, the ten-foot-high roller coaster freaked him out, and when I volunteered to pop for his ice cream cone and he thumbed it down for a Häagen-Dazs bar (for $3.99!), it turned out he didn't like the chocolate coating after all, so I had to peel it off before he'd eat it. And that was just for starters. Because before Mrs. Jordan told us it was time to leave, I noticed one booth that we hadn't seen before. Balloons. Ten feet ahead of us. Balloons.

Oh Mama, why did I even go there? Remembering you and me, I bought him a purple one and tied the string around his wrist so he wouldn't lose it like *I* did—but instead he spent the next ten minutes trying to get it off, the same way people usually do when they have gum stuck to their shoes. By then I already knew it was going to turn out that way. It's like baseball. When you're on a losing streak, you can always tell what's coming next. Proof? As we were walking back across the field with Mrs. Jordan toward the bleachers and I was figuring that this whole experiment had been a bigger bust than the National Recovery Act, I decided that maybe I could teach him a history lesson he'd never forget. Even if my fingers didn't have much of a clue yet, at least we'd be talking about *some*thing. And nobody fits that bill better than Carlton Fisk.

OCTOBER 22, 1975

The most important date in New England. Ever. And the reason is Carlton Fisk. It was Game 6 of the World Series at Fenway Park, and the Sox couldn't afford to lose it because that would have been the end of everything. So they hung on for 12 innings with a 6–6 tie until Fisk came to the plate with no one on and nobody out. Then Pat Darcy threw a sinker and Fisk sent it over the wall to New Hampshire.

"You should have seen the fans," I said, dropping to the grass and pulling him down beside me. "Holy crap, they couldn't believe it! Want me to show you what they saw?" Figuring I'd better not wait for a "no," I hopped up onto my feet and crouched over a make-believe home plate—just the way Fisk used to crouch over the real thing at Fenway. Then I took some pretend practice chops just to get Hucky ready, and when I was positive I had him holding his breath, I let loose with a swing that even Fisk would have been proud of. I bounced along the first-base line waving my hands like I was yelling "Stay fair! Stay fair!" to the ball—and as soon as it cleared the Green

Monster, I jumped in the air with a "Yes!" and circled the imaginary bases with a victory fist spinning around over my head. Since Nehi's seen me do my Fisk routine 100 times before, he knew enough to be waiting for me back at the make-believe plate so he could jump all over me. That's when I checked over my shoulder to see if Hucky had been impressed. Some impressed. While he wasn't watching, he'd found a sharp rock that he used to cut the string off his wrist, and then just for good measure he killed the purple balloon with it. You could hear the pop in Salem.

By the time we got back to the bleachers we weren't speaking to each other. Mrs. Jordan went up into the stands to talk to Pop, I picked up my glove and lit out to second base, and Hucky took his usual seat by the on-deck circle. For some like totally clueless reason, I thought this meant we were back on track again. Instead he made me strike out four times.

AND I STILL DON'T KNOW HOW HE DOES IT!

I love you,

T.C.

P.S. Hucky sort of reminds me of the day I first came back to school after you were gone and how I suddenly noticed the way Augie was always by himself. It wasn't that nobody liked him, but that he always kept his distance—probably because he knew already that he lived in a whole other world from everybody else. That's why I wonder if Hucky ever feels the same way. Did people treat him like a regular kid or just a deaf one? And why would anybody think it makes a difference?

Student/Adviser Conference
Lori Mahoney/Anthony C. Keller

T.C.:   I need to learn sign language.

LORI: What?!

T.C.:   I mean it. This is really important.

LORI: What about French?

T.C.:   *J'ai besoin de, tu as besoin de, il a besoin de.* Please?

LORI: I don't know if I can get you credit for it.

T.C.:   I don't need credit. I need to learn sign language.

LORI: Maybe next semester.

T.C.:   No, now. You told me to apply myself, so I'm applying.

LORI: Anthony—

T.C.:   Look, I just want to know the alphabet and how to say "How did you know what pitches I should swing on?"

LORI: That's all?

T.C.:   Until next week. So you have a small window.

LORI: Thank you. Incidentally, how's Hannah working out?

T.C.:   Who?

LORI: Your father's girlfriend.

T.C.:   Oh. She's history. The new one is Amber. We think
          she used to model for *Playboy*.

LORI: Isn't that lucky?

Dear Mama,

We have a science teacher at Laurents named Mr. Landey, and since his father is deaf he knows American Sign Language (they call it ASL). So I've been learning it from him every day after sixth period. I've already nailed the whole alphabet, even though I still get D and F mixed up (which isn't really a problem as long as I stay away from "duck"). I also learned how to say "My name is T.C.," "I live near the park," and "How did you know what pitches they were going to throw me?" When I asked Hucky the last one, it took me two hours to get an answer from him—but he finally spilled out a whole mess of hand signals that I didn't understand, so I copied them down and showed them to Mr. Landey the next afternoon. Once he'd watched me repeat them, he said, "He's telling you that he can read lips and steal signs."

Hucky Harper might not play well with others yet, but maybe I can get the Red Sox to hire him as a really short batboy anyway. Whatever works.

I love you,
T.C.

From: TCKeller@earthworks.net
To: AlePerez@earthworks.net

Whenever you decide to start speaking to me
again, you're going to have to learn sign language.
I can teach you myself if you want.

From: AlePerez@earthworks.net
To: TCKeller@earthworks.net

Is there a sign for "um"?

From: TCKeller@earthworks.net
To: AlePerez@earthworks.net

Oh, give it up. It's just a syllable. You liked dancing
with me almost as much as I liked dancing with
you. What difference does it make how we got
there?

From: AlePerez@earthworks.net
To: TCKeller@earthworks.net

You're not really learning sign language, are
you?

From: TCKeller@earthworks.net
To: AlePerez@earthworks.net

I have to. Hucky is Augie 8 years ago, only without

the bok choy sandwich. I *know* I can get through to this kid.

From: AlePerez@earthworks.net
To: TCKeller@earthworks.net

Are you manipulating me again?

From: TCKeller@earthworks.net
To: AlePerez@earthworks.net

Yeah. Try not to fall for it. I dare you.

Dear Mama,

Alé's thrown me a breaking curve that I don't know how to handle. The more time I spend with her, the more I want to be with her and the less I think about kissing her. Pop says he knows why, but that I have to figure it out for myself or it won't mean anything. (Glinda said the same thing to Dorothy at the end of *The Wizard of Oz* about the red shoes, and it pissed me off then too.) Did you and Pop like each other first? Or did you fall in love first? Or did they both happen at the same time? Or did Bucky F. Dent's home run screw up the usual batting order?

Before the game today, I gave Hucky one of my Carlton Fisk rookie cards—worth $22.50 on eBay—and reminded him who Fisk was by jumping up and down and circling a fist over my head. (When Grid Tarbell saw me do it, he thought I was on meds that I'd forgotten to take.) Hucky's eyes popped wide open and he asked me how to finger-spell "F-I-S-K." Then "C-A-R-L-T-O-N." Then "P-U-D-G-E," after I told him that Pudge was Fisk's nickname. But I decided to quit before he turned the card over to read the back. If I'd had to spell "Born in Bellows Falls, Vermont," I'd have missed my next at-bat.

Our last game of the fall is usually just before Thanksgiving, since after that it's too cold to play baseball anymore, even in sweatshirts. Carlton Fisk must have put Hucky in a really good mood, because from his new seat in our dugout he flashed me the whole menu of pitches ahead of time so I could have my pick of the litter: Fastball, fastball, curve, fastball, slider. (I even got to decide after ball two that the next one was going over the fence. And which *part* of the fence.) But I couldn't help wondering about Hucky. Even for a spooky little deaf kid, he has more on the ball than Augie and I did at that age— and after three weeks, I've finally gotten him to talk (sort of). It was a good start, but now our season was over, and chances were that I wasn't going to be to running into him again. And what would have happened to me and Augie if one of us had moved away before we'd had a chance to play Galaxy Fighters on the ceiling?

It turned out that Pop and Mrs. Jordan were having the same conversation up in the bleachers, but with a game plan of their own. So before the last "2-4-6-8, who do we appreciate?" was even half-finished, I was holding Hucky's hand in the parking lot while Mrs. Jordan was trying to unsqueeze her maroon Mazda SUV out of a space that said "Compact Only." (If *I'd* pulled something like that, I'd have been grounded for two days.)

I guess I thought that the Children's Residence Home at the Deaf Institute was going to be like in that movie *Oliver!* with kids wearing rags and sleeping on wooden mattresses and eating slop and getting their knuckles rapped by wide men in triangle hats when they asked for more. So I wasn't ready for the four-floor house on Beals Street with yellow pillars on the front porch and dark green shingles. It looks like something that belongs in either a garden magazine or on the History Channel. Mrs. Jordan said there were six bedrooms for eight kids and four adults. That's almost a hotel.

Hucky was his usual leave-me-alone self in the van, and by the time we'd walked up the porch steps (also yellow) and through the front door, the way he was glaring at me gave me the feeling I was about to be arrested for trespassing. So it was Mrs. Jordan who conducted the guided tour—starting in the backyard with the swings and the hanging tire and the log cabin and the trampoline. (I SO wanted to get out of my sneaks and show off my jumping somersault, but Mrs. Jordan didn't look like the type who'd appreciate it. Think of Luke Skywalker's aunt Beruh. Not exactly a barrel of laughs.) She ended the first part of the itinerary with the living room and fireplace so big that you could practically imagine one of Augie's singing Christmastime movies happening in it.

Once Hucky realized we were heading toward the stairs that led to his room, he raced up the steps ahead of us, ducked inside, and locked the door. What a shock. Not. Mrs. Jordan looked a little embarrassed while she was fishing a key out of her pocket.

"He has trouble trusting new people," she warned me. Duh. You think?

Hucky shares his room with Mateo, a six-year-old with dark hair and eyes who looks enough like Alé to be her baby brother. (Hucky was nowhere to be found, but Mrs. Jordan tried to make me feel better by telling me he was probably hiding in the sheet cabinet again. Like this is supposed to come off as normal.) So between Mateo and Mrs. J, I got the whole inventory:

Hucky's bed by the window (Mateo says that Hucky likes watching it rain and snow at night)

His Luke Skywalker sheets (Mateo showed me how to say "The Force is with you" in sign language)

Hucky's brown stuffed puppy (named Shut-the-Door)

His sock and underpants drawer

His pajama drawer

His shirt drawer

His pants drawer

His closet and his shoes

The little TV/VCR that his last foster parents gave him (before they sent him back)

His bulletin board with his baseball drawings on them (is that me at the plate??)

His desk and his pens and pencils

The Pawtucket Red Sox pennant on his wall

His glove with a baseball in it (he's a *lefty*??)

Mrs. Jordan left us alone by promising that Hucky would come out sooner or later, because he usually did. (If the "usually" was supposed to make me feel confident, it didn't.) For some reason it reminded me of getting Nehi to come out from under the couch at bath time by leaving Snicker Snax on the floor—but this probably wasn't going to work with Hucky. Not that I had to worry. Since he figured that I'd be leaving with Mrs. Jordan, he waited until he could feel the door close, and then he stuck his head out from the sheet cabinet just long enough to catch my eye and freeze in his tracks. *Busted!* Meanwhile, I was preoccupied with Mateo and an obnoxious walking-talking plastic toy called Penguin Pat that somebody really should have melted before it ever got put on the market. But I made sure that Hucky saw that I wasn't paying any attention to him at all, which really began burning his six-year-old ass. (You know this routine, Mama. You invented it. Remember how you got me to come out of the drainpipe?)

Now that I had the home field advantage, he didn't know what he was supposed to do—so he climbed up onto his bed and left an open spot next to him for me to sit down too. I pretended not to notice. *Don't like the 'tude, dude.* Finally, he banged on the night table to get me to turn around, which I did eventually—but not before Mateo and I wrapped up our last round of Penguin Pat. *Take your time, kid. This is working.* So I got up to stretch like I had nothing better to do and wound up plopping down on the bed next to Hucky. By then he was so pissed, his arms were folded, his scowl went up past his nose, and his ears looked like they were going to blow off. But he *still* wouldn't connect eyes with me. Instead, he pulled open his night table drawer, took out a videotape, and popped it into the VCR. *Mary Poppins.* We watched it twice and his attention stayed glued to the screen. Even during Rewind. (Mateo lasted twenty minutes and then went to swing on the tire in the backyard. I got the feeling he's seen this movie a lot more than he's wanted to.) Shut-the-Door was in Hucky's lap, his head was almost-but-not-quite resting on my arm, and he was tugging on his favorite piece of hair—but nothing could have pulled him away from those two English kids and their nanny. So halfway through the second run-through of "A Spoonful of Sugar," I pointed to Julie Andrews and said "You like her, huh?" When Hucky answered back with more hand signals I didn't understand, I knew I was going to have to copy them down and run them by Mr. Landey again.

> MR. LANDEY: He says he's been waiting for Mary
> Poppins to come live with him since he was four.

Mama, I may need some help here.

Laurents School
Brookline, Massachusetts

VIA E-MAIL

Dear Ted:

I just got a call from Elizabeth Jordan, the social worker over at the Boston Institute for the Deaf. Apparently there's a six-year-old boy named Hucky Harper who's secretly expanded his roster of potential heroes to include Anthony Keller (thus providing Mary Poppins with her first serious competition). Now I know why your son is so desperate to learn sign language.

Liz needs me to send a formal note over to the Institute vouching for Anthony's character and his sense of responsibility—and since Anthony and his brother are all but biologically inseparable, I'm including one for Augie as well. Let me know if anyone else should be added to the short list of junior guardians who'll likely be hanging out with the new Batman and Robin.

Ted, please make sure Anthony realizes that this isn't a game you give up on after it gets old, or something you do to get the girl. According to Liz, Hucky hasn't had an easy time of it. His mother put him up for adoption at birth, but since the pendulum is still stuck on "Too Many

Deaf Kids/Not Enough Available Parents," she's only been able to manage three short-term foster situations for him. For the past year he's opened up to practically nobody—until he began communicating with your son (granted, via tactics that would have gotten them both bounced off the 1919 White Sox). So he doesn't need to lose anyone else from his life whom he expects to have around for a while. Especially Mary Poppins and Anthony.

Incidentally, did you know that you're dating a former *Playboy* model named Amber?

Lori

KELLER CONSTRUCTION
BOSTON · GLOUCESTER · WALTHAM

ELECTRONIC TRANSMISSION

Dear Lori:

How do you know I'm not? While I'd prefer moping around like a lost puppy until the next time I "accidentally" run into you while you're proofing progress reports alone in Southie, that wouldn't be mortal of me. And incidentally, I'm dropping off my son's diorama on Monday. How big is your loading dock? (I'm kidding. Marginally.)

Tony C understands what's at stake here. That's what happens when you grow up without a mother. Besides, you should have seen the two of them from where I was sitting in the bleachers—my son pretending he was Carlton Fisk and Hucky pretending he didn't care. (Not for publication, but Tony C swung on the wrong invisible pitch. We don't need to tell him that.) And I think the lifelong Anthony Keller–Augie Hwong Fraternal Confederacy is enough proof that these kids know how to stick to anything and anyone they care about. But just to play it safe, add Alejandra to your bill of lading. Her resistance to Tony C is collapsing under its own weight.

I have two tickets to the Celtics-Clippers game on December 9. If I give you one of them in advance, we can run into each other spontaneously again. It's a small world.

Ted

P.S. We're having about twenty people over for Thanksgiving on Thursday, so there'll be enough food for the entire Colonial Army. You can always pretend that you're just stopping by to wish two of your students a happy holiday—or to preview the diorama so you won't need pulmonary resuscitation on Monday.

P.S.2. I didn't realize what a bad influence you're turning into until they wrapped up Tony C's last baseball game of the season with the traditional "2-4-6-8, who do we appreciate?" Would it have been appropriate to point out that it should have been "2-4-6-8, *whom* do we appreciate?" and then make them do it all over again?

LAURENTS SCHOOL
BROOKLINE, MASSACHUSETTS

VIA E-MAIL

Dear Ted:

Yes.

Lori

Augie

DIVA OF THE WEEK

Lauren Bacall

("You know how to whistle—don't you, Steve?")

Dear Betty,

Leave it to the uninitiated to think that "Lauren" is your real name.

The bad news is that my brother is forcing me to take sign language with him after school in case I ever need to have a conversation with Hucky Harper, who didn't turn out to be a delusion after all. This is the price I pay for making Tick listen to *Cabaret* with me in 1999. When he said, "You owe me big time" after the sixteenth replay of "Don't Tell Mama," I knew he wasn't kidding. The good news is that even though Mr. Landey never saw *All About Eve*, he still taught me how to sign: "Fasten your seat belt—it's going to be a bumpy night." I might as well get the kid started in the right direction. He's six years old, he looks exactly like Tick did when we first met, and he probably doesn't know who Bette Davis is either. If you can imagine.

What was it like when you and Bogey first set eyes on each other? Did you know right away? Because I think that's what's happening to me and Andy. I mean, as long as he was calling me Spidey and Wonderboy, how could I not call him Bright Eyes and Lightning Lad? (I think I'm going to switch to Aquaman once he joins the swim team.)

So far, these are the facts:

1.   When we went to the movies together, I waited in line for our popcorn and Slurpees so he could go inside to find seats. Then he called me on my cell phone from the tenth row center and said, "Hurry up. It's *lonely* in here."

2.   When he came over for dinner, he paid as much attention to my parents as he did to me. He helped Mom make the chin-chiang salad, he asked Dad to show him a couple of t'ai chi moves, and then they watched the first inning of the Pats game together. If you didn't know any better, you'd swear he was auditioning for the role of their son's fiancé and they were ready to cast him.

3.   I can't stop staring at the dimple in his chin and if I think about touching it one more time, I'm going to buy a bag of hammers and break all ten of my fingers.

4.   We both agree that if there's really a Hell, all they feed you there is cilantro and calves' liver.

5.   I've gotten into the habit of watching him across the classroom during third-period American history, when he's least likely to get bored and catch me staring. I love the way his eyebrows squish together whenever he doesn't understand something and how he runs his fingers through the hair on the back of his neck if his hands get fidgety. I also love the way his ears blend into his cheeks without any kind of a dividing line (how come I never noticed ears before?) and how wide his eyes open just before he sneezes. I guess there are plenty of handsome guys walking around if you just take the time to look, but if any of them are more handsome than Andy, they sure don't live in Brookline. I really need to be more careful, though. Once when he was wearing a baby blue sweater, I left the real world so far behind that when Ms. Reed asked me a history question, I gave her an algebra answer. These days, Tick allows me five minutes of Andy-gazing before he shoots a spitball at my neck to snap me out of it.

6.   He's sometimes afraid to sit too close to me, and I love that. And when he gets flustered, he makes every part of me light up. Yesterday at The Word Shop Café, Kathy Fine was having trouble remembering all of the words to her *Kiss Me, Kate* audition song, "I Enjoy Being a Girl." So I routined it for her right there and even taught her the second verse just for the hell of it. And when I sang, "I turn and I glower and I bristle, but I'm happy to know the whistle's meant for me" right to Andy, he blushed.

7.   Ever since Lee Meyerhoff snaked us into dancing together the night of the talent show, we haven't been able to stop talking

to each other: on our cell phones, online—everything but face-to-face. No topic is too out there. It can be cornbread in the cafeteria, the potholes on Longwood Avenue, or whether farts float in zero gravity. But no matter what we're discussing, every night before we hang up or log off, the last thing he says to me is "Sleep well." Which only keeps me awake until 4:00 in the morning while I play those two words over and over in my head. Nobody ever told me to sleep well before.

8.   The only thing we never talk about is us.

Okay, I'll admit that the greatest romances of all time probably started like this. But lifelong friendships start that way too, and I'm not about to make a wrong move and scare him off. I love Andy with my whole heart (oh, my God, I actually *said* that??), and if I have to settle for having him in my life as just a buddy, I'll take it.

Remember what Judy Garland said at the end of *In the Good Old Summertime*? "Psychologically, I'm very confused—but personally, I feel just wonderful."

Here's looking at you, kid,

Augie

> **INSTANT MESSENGER**

AugieHwong: Andy's coming to auditions with us on Tuesday for moral support. I've gone through the *Kiss Me, Kate* CD and decided I'm going to sing "So in Love With You Am I" while I'm staring at him in the front row. If he runs screaming into the night, I can always claim I was

just nervous and knew he'd give me
confidence. If he doesn't, we ought to
be back from our honeymoon in time for
rehearsals.

AlePerez: "So in Love With You Am I" is a
woman's song.

AugieHwong: And your point would be?

AlePerez: *I'm* singing it.

AugieHwong: I don't suppose they'd let
me try out for Bianca and cast a girl to play
Bill, do you? Or at least give me "Always
True to You in My Fashion"?

AlePerez: You're singing "Too Darn Hot."
You're also going to be wearing royal blue
tights that Lee Meyerhoff is lending you
and a gorgeous red and gold sash that's
coming off the end of a hideous red and
gold tablecloth that President Fox gave
Mamita in Mexico.

AugieHwong: This is all about getting
even with me for blackmailing you into the
talent show—*isn't* it?

AlePerez: Oh, honey, I haven't even
warmed up yet. And by the way—you're
coming over to the Lycée with me so Mrs.
Salabes can teach you a basic tap break
for the bridge of the song. If you want that
part, you'll do as I say.

AugieHwong: By the way. Making somebody you love blush is a *good* thing—isn't it?

AlePerez: Nine times out of ten.

AugieHwong: Thanks for the non-answer.

AlePerez: You're welcome.

Dear Betty,

You're not the only only one who knows how to pick her scripts well.

THANKSGIVING AT TICK'S

A Play in Two Acts

PROLOGUE

I stay at my brother's house on Wednesday night, the way I always do. Before we go to sleep, we lie in our beds and go over a list of candidates for the new things we're grateful for this year, since Pop is going to ask everybody to name one of them when he starts carving the turkey.

AUGIE'S LIST

Andy

Alé

Judi Dench's interview in *People* magazine

Directing my first show

Getting asked to audition for *Kiss Me, Kate*

TICK'S LIST

Alé

Hucky

Augie coming out

American Sign Language

A hard and bitter peace

ACT I

By the time Tick and I have set the table and changed out of our pajamas into our good clothes, Pop's already lit the fire in our big stone fireplace—and just as the house is beginning to smell like turkey, Aunt Babe (in her usual navy blue) and Aunt Ruth (in her usual yellow) show up from Washington. (They would have come in last night, but Aunt Ruth got out of Congress too late.) Since Aunt Babe made herself the family archivist years ago, she pulls out her digital camera and begins snapping before she's even taken her coat off. In the meantime, Aunt Ruth makes me and Tick sit on the ottoman together while she opens up a Bloomingdale's Big Brown Bag and gives us our Thanksgiving presents. We nearly don't survive the shock.

"Holy crap!" we gasp, practically at the same time, with silver wrapping paper still stuck to our fingers. "iPods!!" Aunt Babe warns us not to confuse them with our Christmas presents, which we start getting tomorrow. Even after eight years, it's all still a little overwhelming, especially for a kid who inherited this half of his family by default. *Andy's not here yet. But that's okay! His family is probably just sitting down to dinner.*

Phyllis comes through the front door with a fruit compote, a casserole dish, and two of her kids: eleven-year-old Jeremy (who immediately goes outside with Tick and Nehi for a game of catch—another tradition), and eight-year-old Chloe (who's actually heard of George Gershwin). Then she takes over the kitchen by chasing Pop out of it.

"The only thing a man understands about an oven is how to clean it," she says, shooing him away. "Now go and watch football." *Andy ought to be starting on seconds. It won't be long. Assuming he meant what he said and wasn't just being casual. I don't do "casual" well. He ought to know that.*

Mom and Dad pull into the driveway with Grandma and Grandpa Der and Grandma Lily at the same time Uncle Piersall and Aunt Donna get there with their kids, Cy Young and Dennis Eckersley. Mom hands over her Dan-Dan noodles and String Bean Special to Phyllis, who's become sort of the commander in chief of anything that has to do with food. *Okay. Andy's probably getting into the car as we speak. Unless he's having second thoughts. Or fifth ones.*

Lori stops by to wish me and Tick a happy Thanksgiving, and Pop takes her to the garage so she can see the diorama that the three of us finished last night. (They're out there for twenty-five minutes. Don't tell me they've been discussing the Treasury Building for *that* long.) Lori says she's really got to go, but she says it at the same time she's taking off her coat and helping Pop set an extra place at the table. Tick's right. Boys are like *so* much easier to figure out than girls.

Tick and I decide it's a good time to call Alé to wish her a happy holiday. She doesn't sound like she's having all that much fun. They've made her wear a formal dress, the only thing on their TV is CNN, and Carlos brought home a visiting delegation from Nigeria.

As soon as Tick leaves the room, I let myself get neurotic over the phone. *"He despises the earth on which I walk. Otherwise why isn't he here yet?" "Because he only said he might come over. Snap out of it. It's Thanksgiving. Give yourself the day off!!"*

Phyllis steps out of the kitchen and hands us our assignments:

Augie	mashed potatoes
Tick	noodles
Aunt Babe	string bean casserole
Aunt Ruth	gravy boats
Lori	three-bean salad
Dad	yams
Mom	open the cans of cranberry sauce
Uncle Piersall	stuffing
Jeremy	biscuits and butter
Cy and Dennis	do *not* shoot Smurf balls into the cornbread
Dad	turkey
Chloe	put our Thanksgiving CD into the changer
Grandma and Grandpa Der	exempt: over 65

Grandma Lily and Aunt Donna	previously drafted for pie prep
Nehi	stay off the table

Then I give myself one additional task:

Augie	Look out the window again to see if anybody's pulling into the driveway.

By the time we've all been checked off Phyllis's list, everybody is seated. Everybody. Eighteen people, a cocker spaniel, and one empty chair. Immortalized for all time when Aunt Babe's camera flashes. I've never felt worse in my life. Oh, Andy. Where are you? *Color him gone.*

"It's still early," Tick whispers into my right ear. "He'll *be* here." *No, he won't. Cry me a river.* After we bow our heads, Pop says grace. This is a prayer we all worked on together so that no matter who joins our family, there won't have to be any rewrites.

> On this Thanksgiving Day, may we each and every one of us remember the many blessings we've received for ourselves and the many blessings we've tried to bestow upon others, and hold close to our hearts those we love and cherish—in life and beyond—and those we shall come to love and cherish before our next Thanksgiving together.

After the "amens" and the "l'chaims" and the "when do we eats," Pop kicks off the Thanksgiving ritual: As he begins to carve the turkey (Nehi always gets two preliminary slivers first), he points to Phyllis and asks her what she's thankful for. But before she can answer, two things happen: (1) the doorbell rings, and (2) my heart smashes headfirst into my sternum. *Let it be him let it be him let it be him let it be him.* Mom gets up to answer it and I can hear a voice mumbling from the hall. Meanwhile, I go through a fast inventory in my head: *UPS, FedEx, and the post office don't deliver on Thanksgiving Day. So who else could it be??* When Mom comes back into the living room, she's got an arm around Andy—who's wearing a suit and carrying a bowl of homemade cranberry jelly. Tick elbows me with an "I told you so" sharp enough to break a rib, while Dad introduces Andy to the rest of the family.

"Uh—sorry I'm late," he mumbles, staring down at the floor. "My father's car wouldn't start." As he slides into the chair next to me, we have just enough time for a "Hi, Augie," "Hi, Andy" before Phyllis tells us that she's thankful for healthy kids and (with a nod to Andy) cranberries that don't come from Ocean Spray. Then it was *our* turn.

"Andy and Augie?" asks Pop, coming around the table to stand behind us. "What are *you* grateful for?"

"New friends," says Andy, glancing over at me with a shy smile.

"Doorbells," I blurt automatically while the whole table breaks into laughter at the same time. *Does everybody know??*

* * * * *

The dinner plates have been cleared and we're waiting for

three different kinds of pie. Tick and I are arguing about whether wishbones only count if they come from turkeys or whether chickens rate too, at the same time Dad and Andy are reviewing the backfield for today's Packers game over a bowl of carrots. By complete accident, Andy's right hand bumps against my left one down between our chairs, and all of a sudden the fingers tangle up together. Then it hits me. *Oh, my God! We're holding hands. The two of us. Under the table. Me and Andy Wexler. And _he_ started it!* Okay, maybe it's just for a second, and maybe that's only long enough for one quick squeeze—but it's out there, and nobody'll ever be able to take it back. *HOLY SHIT! WE'RE ACTUALLY HOLDING _HANDS_!! ON _PURPOSE_!!*

ACT II

I know there must have been more things that happened after 4:32 p.m., but who remembers? It was like the anesthetic I got before my appendix operation, except it lasted six hours and there were only dim flashes of reality: Tick took one of our chocolate turkeys over to Hucky, and the Dolphins won 40–21. People ate, people left, Andy and I avoided eyes, and Dad drove the Hwong family home. Next thing I knew it was dark and I was in bed. So I dropped a Barbra Streisand CD into my Discman and played myself to sleep with a song I used to hate. "He Touched Me." It actually isn't half as cheesy as I thought it was.

Love,

Augie

INSTANT MESSENGER

AugieHwong: When he made sure our fingers were locked together, I figured it probably qualified as hand-holding.

TCKeller: Nothing gets by you, does it?

AugieHwong: "It wasn't accidental, no, he knew it." I wonder how Barbra Streisand knows Andy Wexler.

TCKeller: Dude, you'd be like so easy to barf on. I'm worried about Alé.

AugieHwong: Don't be. Maybe we had to drag her by the hair into the talent show, but notice how she didn't exactly put up a fight when they asked her to audition for *Kate*. Now she's snapping orders at me like she's Ethel Merman on speed.

TCKeller: How do we get her away from her family long enough for her to figure out that she doesn't need prime ministers or Imelda Marcos half as much as she needs *us*?

AugieHwong: It's a two-part program. I got her onstage and you were supposed to make her fall for you. (Can you spell "slacker"?) Because when you're in love, you can be talked into anything. Trust me. I'm an authority on this.

TCKeller: Hello? I'd have gotten there first if some gink hadn't kept putting roadblocks in my way. (Can you spell "um"?) BTW, Hucky had a pretty lousy Thanksgiving, even with our chocolate turkey. Since he's the littlest kid there, they let him win the wishbone tug. Then he spent the rest of the afternoon looking out the window and waiting for Mary Poppins to come live with him. She didn't.

AugieHwong: Ouch.

TCKeller: Tell me about it.

Dear Betty,

When Aunt Babe tells us she's taking us out to buy our first couple of Christmas presents, she doesn't mess around. But there are two rules that drive our parents crazy in the don't-spoil-the-kids category: Rule 1: "If it's something you want, it's a Christmas present." Rule 2: "If it's something you didn't ask for but that I think you should have anyway, it doesn't count." Technically, Tick's Red Sox DVD and "1918 World Champions" sweatshirt clock in as genuine stocking stuffers, just like my Betty Hutton CD and the *Inside Daisy Clover* poster do. But the shirts and the slacks and the bomber jackets and the blue and gold wristwatches and the inkjet color printers don't. It's a good thing she rented a car. We never could have gotten all this stuff onto the Green Line.

Aunt Babe used to live five blocks away from Tick until Aunt Ruth was elected to the House of Representatives when we were eight. After that they had to move to Washington—which is only a short shuttle flight, but it's still too far when you miss somebody. Tick took it harder than I did because Aunt Babe was the one who stepped into the mother part of his life after his mom died—but we promised each other that when we grew up, we were going to buy an apartment near Congress so that we could have everybody we loved in our lives whenever we wanted, and not just on holidays.

The first time I met Aunt Babe was right after Tick and I decided to be brothers, which was the same week Aunt Babe opened her own law practice downtown. Pop took us to her office-warming, and to tell you the truth, I didn't know what to expect. The only lady lawyer I'd ever heard of was Katharine Hepburn in *Adam's Rib*, and you know how intimidating Katie could be. But I didn't need to worry. It was a pretty big party with lots of important people there, but when Aunt Babe saw us step out of the elevator and onto the polished wood floors of the reception area (*great* place to sock-surf, by the way), she left the group of senators she was talking to and came toward us with her arms open wide. Guess who got the first hug?

T.C. AND AUGIE—SHOPPING TRIP

1. Breakfast at the Brookline Café (where, incidentally, Bobby Kennedy used to eat when he was attorney general)
2. Pick up Hucky at Children's Residence
3. Red Sox Store
4. Tower Records
5. Filene's Basement
6. Lunch at Pizzeria Regina

7. Cinema Collectibles
8. Faneuil Hall
9. Best Buy
10. Toys "R" Us
11. Dinner at Legal Sea Foods, Park Plaza
12. Surprise

Hucky was a last-minute addition because he's not even all-the-way sure of Tick yet, let alone strangers. My brother was right. Communicating with him was like trying to get a reaction out of the drapes.

"Honey, did anybody ever tell you that if you were any cuter, you'd be a cartoon?" asked Aunt Babe, buckling his seat belt and re-tying one of his sneakers.

Silence.

But this is a tough group to stay shy around, and Hucky was no exception. Everything turned around at lunch when he stole an anchovy off my brother's plate, realized what he'd gotten himself into once he'd started chewing it, and then got angry at the plate for fooling him. Literally. I mean, he stood up, stuck out his bottom lip, put his hands on his hips, furrowed both eyebrows together, and glared at it. This was how Aunt Babe and I learned that it's not a good idea to laugh when you have a mouth full of food, because we sprayed everything within range. (The people in the next booth *hated* us.) You could tell that Hucky didn't know whether to be flattered or insulted, but as soon as he realized he was in his own spotlight, he figured out pretty quickly how to play a room.

"Show me your mad face," Aunt Babe kept begging.

No.

"Please?"

Okay. Here. I'm doing it. Now laugh again. We did. I mean, you couldn't exactly help it.

During dessert Hucky taught us how to say "mad face" and "show me" in ASL, and we even found out that there's a sign for "gink"—probably the same one as for dork, cheeser, and anything that ends in "hole." Actually, Tick's gotten pretty fluent with his hands. I couldn't tell you for sure how he's managing to pick it up so quick, but after you've seen how Hucky stays glued to his side while they're walking down Congress Street together, it isn't too hard to understand the why. Especially from my brother's point of view. Does he have any idea how much he and Hucky could have been six-year-old twins? Or is that my job to notice these things? They'd have shared the same way of pretending that nothing's wrong, and they'd have both lived in the same bubble that nobody else was allowed inside of. It may just be a coincidence, but most of what Tick talks about these days is his mother. And it doesn't make him sad anymore either. Yesterday he told me the story about the time she wanted to surprise Pop by making lobster bisque for his birthday but didn't realize when she got them home that the lobsters were still alive. When she came back to the kitchen after a long phone call, they were gone. Pop found one of them behind the dryer, Tick turned up another one in the geraniums, and his mom used to say that the third one was still growing somewhere in the basement. I feel like I know her the same as I would have if she'd always been a part of my life.

Once we'd discovered his mad face, Hucky was the center of

everybody's attention for the rest of the afternoon—and he played the part like he'd been waiting to do it all his life. *Hasn't anybody appreciated this kid before? How could they not??* Whether we were chasing him through Faneuil Hall while he tried to hide-and-seek from us, or watching Aunt Babe plop him onto a shiny blue bicycle at Toys "R" Us, or seeing his face light up like a supernova when she bought him a production shot of Julie Andrews as Mary Poppins at Cinemabilia, you had to wonder how he got to be such a regular six-year-old without being able to hear. Or maybe being deaf doesn't matter after all.

"Who's your favorite friend at school?" I asked, while Tick translated.

"My 'loving girl.'"

"What's her name?"

"I don't know."

"Who *is* she?"

"She sat down next to me on the bench. So I kissed her on the head and then I farted."

After twenty-one purchases and dinner at Legal Sea Foods (where we all gave our crab legs to Tick and Hucky so they could fight each other with them), the "surprise" at the end of Aunt Babe's list turned out to be tickets to a preview of *Hello, Dolly!* at the Harborside Arena—which she somehow managed to keep a secret from us right down to the wire.

"You'll have to guess," she insisted, turning right onto Saint James Avenue.

"Movies," said Tick.

"Fireworks," said Augie.

Ice cream cones! signed Hucky, once he'd figured out what was going on. We'd already snaked through half of Boston's curvy downtown streets—still clueless—when Aunt Babe suddenly yanked the steering wheel to the right and pulled our green Hertz Saturn into the theatre's parking lot. Out of four people in the car, one of us went nuclear.

"Oh, my God," I shrieked, when I saw the marquee. Aunt Babe winked at me in the rearview mirror (letting me know that this was a special present from her to me), while Tick and Hucky turned to each other in the backseat.

What's going on? signed Hucky. *Where's my ice cream cone?*

"Sorry, dude," groaned Tick in reply. "It's one of my brother's musicals. But we can go to sleep in there if we want to." I'm pretty sure that Hucky understood the "go to sleep" part.

Hello, Dolly! turned out to be the perfect ending to a day that deserved it. The Arena is one of the biggest theatres in Boston, but Dolly Levi didn't have any trouble filling either the stage or the house. The sets were pink and white, and the lights made everything look like cotton candy and Valentine's Day. But I think I got my biggest kick watching Hucky. He was too short to see anything from his seat, and he squirmed out of Aunt Babe's lap (Hucky doesn't do laps), so he stood between me and Tick for the entire performance with his eyes riveted to the stage and his mouth hanging open. Especially during the title song in the second act—with thirty waiters dancing around the orchestra pit and Dolly coming down that long red staircase—when he actually stood on his tiptoes in order to get a better view.

Look! Look! he signed to Tick.

"I know, I know," mumbled my brother. "I've lost you to the Dark Side." When the nine curtain calls were over and the house lights finally came up, the vote was pretty unanimous: three raves and one favorable. Aunt Babe told us how impressed she was, Hucky finger-spelled *W-O-W*, and even Tick had to throw in the towel.

"Not bad," he conceded, as we were making our way up the aisle. You have to understand what this means coming from my brother, who thinks Rodgers and Hammerstein is a furniture store. "'Not bad'—T.C. Keller" is an ad quote that would have kept it running on Broadway for twenty-three years.

And Aunt Babe had planned it all just for me.

I mean it, Betty. As soon as I'm old enough to have a driver's license, Tick and I are moving to Washington.

As time goes by,

Augie

The Word Shop
BROOKLINE'S FAVORITE BOOKSTORE

E-Memo From the Desk of
Craig Hwong

Hey, Teddy.

You know you've earned your wings as a father when you drop by your kid's bedroom to kiss him good night and on your way out the door he stops you cold with "Dad? Is love supposed to hurt?" I'm not sure if there's an easy answer to that particular riddle (yes, I am— there isn't), but hearing that question from my son is the reason I wanted to be a parent in the first place. How did he know?

So I asked him to tell me all of the things he feels when he thinks about Andy, and I'd tell him what it was like when the same roller coaster got ahold of *me*.

"I'm afraid he doesn't love me back." (That was Alene. And she was worried that I didn't love her either. Yikes! Kids.)

"If he doesn't answer my e-mail right away, I panic." (Marta. She'd always wait a day to return my phone calls, and it was always deliberate. She knew how to play me like a 1959 Buddy Holly Fender Stratocaster.)

"He's going to get tired of me." (Laura. Actually, all she got tired of was me whining about how she was going to get tired of me. That's why she started dating Eduardo Cué.)

All he really needed to hear was that he's not the first kid who's had to go through this. (Isn't that usually what it takes?) By the time I came back from the bathroom with his glass of water, he was already out like a light. And while I was tucking him in, I realized that we'd never had the "I'm gay" conversation. Has this generation finally made it superfluous? If only.

Anyway, thanks for walking me through the minefield. When Alejandra holds T.C.'s hand for the first time, I'll brief you on the running order.

Craig

P.S. I saw Lori accept the Celtics ticket when you handed it to her, which probably qualifies me for the witness protection program if she ever finds out. Suggestion: Don't pull the usual sneaking-down-to-the-empty-courtside-seats-at-halftime routine. She doesn't strike me as a willing co-conspirator in that kind of larceny.

ALEJANDRA PEREZ

Mr. Fred Hoyt
Assistant Superintendent
Manzanar National Historic Site
Independence, California 93526

Dear Mr. Hoyt:

I read with interest an article in today's *Boston Globe* regarding the restoration of the Manzanar National Historic Site as a permanent memorial to the internment of 120,313 Japanese Americans during World War II.

While I appreciate the plans for a museum, the display

of some of the camp's artifacts, and a reconstructed barracks and guard tower, don't you think it's all perhaps a little bit gloomy? These people weren't exactly passive victims, you know. Even with guns pointed at them by their own military, they built a community that included a K-through-12 school system, fully equipped hospitals, professional dance bands, lavish productions in their new auditorium, and baseball diamonds every few blocks. (Manzanar alone had over thirty baseball teams. Some of them—such as the Gophers, the Pioneers, and the Señors—were made up in camp, and some of them—like the San Fernando Aces—were already existing teams before they were sent away. Their diamond was on Block 25, near the fire break.)

Please consider amending your plans to include a more uplifting portrayal of the way our country's citizens of Japanese descent continued to celebrate their lives as Americans, even under such appalling circumstances.

Very truly yours,
Alejandra Perez

The Globe

EMAIL FROM   *LISA WEI HWONG*

Dear Alé,

Bravo.

Don't expect too much from your letter alone. Communicating with the federal government is like talking to a computer that's crashing. So you might want to explore a few ideas of your own, e.g., rebuilding the auditorium or re-creating one of the camp's Christmas shows. That way you'll have a more specific battle plan to pursue in the event you receive a stuporous and non-responsive response from Mr. Hoyt.

Incidentally, where did you learn so much about baseball? You're beginning to sound like T.C.

Wei

Dear Jacqueline,

Consider yourself fortunate that Jack's most serious offense was not getting rid of his girlfriends' panties before you found them under the love seat. Tacky, but at least ironic. Instead, you might have been married to Franklin Roosevelt, who ended a Depression, revived the economy, won a two-ocean war, and used the Constitution to light his cigarettes. Without even *blushing*:

PRESIDENT ROOSEVELT SENDS
AMERICAN JAPS TO CAMP

President Franklin D. Roosevelt today signed Executive Order 9066, calling for the designation of "military areas" along the west coast of the United States, from which "any and all persons" may be excluded in the interests of national security. The measure has been urged by California attorney general Earl Warren and Gen. John L. DeWitt, who are now free to implement the round-up of the approximately 120,000 Japanese Americans residing in California, Oregon, and Washington.

"A Jap is a Jap," said DeWitt. "And it doesn't matter where he was born."

FDR stated that E.O. 9066 would take effect immediately.

Even Eleanor was shocked. And she already *knew* he was a schmuck.

I'm sorry. This is supposed to be the season for giving thanks, not for maligning an amoral dead president—although on Thursday, the only thing I was grateful for was that I didn't know how to speak Nigerian. Papa and Mamita had planned a quiet cocktail party for 200 of their most intimate titled friends, which meant that I was expected to circulate amongst the diamond tiaras and ruby-studded cufflinks in our gold and white living room while wearing an ivory lace gown from the president of Greece, with a décolletage that would have made a nudist blush. Happy Thanksgiving. What's wrong with this picture?

"*Alejandra, tu es ravissante.*"

"*Merci, Mme. Alphand.*" The French ambassador's wife is a particular thorn in my side. She's been attempting to arrange a marriage between me and her evil son Philippe since we were both four years old and playing in the same sandbox on Massachusetts Avenue in Washington. As I recall, Philippe's most enduring adjectives, in no particular order, included venal, selfish, ignorant, petulant, narcissistic, malicious, and (by way of summary) ghastly. So as his mother and I made small talk over canapés and sparkling cider, I lied through my teeth at the first opportunity and mentioned that I already had a boyfriend—but I was sure that Philippe would make someone a very special husband (which is entirely true, given that one of the key synonyms for "special" is "abnormal"). Mme. Alphand didn't accept the news with much grace; the third degree that followed made me suspect that she was determined to find out who the miscreant was so that she could drag the guillotine out of cold storage.

"*Tst, tst, tst. Un autre beau? Quel dommage.*"

"*Oui.*" I smiled, both demurely and insincerely.

"*Et il s'appelle—?*"

"Anthony," I blurted automatically, horrified at myself. *Where did that come from?*

Fortunately, in putting together such a glittering and exclusive R.S.V.P. inventory, my parents had forgotten that Carlos collects stray consul generals the way other people collect homeless cats and failed to allot the square footage necessary to accommodate this little quirk. In fact, having gone out for cigars twenty minutes earlier, he returned with a box of Havanas and half the Nigerian embassy. Nobody knew quite where to put them. It was just the diversion I needed to sneak up the back stairs to my bedroom, change into my jeans and sweatshirt, flop face-first onto my pink bedspread (God, I hate pink), and listen to Carly Simon on WQSX. As I saw it, I had two options for the remainder of the afternoon, and both involved climbing out the window: (1) stopping by the Kellers' to see if Augie needed any Andy support; or (2) running away from home and joining a circus. *Any* circus.

Instead, I fell asleep and dreamt about Anthony.

Amory Park, late afternoon. I'm on my way home from school when I pass the baseball diamond. It's empty except for a lonely figure seated in the front row of bleachers. Anthony. His head is down and his shoulders are hunched. Since I've never seen him bereft before, I cross over the base line and sit down next to him.

"Are you okay?" I ask hesitantly, putting a hand on his forearm. When he looks up, his face is streaked with tears. (Oh, my God. He cries??)

"I can't find my mother," he sobs. "She was supposed to meet me here. What am I going to do?" I search for the right words to comfort him because he's breaking my heart. But when I

realize there's nothing I can possibly say, I pull out my cell phone and flip it open. (Reliably practical Alejandra—she doesn't hug, but she's always got a plan.)

"Don't worry," I promise him, punching 4-1-1 on the keypad. "We'll track her down." I call the airport, Tower Records, and Nikita Khrushchev, but nobody's seen her. In despair—since Anthony is staring at me with such hope lighting his face—I try Phyllis at The Word Shop. She knows everything.

"Anthony's mother?" she confirms matter-of-factly. "She's working the register, honey. It's Tuesday, remember?" Since by now her voice is coming through the speakers attached to the backstop, Anthony hears every word. He's overjoyed. Grabbing my hand, he pulls me to my feet, and we race across Mexico City together before it gets dark. After all, he wants to be able to see her.

"Say 'Kenmore Square,'" I insist.

"Kenmaw Sqway-ah."

"Say 'Nothing could be finer than to be in Carolina.'"

"Nothing could be finah than to be in Caroliner."

"You're doing that on purpose."

"I'm not. I sway-ah."

I woke up startled, wondering why I felt such an unusual (for Alejandra) longing. Then it hit me. *What an idiot I am!* Anthony was right. The "um" didn't have anything to do with it. He hooked me on the "sway-ah." It was so spontaneous, so genuine, so vulnerable, and so endearing, he caught me with my left flank unguarded. The entire United States Marine Corps couldn't have defended against it, even if they'd been on the dance floor with us. Jacqueline, did you ever have a similar epiphany with Jack? When something as simple as a twisted verb made you forget everything you thought you didn't like? Because it was the gold medal 10 of all possible boy-moments, especially for Anthony—and it instantly made me wonder whether there were any other qualities equally worthy of a Cole Porter lyric that I might have misjudged.

ANTHONY STATUS REPORT—SEPTEMBER

THINGS I HATED	*THINGS I COULD TOLERATE*	*THINGS I LIKED*
His hideous accent	He's cute	Things he hated
His gray T-shirts		
His confidence		
His stubbornness		
Most of his opinions		
Things he liked		

ANTHONY STATUS REPORT—DECEMBER

THINGS I HATE	THINGS I CAN TOLERATE	THINGS I LIKE
Some of his opinions	His gray T-shirts	He's cute
	His stubbornness	His hideous accent
	Things he likes	His confidence
	Things he hates	When he's embarrassed

I knew I was in deep trouble during American history yesterday, when Anthony and his father brought their diorama to school. (At first it appears to be a study in obsessive-compulsive disorder: They included valet parking in front of Union Station.) Since it has six legs and takes up a good third of our classroom, we had to spend fifteen preliminary minutes rearranging our desks before they could get it through the door—so I used my downtime to remember one reassuring fact: *Just because you discover that you may like somebody after all, it doesn't necessarily mean there's any attraction. That's a whole other hemisphere.* Then Anthony crouched down and bent over to plug in the diorama. As it happens, he was wearing his favorite pair of worn jeans, which, from the back, fit so well that they leave nothing to the imagination. Like a witness to a natural disaster, I was physically incapable of turning away from the view. I may even have gasped. *Now, that's Louvre-worthy art.* To my left, of course, I could feel Lee's eyes boring into me, but I wasn't about to give her the satisfaction of boring back. If I need a Butt-Junkies Anonymous sponsor, I'll ask for one.

> Fondly,
> Alejandra

P.S. I terrorized Augie into a dance lesson he didn't really need, because it was supposed to be his penance for pulling a fast one on me. Instead, he learned the tap break in ten minutes flat, asked Mrs. Salabes to teach him two more of them, and then began improvising a pair of Gene Kelly routines from *An American in Paris*. I've created a monster.

Alé,

I happened to notice that you couldn't keep your eyes off of you-know-who. It kind of reminded me of fifth grade when we put on a couple of scenes from the musical *Brigadoon*. Quita sang a song called "Almost Like Being in Love." Would you like me to print out the lyrics for you? It looks like you might be needing them. And not for the *Kiss Me, Kate* audition either. Passion, thy name is Anthony.

> —*Lee*

Lee,

Assuming you're not inventing all of this as you go along (which is so like you), I'm trusting you to keep your mouth shut. The last thing I need is for Anthony to find out. I feel like I've caught the Ebola virus and there's nothing I can do about it.

—*Alé*

Alé,

Don't worry—some people develop antibodies. I would have grabbed him myself when we were eight, except by then we liked each other too much to fall in love.   —*Lee*

Lee,

Remind me again. Why doesn't he impress me?

—*Alé*

Alé,

Because you've still got it in your head that you're supposed to marry a prince. Know what? The only thing T.C. doesn't have is a sword and a battleship named after him. Everything else is Royal Family. Think it over.

By the way—am I the only one who's noticed that Andy Wexler's turned into a walking anxiety attack? Half of him may be in love with Augie, but the jock half is freaking out. Maybe Augie should tone down the Mary Martin routine until Andy drops back to Defcon 5.   —*Lee*

Lee,

Yes. You're the only one who's noticed. Do you *enjoy* cackling?   —*Alé*

INSTANT MESSENGER

AlePerez: Stop hyperventilating! You survived your first day on the swim team with Andy, didn't you?

AugieHwong: Barely. We sat next to each other in our black-and-white-striped Speedos with our legs dangling over the edge of the pool, and my body managed to behave. That was the best I could have hoped for.

AlePerez: I can't imagine why anyone would choose to be male. It's just so unsubtle. Women only have to deal with breasts, which are what they are. They don't suddenly stand up whenever they feel like it and begin pointing at something they want.

AugieHwong: You SO don't know what you're missing.

Andy hasn't said much to me since we

held hands. And whenever the other guys are around, it's almost like we never met before. Dad says it's because the one who makes the first move always gets scared until the other one makes the second move. Is he right? I mean, in the minute and a half between my brother asking you to dance and you saying yes, did he look afraid?

AlePerez: Wait a minute. That didn't qualify as the first and second moves—did it?

AugieHwong: Duh.

By the way, I tried on my *Kiss Me, Kate* audition costume and ran through "Too Darn Hot" for Mom and Dad. (Dad made me do it again so he could videotape it for Grandma Lily.) Am I really cute?? Or was Mom just saying so because she had to?

AlePerez: You mean you didn't *know* that?!

AugieHwong: Thank you for the italics and the exclamation point. My self-esteem issues just kissed my ass. Sort of. I mean, why does he pretend he doesn't know me in front of other people?

Dear Jacqueline,

I'm a little dazed and confused, but I know all of the lyrics to "So in Love With You Am I" in sign language. This has been a very peculiar day.

I stopped off at The Word Shop to pick up my copy of *Voices of the Civil Rights Movement* that I'd asked Phyllis to order. Usually she's handling two phone lines and the register, but that never stops her from seeing right through me.

PHYLLIS: Good Lord, *more* civil rights? Honey, even Dr. King had a hobby. Here. Read *The Amazing Adventures of Kavalier and Clay*. On the house.

ALEJANDRA: I've already read it. Maybe I'll just browse the New Fiction table and—

PHYLLIS: He's in the café.

ALEJANDRA: *Who's* in the café?

PHYLLIS: Alejandra, your face may be pointing straight ahead, but your eyeballs are looking for Anthony Keller.

Naturally, I laughed it off as though this were the most implausible scenario I'd ever heard—then I thanked her, picked up my bag, and left the store. Besides, the café has its own entrance on Babcock Street.

Anthony was seated in the rear booth seemingly by himself, but that was only because Hucky is so short, it takes a while to notice his little blond head sticking up over the table. Judging by the foam on the end of his nose, I took it that Anthony was introducing him to that most unsavory of diets, hot cocoa and chocolate chip cookies. (Why he and Augie haven't come down with rickets is an enigma far beyond me.) Since late afternoon is the café's busiest crunch time, it took me ten minutes to work my way through the crowd and find an empty stool at the counter—but once seated, it was easy to keep an eye on them through the mirror on the wall behind the cappuccino machines. *Perfect. I might as well be invisible.*

"Are you Alejandra?" asked a harried café manager, tapping me on the shoulder.

"Uh—yes," I replied, startled. "Why?"

"Gentleman in the back booth wants to know if he can buy you a drink," he said impatiently. "And I could really use the stool." I turned around to glower at Anthony. His chin was in his palm and he was shaking his head as if to say, "You know, it *really* doesn't have to be this difficult." Why was everybody ganging up on me??

"The only thing T.C. doesn't have is a sword and a battleship named after him. Everything else is Royal Family."

So I gave up the stool. I figured I could handle a walk on the wild side. And I wasn't wrong:

- When I sit down next to Anthony, he teaches Hucky how to spell "Alejandra" and "Alé," and he teaches me how to say "I live near the park" and "I sing and I dance." I learn that when I speak, I have to do it slowly so he can read my lips. I say "square" and Hucky draws one on a napkin. Then I make Anthony say it too. "Sqway-ah." Hucky draws another square.

  "He can read accents," says Anthony proudly. Maybe, maybe not. But he can definitely read Anthony.

- Hucky wants another cocoa. Anthony says no. Hucky sticks out his bottom lip and looks sad. Anthony says no again.

Hucky draws a picture of a cup of cocoa with Anthony's head popping out of it, then glances up disarmingly with a calculated smile. It's so obviously manipulative, I can barely keep a straight face. But Anthony still says no. Hucky figures out who's boss. He also figures out that there's a weak link in the chain of command, because he turns to me with an angelic twinkle and twists his fingers into a pair of gestures that Anthony translates as "Please?" and "Pretty please?" I had no idea I was such a pushover.

"Why can't he have another one?" I demand of Anthony, charmed off my feet.

"Because it'll ruin his dinner," he grumbles, like it's the dumbest question on earth. "I'm surprised at you." I decide it's time to bring in the heavy artillery.

"You know you're talking like a parent, don't you?" I retort accusingly. That does the trick.

"EWWW! GROSS!!" Hucky gets his cocoa. Then he makes me come around to his side of the booth and sit next to him. I'm his new best friend.

• We leave the café and turn down Harvard Street toward Amory Park. Anthony and Hucky are both carrying their gloves, but Hucky is also holding Anthony's hand as well. Since Anthony is preoccupied with walk signs, green lights, and crosswalks, he doesn't notice that Hucky is staring up at his face, oblivious to anything else in his world. I'm ashamed of myself for once thinking he was using Hucky to catch my attention. Get over yourself, girl!

• As it's 31 degrees outside by the time we reach Amory Park, we have the diamond all to ourselves. I deliberately sit in the bottom row of bleachers, where Anthony was sobbing in my dream, because an exorcism is definitely in order. Meanwhile, the team has taken the field. Anthony lobs a couple of easy tosses to Hucky, who only drops one of them. But when he does, he puts his hands on his hips and glares.

"That's his mad face, Alé," calls out Anthony. "You're getting it for free. He usually charges admission."

"Dish it back!" I shout. "Kids love it when you do that!" So Anthony puts his hands on his own hips and glares at Hucky, who promptly turns around so Anthony can't see him losing the battle not to smile. He also shoots me a six-year-old wince that needs no translation at all. *Did you tell him to do that? Did you? I thought you were on my side!*

But Hucky gets even. When it's his turn to throw, he pitches the ball straight up in the air as though it were a pop foul. In all honesty, it's the kind of catch that Augie's grandma Lily could probably make with her eyes closed, but Anthony frantically races back and forth underneath it as though it had been hit by Willie Mays. Finally he takes a belly dive by third base and goes skidding on his stomach toward the outfield with his gloved hand outstretched—while the ball drops harmlessly to the grass ten feet behind him. He pounds the ground in mock anguish as Hucky raises a triumphant fist. He's invincible.

We detour by Toy Mart on the way home to find Hucky

his Gold Glove present. (Requirement: under $2.00.) He heads directly for the rabbit's foot bin, but once there he can't decide whether he wants a blue one or an orange one.

"He's playing us," warns Anthony. "He thinks that if he can't make up his mind, we'll buy him both."

"He's right," I reply. "I'll get the blue one."

"I'll get the orange."

We take Hucky back to the Children's Residence, but since it's still early, we go up to his room to watch *Mary Poppins*. His roommate Mateo hastily turns down our invitation to join us, though his eyes light up when Anthony hands him a blue rabbit's foot. Then he hesitates nervously.

"*Was this a real rabbit?*" he signs.

"No," says Anthony, shaking his head for emphasis. "Just pretend." Relieved, Mateo races downstairs to show off his brand-new present, while Anthony and I sit on the bed with Hucky in the middle, as he scrutinizes Mary Poppins powdering her nose on a cloud. A good forty minutes passes in silence, but somewhere during "It's a Jolly Holiday With Mary," Anthony reaches out to hold Hucky's right hand— checking on me out of the corner of his eye to see if I've noticed. I have. So I grab on to Hucky's left one. According to certain principles of algebra and math, this means that Anthony and I are holding hands as well.

And with all due respect to Augie, *that* was the first move.

Fondly,

Alejandra

INSTANT MESSENGER

AlePerez: This is the one and only favor I'm ever going to ask you.

TCKeller: you don't have to set a limit. but i'm flattered anyway.

AlePerez: Is your shift key broken?

TCKeller: no. there's an ace bandage on my right hand so i have to type with my left. i don't do question marks or exclamation points either, so keep that in mind.

AlePerez: What happened to your right hand?

TCKeller: hucky made me finger-spell supercalifragilisticexpialidocious until he got it right. it took an hour and a half. i still can't hold a fork. what's the favor.

AlePerez: You know how baseball players have superstitions?

TCKeller: yes. bo belinsky wore the same jockstrap for 23 days until he started striking out again.

AlePerez: Thanks for the word picture. Don't take this the wrong way, but it helped having you there at the talent show, so I want to make sure you're at the auditions tomorrow. Someplace where I can see you.

TCKeller: augie's already got dibs on
my karma, but you can have whatever he
doesn't use. should i be reading anything
personal into this.

AlePerez: No. I want that part, and you're
good luck. A horseshoe would probably
work just as well, but I wouldn't know
where to find one.

TCKeller: you just made me hit my hand
on my desk. ow.

Dear Jacqueline,

At breakfast this morning, my parents asked me if I'd thought
about how I intended to spend my summer vacation. This is usually
a prelude to announcing the plans they've already made for me,
but they like to pretend that the whole thing was my idea—as if a
ten-year-old is really going to choose eight weeks in the Ukraine
with the Peace Corps on her own. Mamita suggested that I intern
at the French embassy (translation: Mme. Alphand promised her
that the charm-challenged Philippe would be visiting from Hell for
the season and probably dangled a Newport wedding as bait); Papa
recommended an assignment with the Harvard history department
(translation: Their filing has been backlogged since 1968 and they
can't even get a temp to say yes); and Carlos glanced up from *The
New York Times* long enough to utter the ten most astonishing
words I've ever heard him speak.

"Why don't you ask Alejandra what *she* wants to do?" he asked
casually before going back to the Arts & Leisure section. I nearly

dropped a soft-boiled egg into my lap. *Carlos??* Papa and Mamita were evidently as flustered as I was, because they immediately changed the subject to Yugoslavia. They always do that when they're in conversational denial.

Twelve minutes later I was halfway up Ivy Street on my way to school, still so bewildered that I hadn't even noticed the season's first real snowfall already beginning to swirl through Brookline. *When was the last time Carlos stood up for me? Uh, October 15, 2000. I'd just mistaken President Chirac for a waiter and asked him for another Diet Coke. But before France could secede from the U.N., Carlos cut in front of me and congratulated His Excellency on delivering such a stirring address at the Earth Summit, which gave me just enough time to sneak away and hide in a closet until it was time to go home. Papa and Mamita never found out about it.*

"Hey, Alé! Slow down!" I turned around just as Carlos caught up with me and pulled a familiar-looking flyer out of his chocolate brown Armani coat pocket. "Here," he said brusquely, handing it over. "You dropped this in the hallway outside your room." As soon as I recognized the logo, my face drained of color.

THEATRE-BY-THE-SEA
Matunuck, Rhode Island

SUMMER APPRENTICE PROGRAM

"Are you crazy, sis?" he demanded, brushing half a dozen snowflakes out of his eyes. "*Never* leave anything like this lying out in the open. If you want to work in summer stock, just tell me. I'll only need about four weeks to get the parents with the program. But *talk* to me first, would you?" He looked so worried, and we were both so snowy, and his usually perfect curly black hair was so uncharacteristically asymmetrical, none of it made any sense. *This simply can't be happening. The pod people got ahold of my brother.*

"It wasn't— I mean— It's just a thought," I stammered.

"Yeah?" he retorted. "Like the dance classes and voice lessons at the Lycée? You're lucky I check the bills first. Papa'd have a coronary if he ever saw that." Then he pointed me toward the school and gave me a small push in the right direction. "Now go learn something," he said firmly. "And break a leg at the audition."

He left me standing on Longwood Street with my mouth hanging open.

AUDITIONS
KISS ME, KATE

Sign the list and make sure you have
a song prepared to sing.

—Mrs. Packer

Since you were in Paris in 1948 and may have missed the original run, *Kiss Me, Kate* is about a touring theatrical company that's putting on a production of *The Taming of the Shrew*. The two leads are Fred and Lilli, who play Petruchio and Katharine in *Shrew* and who used to be married but aren't anymore. (Obviously, you don't have to hear much more than one verse of their "Wunderbar" duet to know they're going to wind up together again before the show's over.) Meanwhile, Bill and Lois are a couple of chorus gypsies who fall in love too—he plays Lucentio, she plays Bianca, he gambles, and she flirts. (They have all of the comedy numbers.) So if I was going to get my feet wet in show business, this was definitely the musical to do it with.

The auditorium was jammed with more kids than Mrs. Packer could handle, so she had to keep the auditions moving pretty quickly. Inside of the first three minutes, Lee Meyerhoff and Andy Wexler had earned applause for "Soak Up the Sun" and "Can't Get You Out of My Head" (which Andy actually delivered without looking at Augie even once), Stu Merliss had been thrown out on his ear after five syllables of the lyrically restored "I Feel Like a Dick," and Augie—in Lee's tights, a shirt borrowed from Carlos, and Mamita's tablecloth—stopped the show cold with Cole Porter's "Too Darn Hot." Mr. Disharoon was only supposed to play the first sixteen bars of each song, but everybody so thoroughly enjoyed the swinging-tapping-finger-snapping combination of Hwong and Porter that Mrs. Packer let him finish—and then asked him if he knew "Make 'Em Laugh" from *Singin' in the Rain* (!!). He did, and he proved it.

"What a ham," I whispered to Anthony as we stood at the back of the house together watching the Augie Hwong Show.

"That's nothing," he whispered back. "You ought to see what he does with 'You Can't Get a Man With a Gun.'"

By the time my name was called and I'd walked up the steps toward the footlights, the stage fright I'd been expecting for two days still hadn't materialized. And it wasn't difficult to figure out why. True to his word, Anthony had taken a seat smack in the center of the front row next to Augie, Lee, and Andy—who were smirking, leering, and grinning, respectively. I wondered if this was what Carlos had meant when he told me to "go learn something." Not only did I have each one of my friends in my corner, but it also turned out that I had a big brother who was taking care of me after all. *"If you want to work in summer stock, just tell me. I'll only need about four weeks to get the parents with the program."* So what on earth was there to be nervous about?!

Then I nodded to Mr. Disharoon, took a deep breath, and began to sing "So in Love With You Am I."

KISS ME, KATE
Cast List

Fred Graham/Petruchio .... KEITH MARSHALL
Lilli Vanessi/Katharine .... ALEJANDRA PEREZ
Lois Lane/Bianca .... LEE MEYERHOFF
Bill Calhoun/Lucentio .... AUGIE HWONG
Harry Trevor/Baptista .... TOMMY LEE
Gremio .... ANDY WEXLER
Hortensio .... BENJI BENNETT
Paul .... NEIL REIMAN
Hattie .... NANCY BULL
Harrison Howell .... BILLY MODINE
Doorman .... SAMMY SHEA
Haberdasher .... RICARDO BARRERA

REHEARSALS MONDAYS, WEDNESDAYS, AND
THURSDAYS AT 4:00 P.M. SHARP;
SATURDAYS AT 10:00 A.M.

INSTANT MESSENGER

AlePerez: Did you see Andy's face when Augie was singing "The Hostess With the Mostes' on the Ball"?

TCKeller: was that before or after he hid under his chair.

AlePerez: I know Augie takes a little getting used to, but Andy had better sign up for the program before he misses too much.

TCKeller: this is going to sound like i need to get over myself, but when mrs. packer asked you to sing another song and you picked 'were thine that special face,' i got the feeling you were sending me a message. i mean, you were looking right at me for most of it.

AlePerez: I had to look *some*where. Trust me, Romeo. I wasn't sending you anything.

Not much I wasn't.

And that was the *second* move.

Fondly,

Alejandra

SportsAmerica

<u>ON DECK</u>

KELLER vs. LANDIS
ONE BOY'S CRUSADE TO CLEAR BUCK WEAVER

by Colleen Wilson

I n September 1920, the sports world in general and Chicago in particular were shocked to discover that eight members of the Chicago White Sox—arguably the best team in baseball—had deliberately thrown the 1919 World Series in the most notorious gambling fix of its time. Though a jury acquitted all eight players— Swede Risberg, Chick Gandil, Eddie Cicotte, Joe Jackson, Buck Weaver, Happy Felsch, Lefty Williams, and Fred McMullin—the newly named Commissioner of Baseball, Judge Kenesaw Mountain Landis, declared that "no player who throws a ball game will ever play professional baseball" and banned all eight Black Sox players for life.

Third baseman Buck Weaver had played his heart out through the entire World Series of 1919. His only "crime," as it were, was flat-out rejecting an offer from Gandil to participate in the double-cross. However, since he had, according to Landis, "sat in conference with a bunch of crooked ballplayers" and not ratted on his teammates, he was banished under the same cloud of shame that forever shadowed the remaining seven.

Like many others since 1920, ninth grader Anthony Conigliaro Keller believes that Weaver was handed a bum rap. But he's doing something about it. His "Free Buck Weaver" website has attracted fan support from all across the United States, and it will only be a matter of time before Major League Baseball is forced to take notice.

We recently caught up with Anthony (who prefers to be called "T.C.") at his home in Brookline, Massachusetts, in order to ask him a few questions about Weaver, loyalty, believing in the impossible with all your heart, and—inevitably—the Boston Red Sox.

Dear Mama,

Boy, would you be proud of me. *SportsAmerica* hit the stands yesterday, and my interview about Buck Weaver is four pages long (including a picture of me and Pop in our 1918 World Champion sweatshirts and one of me and Nehi playing catch). Pop bought 50 copies to mail to all our relatives and friends, Aunt Babe is having it Perma-Plaqued for one of my second-level Xmas presents, and we've gotten over 20,000 hits and 6,400 new signatures on our website. I just wish Buck Weaver was around to see how many people believe in him.

It made me a superstar at school too, even though I'm not in *Kiss*

Me, Kate. Mrs. Fitzpatrick bought the magazine for the class to see, and then she passed around Xeroxes of the interview for everybody to take turns reading the T.C. parts out loud. Augie had my voice down perfect (like he shouldn't by now?), and Lee Meyerhoff hit one over the wall when she decided to work the body language too—she sat back in her chair with her legs sticking straight out and her feet crisscrossed over each other while she ran her fingers through her hair. (Do I *do* that??) The only ugly part came around when Andy Wexler read the section about my family and got to the line that said "my dad and my brother Augie and my cocker spaniel Nehi and my girlfriend Alé" (which they spelled wrong). Every eyeball in the classroom turned to Alé, and meanwhile all I wanted to do was stick my head in the trash can. How come whenever I start to make progress, something happens to end the inning?? Kind of like what Bucky F. Dent did to the Red Sox—only I keep doing it to myself. First I get her to dance with me, and then I blab to Augie about the "um." Then she calls me her good luck charm, and I get snaked by my own words in *SportsAmerica.* I'll be lucky if she talks to me before 2010 (partly because I said she was my girlfriend, and partly because she got billing after a dog).

Oh, yeah. At the *Kiss Me, Kate* auditions, she sang a love song to me for three solid minutes and then said it didn't mean anything because she'd have sung it to a horseshoe too. Does she think I was born yesterday? I know exactly what she's trying to do. She's trying to make me crazy on purpose. The only problem is that it's working.

I love you,

T.C.

From: TCKeller@earthworks.net
To: AlePerez@earthworks.net

Reminder. We live in a nation where every man
is innocent until proven guilty, and where most
of us have been tempered by a hard and bitter
peace. You could at least hear my side of it.

Dear Mama,

After 14 times through *Mary Poppins*, I now know the words
better than Augie knows *All About Eve*. Hucky and I even began
signing parts of it to each other, usually after he deliberately lets his
bottom jaw drop open and hang there.

ME: Close your mouth, Hucky. We are not a codfish.

HUCKY: *Spit-spot!*

Tuesdays are when we always to go to Amory Park and re-play
Game 3 of the 1918 World Series (unless it's snowing, and then we
just sit in The Word Shop Café and draw pictures of it). I'm Wally
Schang, Hucky is Stuffy McInnis, and I get to single him home from
third. But today Hucky had other ideas. Once we'd hit the sidewalk
in front of the Deaf Institute, he grabbed my hand and began
yanking me in the opposite direction, while Nehi pulled the bottom
of my pants leg toward the park. (I felt like Play-Doh.) I should have
known better. Nobody argues with Hucky when his mind is made
up. So we followed his lead all the way down Sewall Street, through
an outside fruit market, past Brookline Hardware, right up to the

double glass doors in front of Toy Mart. That's when I had to put on the brakes. *Uh-oh. Look at that face. He's wearing "cute and hopeful" all of a sudden. Remember, T.C.—you're the grown-up. If you have to play Bad Cop, it comes with the turf.*

"Sorry, dude," I said, yanking him away from the red wagon display in the window. "Christmas isn't for another two weeks. No toys till then, all right? Peace out." I turned us back toward Amory Park, but Hucky had already squiggled his way out of my grip.

"*This is different,*" he signed furiously. "*And I have my own money—look!*" He pulled a chocolate-covered hand out of his pocket and showed me two nickels and a penny. Holy crap—I didn't realize he was loaded. So I glanced down at Nehi for a second opinion before I changed my mind.

"Should we?" I asked. *Double-bark and a tail wag.* Like he'd ever say no. Hucky's the one who feeds him potato chips.

Even though it was a pretty gray day and the leaves were gone from all of the trees, fifteen minutes later we found ourselves sitting in the middle of a walkway in Emerson Garden. Hucky was opening up his brand-new box of colored chalk—which I let him pay for with one of his pennies and 116 of mine—and I was feeling like a pretty cheap gink (who knew that all he wanted was *chalk*?). I probably should have guessed what he was up to, but when you're busy watching your dog to make sure he doesn't pee on a wheelchair with an old lady in it, you're not always in peak form. So by the time I turned back to the pavement, Hucky had already drawn a picture of a park, a stream, a bridge, and a red-and-white-striped merry-go-round right there on the sidewalk. (Reminder: Teach him how to finger-spell "vandalism.") Once he'd added a blue and orange frame around the whole thing, he pulled back to make sure it looked just the way he wanted—and then he stood up and jumped right into the middle of it, both feet first. For a second he just kept staring down with half a smile on his face like something was supposed to happen—and when it didn't, he turned his head to me with hurt little question marks in his eyes, as if he was saying "Hey, you. What gives here?"

Suddenly it made sense. *Oh, duh. Mary Poppins. The part where Bert draws a chalk pavement picture and the kids and the nanny hop into it with him.* But figuring it out didn't mean I had an easy answer for him—it just meant it was time for the man-to-man talk I've been afraid of ever since the eighth time we watched that movie together. (It's still a little hard to have a whole conversation with Hucky when I only know how to sign every other word—but our imaginations help us understand most of the rest, and this time it was especially important.)

"Come here, dude," I said, pulling him down beside me. "You can't get pissed off at a chalk pavement picture. It has the home field advantage."

"*Oh, no? Watch me!*" He struggled to stand up and jump into it again, but I held on tight.

"Hey! Look at me," I ordered, turning his face in my direction. He looked. He wasn't happy about it, but he looked. "Remember when you were afraid of the dragon in *Shrek*?"

"*So?*"

"What did we learn?"

"*It's only a movie.*"

"What about the kid with donkey ears in *Pinocchio*?"

"*Only a movie.*"

"Right. So isn't *Mary Poppins* only a movie too?" Hucky pulled away from me like I'd just grown Lampwick's ass ears myself. I mean, he was *scared.*

"*No! She's magic! Why are you asking me that?*"

Mama, as soon as I saw the panic start and the tears happen, I forgot all about the man-to-man thing and went right back to boy-to-boy again. I'm too young for this gig anyway. If somebody has to play Bad Cop or tell him the truth, they'd better pick a different hoser because it sure isn't going to be me. "T.C.! Come quick! Look who's here! Your balloon came back!" I believed that until I was ten, didn't I? Then why can't Hucky have Mary Poppins for as long as he needs her?!

So instead, I told him he was right—*Mary Poppins* couldn't possibly be a movie like *Pinocchio* and *Shrek,* because they were cartoons and she wasn't. And the only reason we wouldn't be able to jump into the chalk picture ourselves is because nobody but Mary Poppins knew how to take us there. Which wasn't exactly the greatest news Hucky'd ever heard, but at least we were back on the right track.

"*You mean we can't ride on my merry-go-round?*" he signed, staring down at his feet glumly.

"Not today," I blurted, hoping I wasn't about to lie as bad as I thought I was. "But we can draw a couple of other pictures instead so that she'll have lots of different places to take us when she gets here." *T.C., you're like SUCH a low-life! What if he believes you??*

He believed me. Before we left, there were eight more chalk drawings on the sidewalk.

On the way back home, I watched Hucky and Nehi play Got You Last up and down Cypress Street, and I remembered the day I taught it to him. It seems like such a long time ago. Was it really just a *week*? I also noticed how certain things have been adding up a little differently ever since the first time the short little blond kid with frowny eyes told me what pitches to hit.

1. I don't worry about things like making up fake girlfriends for Pop so Lori can get jealous or writing obnoxious notes to Alé or people thinking I'm a poser if I get an A instead of a B+. There's just no time for stuff like that anymore.

2. Nehi has a new best buddy. If Hucky gets up and walks three feet across the room, Nehi gets up and walks three feet across the room. If Hucky has to go pee, Nehi waits for him outside the bathroom. If Hucky dozes off during *Mary Poppins*, Nehi falls asleep with him. If Hucky gets too close to a street corner and I'm not holding his hand, Nehi grabs on to him and pulls him back.

3. I'm not afraid to try things I would have stayed away from before. I can't believe I'm actually letting myself fall in love with Alé before I even find out if she could ever feel the same way back. It's like asking for trouble—but the good kind.

4. I dream about you all the time. Before, the only thing I used to keep in my head was the purple balloon—but now I can remember most of our Christmases and summers, our favorite Red Sox games at Fenway Park, the trip to

Nantucket on the boat, sitting in your lap on my first plane trip, and you sleeping on a futon by my bed when I had the flu. Why didn't I remember any of these things before??

We finally made our way back to the Children's Residence (with only one detour to peek through the fence around the Fenway Park outfield—how could we *not*?) and I wasn't looking forward to it, because dropping off Hucky is always the hardest part of the day. He stalls so much that I learned pretty quickly how to get him home half an hour early so he'll think he's putting one over on me.

"*Come look at the new rock in our backyard!*" "*Want to see where Mateo threw up in our room?*" But you can tell when he realizes the clock's run out, because we're standing in the hallway by the front door and he's tugging nervously on his favorite piece of hair.

"*Are you coming back?*"

"Tomorrow."

"*You promise?*"

"I promise."

How could he think I wouldn't come back?!

> I love you,
> T.C.

INSTANT MESSENGER

AlePerez: I can't believe you told the whole world I was your girlfriend. I didn't even consider *liking* you until Hallowe'en!
TCKeller: I was quoted out of context and

it was 2 months ago. Who knew you could resist me?

AlePerez: Are you interested in making amends? Or at least restitution? Because I have a problem that's right up your alley, and I don't know what else to do.

TCKeller: Shoot.

AlePerez: I got this back from the Manzanar people: "Dear Ms. Perez: Thank you so much for your kind words about our site restoration project. We too are most excited about the way it is shaping up. Please feel free to visit us when we open our gates in 2004. Very truly yours, Fred Hoyt, Assistant Site Superintendent." Hello? Does anybody pay attention? I could have asked him for a toilet seat and he'd have sent me the same letter.

TCKeller: It's your own fault. You're not going to get anywhere yelling $10 words down a tunnel to these people. Sometimes you've got to *do* something.

What about restoring the Manzanar baseball diamond? And maybe having some of the people rebuilding it be the grandchildren of guys who played ball there? Then there could be special games a couple of times a year with white kids and black kids and Asian kids and Latino kids and any other colors they invent along the way. Kind of like a living "I'm sorry."

AlePerez: How long have you been planning this?

TCKeller: Ever since you mailed your letter to the Assistant Gink in the first place. I figured you'd need some Buck Weaver kind of help, so I got a little bit of a head start. Even before *SportsAmerica* made me a household word.

By the way, we're all going skiing in Vermont between Christmas and New Year's. The Deaf Institute might even let Hucky go with us. Want to come?

AlePerez: Get me my baseball diamond and I'll think about it.

Dear Mama,

Remember at the end of the first *Star Wars* when Darth Vader nails Luke's X-Wing Fighter in his sights and says "I have you now"? Alé doesn't know it yet, but she's just been locked into my scope and there's no way out. This is what I told her we're going to have to do.

1. Write a one-page argument on why they have to let us build our diamond

2. Start a website with our contact info

3. Post the one-page argument on our website

4.   Turn the one-page argument into a letter

5.   Find out the names and addresses of all 100 senators

6.   Send the letter to all 100 senators and CC each one of them to Fred Hoyt, the Gink of Manzanar

7.   Turn the one-page argument into a press release

8.   Get the names and e-mail addresses of 500 political reporters and sports columnists from Mom's P.C. at the *Globe*

9.   Send the press release to all 500 political reporters and sports columnists and CC each one to Fred Hoyt

10.   Kiss Anthony

(Since Buck Weaver taught me how to make Major League Baseball nervous in just a couple of months, I figure the U.S. government ought to be a no-brainer.)

Except for crossing out #10, Alé agreed with everything else, so I started a website called www.manzanarbaseball.com and showed her how to use it. Now she calls me at least four times a day with questions. Seeing as she's a rookie and I'm indispensable, how could she *not* know that wearing my sweatshirts comes next??

Q: Why are we copying the senator letters to Fred Hoyt? Won't it make him angry?

A: No, it'll give him the runs. That's what we want. They always move faster with stomach cramps.

Q: Didn't all ten internment camps have baseball teams?

A: Yeah, but Manzanar started it, so that's where the diamond should be. Unless we want to make them build nine more, which come to think of it isn't a bad idea for down the road.

Q: I just got off the phone with Wei at the *Globe*. She can get us a thousand reporters' names instead of five hundred. Is that too many?

A: No. A thousand names is a good thing. Especially if we put Fred Hoyt's telephone number on all of the press releases.

But you know what? She doesn't really have to wear my sweatshirts if she doesn't want to, and the only reason I put in "Kiss Anthony" is because I love watching the way she shakes her head whenever she deletes me. Now I think I know what Pop meant when he said I had to figure it out for myself: I trust her. I've even started telling her things that I never breathed to anybody else except Augie. So who really cares if she winds up falling for me or not?? The friend thing can last forever. Pop says this is called "rationalizing." And it got you to marry him when he figured out how to tweak it the right way.

ME: Pop, you need to teach me how to tweak it the right way. Like now.

POP: Where are you calling from?

ME: The boys' lav. I finished my geography quiz early. Alé

was wearing the flower dress again and wouldn't look at me once. I think I wrote down that Greece was in Spain. Pop, I can't take much more of this.

POP: You're too young to try the "just friends" routine. Because if it backfires—

ME: It won't. Just tell me what the ground rules are.

POP: All right. But listen to me carefully, because there's no margin for error here. Remember when Luke Skywalker only had one shot at the Death Star?

ME: Duh. "It's just like shooting womp-rats in Beggar's Canyon back home."

POP: But first you have to wait for the right moment.

ME: Sweet. I was thinking that maybe at lunch I could—

POP: Hey! I said *wait* for the right moment. That could be tomorrow or in two months. You'll know when it happens. Then you say, "Alé, would it be okay with you if we could rewind to the first day and just be friends? Without all of my secret plans to make you fall for me? Because I think I'm getting in a little too deep here, and it's more important to know that we can always count on each other no matter what."

ME: Oh, that's good.

POP: Yeah, well you'd better be ready to live up to it, because girls like to take their time when it's their move. And if she ever smells that the "just friends" fix is bogus—

ME: She won't.

Today Hucky came over to our house with somebody named Alice Trumbo from Social Services. Mrs. Jordan already said he could spend a weekend with us and go on our Xmas ski trip to Vermont, but first we had to be vetted by Ms. Trumbo. It sounded to me like something they do to pets so they don't get pregnant, but Pop says it just means that Massachusetts needs to check us out to make sure we don't belong to the Mafia or sell stolen cars and children. The only problem with Ms. Trumbo is that she looks pretty much like Miss Gulch before she morphed into the Wicked Witch of the West, and the minute she came through the front door into our living room, Pop and I had to turn away from each other. This was a life-saving routine that we invented when I was eight and we went to Cousin Bobo's wedding in Peabody. The lady minister was a dead-ringer for George Washington on the dollar bill—and even though Pop and I both noticed it at the same time, we behaved ourselves. Then we made the mistake of looking at each other while we were both biting our bottom lips so we wouldn't laugh, and it was all over. After whispering back and forth things like "The Mother of Our Country" and "I do, Mrs. President," we had to go out and listen to the wedding from the lobby. Otherwise we would have ruined the whole ceremony.

We're *so* not a good influence on each other.

I love you,

T.C.

P.S. Hucky taught me how to say "I have you now" in sign language the same way Darth Vader would say it if he was deaf. At least we think so.

INSTANT MESSENGER

AugieHwong: Is she going to let him go on the ski trip with us?

TCKeller: Yeah, as long as Toto doesn't bite her leg again. I invited Alé, but she found a creative way to say no. The "just friends" thing is my last resort. Does Pop really mean it when he says I'll recognize the right moment when it happens? Or is he just saying that so I won't notice that he's just as clueless as I am? Again.

AugieHwong: Andy can't come either. They're going to Cleveland to visit his grandparents. Why do they always keep grandparents in places like Cleveland?? I won't even be able to see him until January.

TCKeller: This is going to be some vacation. You'll be obsessing about Andy for 5 days and I'll be on the phone with Alé.

AugieHwong: What are *you* complaining about? First Alé wouldn't even admit you existed, and now she's got this thing about building a baseball diamond with you in a California desert. I need to borrow your routine, preferably without a cactus in it.

TCKeller: That's easy. But you need to find a political issue that means a lot to him.

AugieHwong: I tried that, and all I can come up with is changing the color of the Patriots uniforms. Somehow it doesn't have the same bite. Even in sign language. And he gets antsy whenever I say things like that anyway.

Mrs. Packer staged three of my numbers already. "Another Op'nin', Another Show," "We Open in Venice," and "Bianca." Since Andy's in two of them, he thinks we should rehearse privately whenever we can. Does this sound like he's waiting for me to make the second move?

TCKeller: No, dude—it sounds like he just made it.

Student/Adviser Conference
Lori Mahoney/Anthony C. Keller

LORI: Show me again.

T.C.: Both hands parallel to the floor, pinkies down and palms facing you, one hand in front of the other. Then tap the hand closest to the body against the other hand. *That* means "near."

LORI: I thought that was "live."

T.C.:   No. No. Remember we said— Wait. What's "re-member"? That one gave you a hard time too.

LORI: Thumb on the forehead, then both thumbs together.

T.C.:   Good. Remember we said that "live" was like zipping up a pair of zippers on each side of your chest at the same time?

LORI: So if I want to say "I live near the river," I'd do it like *this*?

T.C.:   Um, actually you just said "I live in a parking lot." You didn't mean to do that.

LORI: You've never seen traffic on Concord Street at eight o'clock in the morning.

Dear Mama,

I wish somebody could have told me how many invisible land mines there are when you make friends with a little kid. Because if I knew that up front, maybe I wouldn't be doing such a ginky job.

Hucky spent the weekend at our house. Since it was his first sleepover ever, Pop and I decided we were going to make it a special one, but when we saw him waiting for us on the Institute porch— carrying his stuffed dog Shut-the-Door and a suitcase so small you wouldn't figure anything could fit inside—it sort of hit me like a punch in the stomach that he looked really little and really scared. *That's me when I was six. I remember how afraid I was to spend a weekend with Aunt Babe once it was just me and Pop. What was that all about?* The good news is that Hucky is a whole lot braver than I was, and if he really had cold feet, he didn't show them for long. As a matter of fact, he got a handle on the whole sleepover routine in about a minute and a half.

- Before we'd gone even a block, he discovered the Mazda's navigational system, and he never took his eyes off of it. Pop offered to show him Mars, but Hucky didn't believe him until it popped onto the screen. It's a good thing he's never been to Nashua, New Hampshire, or else we'd have been busted.

- When Pop unlocked the front door of the house, Nehi was already waiting for us. He ignored me and Pop completely (like we aren't the ones who've been feeding him for six years) so he could grab Hucky by the left sleeve and drag him up the stairs to my room. Hucky knew right away which bed was his because (a) Nehi was bouncing up and down on it and (b) there was a *Mary Poppins* poster on the wall above it, covering up most of Augie's Bette Davis pictures.

- We all went to the grocery store so Hucky could pick out our menu. French fries, melon, pasta, potato chips, and chocolate milk. (I smuggled in some chicken strips while Hucky was debating about Tater Tots.) Pop was in charge of dinner, but he let Hucky help. Together they invented Cantaloupe Linguini. It wasn't as gross as the hot-dogs-and-maple-syrup that Augie and I lived on for a whole summer, but it was definitely in the same ballpark.

- Pop built a fire after we cleaned up the kitchen and Hucky had his first s'more. Almost. He was a little suspicious when he got a good look at it all glopped together like that, so he insisted on eating each of the ingredients separately—which kind of defeated the whole purpose.

  "Let me just melt it for you," I insisted.

  "*No!*" he signed back. "*I don't like it!*"

  "Do you like graham crackers and marshmallows and Hershey's bars?" I demanded.

  "*Yes.*"

  "Then that's impossible!"

- Pop showed Hucky how much sign language I'd taught him, but he somehow wound up saying "I am a horse." Hucky thought that was about the funniest thing he'd ever heard in his life. So Hucky showed Pop how well he can finger-spell. He did okay with the preliminaries, but then "hamburger" came out "hangabur"—which Pop thought was about the funniest thing he'd ever heard in *his* life. He even got a mad face as a reward.

- Pop tucked Hucky into bed and then we both read him part of *The Enormous Egg*. (Pop's actually a lot better at sign language than he thinks. Somebody must be coaching him. Gee, I wonder who? Am I *really* not supposed to know that he's dating Lori??) But before the baby Triceratops could even hatch, Hucky was already yawning. He grabbed on to Shut-the-Door and turned over onto his side so he could see Mary Poppins on his wall. Then Nehi snuggled up against him, and he was out like a light.

• Pop turned off the lamp, kissed me good night, and I wasn't too far behind.

If it had ended there, it would have been one of the better days of my year. But around 2:30 in the morning—right in the middle of a dream about Augie playing left field for the White Sox—it got really cold at Comiskey Park. That was because Nehi had pulled off all my blankets and sheets while he was poking his nose into my neck like he always does when it's time for me to get up for school. But now he was also yanking on my sleeve too, and by the time I woke up enough to figure out it was still dark, I was also awake enough to hear Hucky crying. It wasn't very loud and it almost sounded like coughing—but it got me up on my feet pretty fast anyway. Nehi had already jumped back onto Hucky's bed and begun pacing back and forth like he was saying "*Do* something!" Do *what*? Mama, his hands were clenched into two little fists and his whole body was scrunched up and shaking like a catcher who's just been really badly hurt—but he was still sound asleep. So I couldn't even laugh him out of it the way you used to do whenever I had a bad dream. The only thing I could think of was to wrap his arms back around Shut-the-Door and then sit on the edge of his bed and keep patting his head to see if it made a difference. *T.C., you're SO out of your league here! Get Pop. Call Mrs. Jordan. Anybody who knows what they're doing!* It felt like we were there for most of the night, but the sobbing finally got quieter and quieter until it stopped completely—and Nehi even lay back down, keeping one eye open like he was still at Orange Alert. I guess I didn't fix what was broken, but it was the best I could come up with in the middle of the night. And any hoser probably could have done better.

Mama, I *really* need some help here.

I love you,

T.C.

---

www.augiehwong.com
PRIVATE CHAT

AlePerez: How many times did it happen?

TCKeller: Three. I finally got the idea to fall asleep next to him and Nehi so he wouldn't be left alone. It worked. At least he didn't cry anymore.

AugieHwong: He could have been homesick. Sometimes you do that when you're little and in a strange bed.

TCKeller: Or maybe it happens all the time, but since Mateo's deaf and can't hear him, nobody knows about it.

AugieHwong: Please don't go there. It reminds me of you when we were seven.

TCKeller: I cried in my sleep??

AugieHwong: All the nights I stayed over you did. I never felt so clueless in my life.

AlePerez: Maybe Hucky misses his mother too.

TCKeller: How? He never knew her.

AugieHwong: No, it's the Mary Poppins thing. He really thinks she's going to rescue him. Tick, remember his face when Aunt Babe bought him the picture from the movie?

TCKeller: That's what I thought. So I tried to hint that maybe she's too busy with kids in England to come to Brookline but—

AlePerez: Anthony, you can't do that. She's all he's got.

AugieHwong: Yeah, but we also can't let him think that she's really going to float down in the middle of Commonwealth Avenue. That's not fair either.

TCKeller: I know, I know. The only person who's going to convince him that Mary Poppins isn't coming to stay with him is Mary Poppins.

AlePerez: You lost me.

TCKeller: Aug, how much do you know about Julie Andrews?

AugieHwong: Real name Julia Elizabeth Wells, born October 1, 1935 with a five-octave range, loves kids, has three of her own, wrote a couple of children's books, and incidentally knows the British version of

American Sign Language (assuming that's what she was doing with her hands while she was singing "My Favorite Things" on the Tony Awards). Why?

TCKeller: Look, I know she's famous and all, but if we FedEx her a letter and tell her about Hucky, she's *got* to write him back, doesn't she?

AugieHwong: First of all, where are we going to find her? You can't send something like that to an agent and think they're going to forward it. I know. I tried writing to Anne Bancroft that way. Six times. I kept getting form letters from the Creative Artists Agency and one of them included an autographed picture of Candice Bergen.

AlePerez: I can get Julie Andrews's home address from the Secret Service. But I'll need a day.

TCKeller: You're kidding, right?

AugieHwong: No, she's not. I've seen her Outlook Address Book. She's got the FBI in there too.

AlePerez: Who's going to write it?

TCKeller: We all are. I don't do well with letters to famous people unless they have batting averages.

Laurents School
Brookline, Massachusetts

VIA E-MAIL

Dear Ted:

Floor-level Celtics seats are the private property of the people who own them, even when they don't show up. Sneaking downstairs at halftime and sitting in the empty ones is no different than breaking into a neighbor's house to use the swimming pool while the neighbors are out of town. See if you can finger-spell M-I-S-D-E-M-E-A-N-O-R. We should have been arrested.

As of this morning, I have half a faculty and an entire ninth grade at various stages of proficiency in American Sign Language—and it's not even on the curriculum. The teachers don't have a choice. Learning it is the only way they can figure out what the kids are saying.

Clayton Landey claims that he's never seen anybody pick up ASL as quickly as Anthony has, which probably accounts for the overall change in his grades. Including yesterday's algebra quiz, his GPA is 98. Evidently, American Sign Language drains all of the energy necessary to keep the lid on a B+ average. Please don't say "I told you so." Just because you wear "stubborn" well doesn't mean you'd look good in "smug."

Lori

KELLER CONSTRUCTION
BOSTON · GLOUCESTER · WALTHAM

ELECTRONIC TRANSMISSION

Dear Lori:

I never attained enough emotional maturity to graduate to the level of smug. The best I can do is "nyah, nyah."

Sneaking downstairs into the expensive seats is a tradition as old as the seventh-inning stretch, Fenway Franks, and tossing out the first pitch on Opening Day. Not only is it an accepted fact of life, it's considered unpatriotic not to make the effort. Get used to it.

Craig, Wei, and I are taking the kids skiing in Vermont from December 26–30. ("The kids" is a category that hereafter includes Hucky, now that I've been deemed morally competent by the Commonwealth of Massachusetts.) We're staying at the Briar Hearth Inn in Woodford, and due to an unexplained mathematical brain fart, I somehow managed to book an extra room by mistake. Gee, it'd be a shame to waste it. "Kids, look who's staying at our hotel!" What could be more credible?

Ted

Augie

DIVA OF THE WEEK

Angela Lansbury

("But darling! I'm your Auntie Mame!")

Dear Angie,

Remember when you started rehearsals for *Mame* and you discovered muscles that hadn't been invented yet? Because I have one in my left butt that even scientists couldn't know about.

In *Kiss Me, Kate* I play a scoundrel who loves Lois (Lee Meyerhoff) but who can't stop gambling—so in between dances, he's dodging mobsters and getting everybody else into trouble right along with him. It's definitely a stretch for me. I mean, the kids are so used to my Katharine Hepburn, they never knew what kind of a range I had before.

But the star of the show is definitely Alé. When Mrs. Packer blocked her in "Wunderbar" and "So in Love With You Am I," me and Andy and the rest of the cast just sat on the edge of the stage to watch and listen. (We found out later that you could hear her as far away as the cafeteria, which is why about thirty civilians snuck into the back of the auditorium for a closer look too.) She has the kind of smoky voice that's part Lena Horne, part Juanita Hall, and the rest of it like nobody you ever heard before in your life. And she knows how to sell "hot." Tick had better move fast before the competition drowns him. And speaking of drowning, I qualified as a near-fatality at swim practice this afternoon. Tick was butter-flying in the lane next to me, but I got assigned a half a lap behind Andy. Imagine the view every time I looked up. I accidentally discovered that it's not a good idea to hyperventilate in eight feet of chlorinated water.

We finished our letter to Julie Andrews. Tick, Alé, and I each wrote our own drafts, but since I'm the authority on divas, it was my job to choose the best parts and put them all together.

Dear Ms. Andrews:

(**ALÉ**)   Please forgive the intrusion, but we're three ninth graders who live in Brookline, Massachusetts, and who find ourselves with a problem that only you can help us solve.

(**TICK**)   When Hucky watches *Mary Poppins*, he doesn't see special effects or make-believe houses. What he sees is a world he thinks is real.

(AUGIE) Sooner or later somebody's going to adopt him—but until that happens, you're all he's got. So if you can remember how Jane and Michael looked up to you in the movie, maybe you'll consider writing him a short note. It could make a lot of difference.

I really hope she comes through. At first I thought Hucky was just another one of my brother's long-term, generally weird projects (e.g., Free Buck Weaver and Save Fenway Park), but the more I hang out with this kid, the more I remember what it was like to be the same age. And since Hucky doesn't have to worry about getting confused by words, sometimes he zeroes in on the bottom line a lot faster than I do—especially when I try to con myself into or out of things.

HUCKY: *Who's in the picture?*
ME: That's Andy and me at Thanksgiving.
HUCKY: *Why are you smiling at him that way?*
ME: Uh, because I love him.
HUCKY: *Does he love you too?*
ME: I don't know.
HUCKY: *Why don't you know??*

Maybe I'd be smarter with only four senses.

Love,

Augie

```
www.augiehwong.com
PRIVATE CHAT
```

AugieHwong: I just e-mailed you the final draft of the letter. I'm signing off on this, so let's rock and roll.

TCKeller: Hold it. I just got to the end. Hucky does *not* need an autographed copy of *Julie and Carol at Carnegie Hall*.

AugieHwong: No, but *I* do.

TCKeller: You said you were going to lose that line.

AugieHwong: I did. And then I hid it in a P.S.

TCKeller: Alé, how does the rest of it look?

AlePerez: If you cut the P.S. and get rid of the question about Richard Burton's drinking, it's a done deal.

TCKeller: Sweet. Then both of you guys e-mail me your signatures so I can paste them below mine. I'll FedEx it out this afternoon. Alé, please thank Clint for Julie's address.

AugieHwong: And while you're at it, find out if he knows where I can get ahold of Carol Burnett.

Dear Angie,

Nobody remembers that when you sang "We Need a Little Christmas," it wasn't supposed to be because you were happy. The stock market had crashed, you had to sell all of the paintings in your Beekman Place apartment, and the only present you could afford to buy your nephew was a pair of long pants. But as soon as you finished the song, the doorbell rang and it was a Southern gent named Beauregard. You both discovered love, got married, and lived happily ever after (until he fell off an Alp).

So while I was standing in front of the Coolidge Corner Theatre yesterday afternoon waiting for Andy, I should have known that everything was going to work out as soon as I heard "We Need a Little Christmas" twinkling through the box office speakers. Up until that moment, my mood was so right out of Dickens and Sondheim, I didn't even notice the first couple of snowflakes, the Xmas lights, or the smell of roasting chestnuts from the vendors on every corner. How could I? *Andy's going to Cleveland tomorrow. For eight days. EIGHT DAYS! That's 192 hours. 11,520 minutes. 691,200 seconds. 1 one thousand, 2 one thousand, 3 one thousand . . .* Right around "103 one thousand," I saw him weaving his way through the crowd of second-to-last-day shoppers on Harvard Street. He hadn't noticed me yet, so it gave me a chance to take my favorite kind of inventory from an anonymous point of view.

1. His hair curling out from under his wool cap.

2. His red nose from the cold.

3. His right hand jammed into his pocket because he's always losing one of his gloves.

4. His scarf hanging around his shoulders because he doesn't understand that you're supposed to wrap it around your neck. ("It's not a fashion statement, you dope—it has a function!")

5.   His eyes darting all over the place—looking for *me!*

6.   His eyes finding me and smiling before his mouth even does.

"Hey, Spidey."

"Hey, Aquaboy." We stood there for a second just looking at each other. How come it's so easy to talk on the phone and online but so impossible in person??

"You get the tickets?"

"Yeah. They're almost sold out."

"We'd better go inside then."

"Let's do it."

As usual, Andy went ahead to find us seats while I stood in line at the concession counter—which gave me a good chance to get unneurotic before the movie started. *Look, it's not like you're going to be sitting on your hands while he's in Ohio. You've got Vermont. Skiing with Tick!! Toboggan rides with Mom and Dad! Snowboarding with Pop! Hot chocolate in front of the fire with Hucky! 691,200 seconds'll be over before you know it. No, they won't. 211 one thousand, 212 one thousand . . .* Just then my cell phone rang.

ME: Hello?

ANDY: Did I tell you I want Junior Mints?

ME: Yes.

ANDY: Did I tell you I miss you already?

ME: No. But it's only for 192 hours. I know. I've been working on this since last week.

ANDY: Dude. Who *hasn't*?

ME: You know, Irving Berlin once wrote this song about us called "My Defenses Are Down" and—

ANDY: Hold it. Did a girl sing that one too?

ME: No. A guy.

ANDY: Then okay. As long as we're on the same page for a change.

Naturally, by the time I got to our seats with the popcorn, the red Twizzlers, the Junior Mints, and the Slurpees, we were back to single syllables again. "Here." "Thanks." "Gum?" "Sure." If you and Beau had started out this way, you'd still be selling off your paintings.

But I finally decided to do something about it. Maybe it was because Hucky had made me realize what ginks we were or maybe it was because I knew I'd never be able to sing a torch song with any real authority until I took some affirmative action. So as soon as the lights went down, I gave my right hand permission to storm the beaches at Normandy. Which is exactly what it did. Reaching across the armrest, it deliberately took hold of Andy's five left fingers—no accidental bumping this time, but sure and confident like it knew just what it was doing. Andy instantly squeezed back, and that's the way we stayed for two and a half hours.

LORD OF THE RINGS: THE RETURN OF THE KING
Reviewed by Augie Hwong and Andy Wexler

PLOT: *Lots of very short people running around onscreen. WHO REMEMBERS??*

RATING: *Four thumbs up. Best time we ever had at a movie.*

When we left the theatre for cookies at the café, the snow was falling all over a winter wonderland of our own, and "We Need a Little Christmas" was still serenading the people lined up to get in. That's when I knew for sure that I was going to survive the 192 hours without him, and that sooner or later we'd wind up as happy as you and Beau (assuming Andy doesn't fall off an Alp). Besides, I'd already started a new page in the Augie Hwong Journal of Modern Anxiety called "Will He Ever Kiss Me?"

The Word Shop
BROOKLINE'S FAVORITE BOOKSTORE

E-Memo From the Desk of
Phyllis Bryant

Augie Hwong, anybody can see how much that boy likes you, so don't go looking for trouble where there isn't any. He's the best Christmas present you ever got, so keep quiet and enjoy yourself.

Phyllis was right. I made it through the first 43½ Andy-less hours without even counting them.

Christmas Day was mostly about getting ready for Vermont, but we had a truckload of packages under the tree that we had to plow through first. Half of them were for me and Tick, and half of *those* were from Aunt Babe—who always finds a way to blend our Christmas presents into our birthday presents without a gap. (Tick is February 16 and I'm March 24, so Aunt Babe's figured out how to blend our birthdays into Easter too.) Best Reactions to Christmas Gifts 2003? Mine when I opened the actual authentic original reproduction *All About Eve* poster from my brother, and his when he got a good look at the autographed photo of Carlton Fisk in the 1975 World Series that I'd even framed in gold. (I still don't know what he sees in that guy. So he hit a home run. Big deal. Isn't that what they're *supposed* to do?) Andy and I already decided that our present to each other was just knowing we'd be together on January 2. Alé thought it was "achingly sweet," but I never told Tick about it. He'd have puked all over me.

Since we're leaving for Woodford early tomorrow morning, Mrs. Jordan brought Hucky over to our house in time for dinner. That's when he scored the bonanza he'd been coveting through three weeks' worth of pilgrimages to Toy Mart: an electronic sing-a-long keyboard with a mike. Go figure. Tick says that deaf people can feel music the way we can hear it, and Hucky proved the point. He gave three sold-out concerts between the plum pudding and bed.

"What song was that"

"'Tenth Avenue Freeze-Out'! Don't you know *anything*?"

I have a boyfriend and I'm going skiing with a 3½-foot Bruce Springsteen. Haul out the holly.

> Love,
> Augie

P.S. By the way, *Hello, Dolly!* finally opened. It's a good thing we saw it over Thanksgiving, or else we'd be out of luck.

The Globe

THEATRE

HELLO, DOLLY! AT THE HARBORSIDE

BY LISA WEI HWONG

It doesn't matter if you're short, tall, quiet, loud, agnostic, asexual, intelligent, a gibbering idiot, an international terrorist, or the Hillside Strangler—Dolly Gallagher Levi will fix you up with a partner whether you want one or not. For a fee, of course. That's because she's a matchmaker. If she were working Tremont Street after 7:00 p.m., she'd be called a pimp.

*   *   *

Here's a woman so greedy, so avaricious, and so lacking any sense of propriety, she drove her husband Ephraim to an early grave—and now, presumably without a hobby, she appears determined to cast a far wider net. By evening's end, she's destroyed four lives and three relationships, lied to twenty-six featured players and an entire chorus, and cost at least seven people their respective jobs. This is a reason to sing?

*   *   *

Jerry Herman's always-endearing melodies should not mislead anyone into thinking that *Hello, Dolly!* actually deserves him. Herman—a national treasure—is perhaps the only composer

now or ever who could just as easily leave an
audience humming the Nuremberg Trials. And
boy, does *Dolly!* need him. All it would take is a
score by Stephen Sondheim to make you want
to kill yourself.

Dear Angie,

Briar Hearth Inn looks like a cross between a gingerbread house and a von Trapp Family guest cottage for 158 of their friends. The outside is made of dark brown logs with pointed roofs, apple-colored shutters on all of the windows, and vanilla icing on the top whenever it snows. Seeing it for the first time in the middle of a curvy driveway lined with pine trees, all you want to do is drink hot cider and sing "It's Beginning to Look a Lot Like Christmas."

My favorite room is the Briar Lounge on the second floor. One whole wall is a stone fireplace that stays lit 24/7, with enough couches and stuffed chairs in front of it to keep you there all day, especially if you have a ginky vacation assignment to read like *Great Expectations*. Best of all is the bay window that looks out across the whole valley, with the kids' slope front and center. This is where we took Hucky as soon as we'd unpacked. Mom and Dad rented him the smallest skis you've ever seen, and Pop walked behind him—hands on shoulders—all the way down the hill, which maybe slants twenty degrees, tops. Dressed in his Red Sox ski jacket (from Mom and Dad), Red Sox ski cap and gloves (from me and Tick), and Red Sox muffler (from Pop), he looked like a frozen little Ramon Garciaparra who was scared to death—but once he'd made it to the bottom in one piece, the cheers and high fives changed his mind. So did the trophy (HUCKY HARPER—BRIAR HEARTH SKI CHAMPION). After that, he wouldn't let Pop help him out anymore. *"But you can watch me."* He figured out the rope pull that took him to the top all by himself, and by the time he'd finished his first solo run, he was on his way to the Olympics.

Tick and I were supposed to practice on the beginners' slope, but we decided that the mountain air had made us susceptible to the cold, so Tick headed off to the Briar Lounge to warm up and I went back to our room.

---

www.augiehwong.com
PRIVATE CHAT

AugieHwong: Know what I really hate? When people use words like "puppy love." What's up with *that*?

AndyWexler: I don't know. Maybe we're supposed to go pee on trees. Spidey, this isn't fair. All there is to do in Cleveland is watch my aunt Ett chew Chiclets or listen to my grandpa remember about when tariffs were paid in gold, so I can *afford* to spend the whole week online with you. But you could be out skiing.

AugieHwong: Does it sound like I think I'm missing anything?

AndyWexler: Just me. :)

AugieHwong: Oh. You noticed. Besides, my brother's been on the phone with Alé a lot longer than we've been online. He's waiting for the magic moment to tell her they should just be friends—which is supposed to make her fall in love with him. What's up with *that*?

AndyWexler: Jealous that you didn't think of it first?

AugieHwong: I never had to.

Dad and Pop had booked a deluxe double for the kids, which meant two big beds for me and Tick, and a cot for Hucky and Shut-the-Door. "*Wow! A little mattress with wheels! Dude! Fold me up inside it and then roll me around.*" In between pillow fights on our first night there—and while Hucky was brushing his teeth with his *Shrek* toothbrush and *Hey, Arnold!* toothpaste—my brother and I decided that if he started crying in his sleep, whichever one of us woke up first would take the shift.

"Like a two a.m. feeding?" I asked, whacking him over the head. Nobody gets the best of Augie Hwong in a pillow fight. My dad teaches tae kwon do. I inherited all the right moves.

The initial tour of duty turned out to be mine. It was around 3:15 a.m. when the whimpering made me open my eyes and figure out what was going on. But Tick had already briefed me on the drill, so I climbed out of bed automatically, sat down next to the cot, and worked the Stuffed-Dog-in-the-Arms/Head-Patting maneuver like I'd been doing it my whole life. Since it only took about ten minutes before he quieted down and I could hit the sack again, I assumed I had the magic touch—until I woke up an hour later to go pee and discovered Tick sound asleep on the floor with his arm stretched across the cot and around Hucky. *This is SO not going to work*, I thought. So while I was dragging him back to his deluxe double across the room, I drafted an emergency battle plan of my own: For the rest of the trip, Tick and I would just take turns sharing our beds with him. It'd be a lot easier on all three of us. And we could always use the cot to fold him up and roll him around in.

"Good idea," mumbled my brother, crawling back under the covers. "G'night."

AugieHwong: After four pancakes and one toboggan ride, Tick pulled a mostly effective "I'm sleepy" routine so he could go back to the Briar Lounge and call Alé. When it worked, I started yawning too.

AndyWexler: Now I've got you all to myself. The whole world is jealous.

AugieHwong: How come we can't talk like this to each other when we're together?

AndyWexler: Maybe because I don't think I'm all the way used to it yet. Not like you. You're sure of everything. And my dad used to be an Air Force pilot. He'd never go along with the program.

AugieHwong: Your dad already knows.

AndyWexler: Knows what? That I'm crazy about Wonderboy?

AugieHwong: Gulp. You said it first.

AndyWexler: But you've been thinking it too.

AugieHwong: Only since October.

AndyWexler: I can't remember October. I got hit in the head by so many softballs from trying not to look at you in the stands that the October part of my brain was damaged. After a while it got pretty annoying. I even thought about kicking your ass. Would you let me teach you how to play football?

AugieHwong: Where did *that* come from?

AndyWexler: Anybody who's good enough to letter in soccer, swimming, and track should be playing football too. It's a boy thing. You practically *have* to.

While we were at lunch in the Lookout Mountain dining room (all four walls are made out of windows), we got a big surprise. Who was eating scallops at the next table? Lori! It turned out that she needed some downtime after six days in Queens with her family, so out of all the places in New England to go to, she just happened to pick the Briar Hearth Inn. What are the odds?

"Ted?" she called out, looking a little startled. Pop turned around at the sound of her voice and smote his forehead as soon as he saw her.

"Oh, my God," he blurted, jumping to his feet. "Talk about synchronicity!" There was a scene just like this one in *Muriel's Wedding*. ("Deidre Chambers! What a coincidence!") I didn't believe it then, and I didn't believe it now. Tick and I swapped fish-eyes with Mom and Dad, and then I whispered to my brother, "How long do you think they've been planning this?" Tick listened for a second to how fast Pop was talking, and then he turned back to me.

"At least two weeks."

As soon as Lori sat down with us, she introduced herself to Hucky in a confident kind of sign language that proved she didn't realize that what she'd just said was "I ate Lori"—but Hucky caught on anyway. And since it was obvious that Pop had other things on his mind for the rest of the afternoon, it seemed like a good idea to go back to the room for a nap while Mom and Dad took Hucky snowboarding. Tick was already in the Briar Lounge. He didn't even wait around for the hangaburs.

Why does Andy want me to play football??

INSTANT MESSENGER

AlePerez: Have you seen *any* of Vermont?

AugieHwong: About as much as you've seen of Mexico City. Why aren't you on the phone with my brother? They've practically bronzed a chair for him in the Briar Lounge.

AlePerez: Our batteries died. We're recharging.

AugieHwong: By the way, last night I wore the brown sweater you gave me for Christmas. When we walked into the dining room, heads turned—and I'm not kidding. Three of them were boys, and one of them had to be at least 16.

AlePerez: I told you I know how to dress men. Wait until you see what Anthony's baby blue sweater does for his eyes. He promised me he'd wear it to dinner tonight. Make sure he does.

AugieHwong: Do you know what you've achieved? My brother hates sweaters the way he says JFK hated hats, but he packed yours anyway. So you've already won the round. And every time he gets off the phone with you, he stares into the fireplace for an hour and doesn't respond to any external stimuli. We're afraid he's going to burn his retinas.

Hucky's teaching himself how to slalom, but he only wants to do it on flat ground and without skis. The hotel's ready to hire him as their mascot. By the time we leave, he'll *own* Vermont. And he stopped the nighttime crying once he realized one of us would always be next to him. We were going to tell Pop, but now we can't find him anywhere.

AlePerez: Check the ski lift, especially if it's stuck. He and Lori'll be in the top gondola, she'll be panicking, and he'll have his arm around her. Adults become so obvious when they're in love.

AugieHwong: Gotta go. IM from Andy.

AlePerez: My cell's ringing. It's your brother.

AugieHwong: Ask him if they're serving hot chocolate yet.

AlePerez: Hello? I'm in Mexico. You're down the hall. *You* ask him.

Alé has a point. This is family vacation. We're supposed to be sharing quality time with each other. Thank God we're leaving tomorrow night. This has been the longest 192 hours of my life.

Love,

Augie

THREE WEEKS ONLY!!!
The Lyric Stage

PRESENTS

FOLLIES

Book by JAMES GOLDMAN
Music and Lyrics by STEPHEN SONDHEIM

✶ ✶ ✶ ✶ ✶

Dear Angie,

What have I done? How could I have been so clueless? WHY DOESN'T SOMEBODY JUST TELL ME TO SHUT UP AND BE NORMAL???

It wasn't Aunt Babe's fault. When she saw that *Follies* was playing at the Lyric, she flew up for a day and a night just to take me to see it. (She knows how I feel about the CD, and Mom once told her that I could pronounce "Yvonne DeCarlo" before I even learned to say "Grandma Lily.") So when Andy and I were at The Word Shop Café this afternoon, it was only a matter of time before I began singing

"I'm Still Here" for him over hot chocolates and lemon loaf cake. I mean, who *wouldn't* share something like that with a boyfriend, right? Pretty soon I had my usual audience, and at the end of it I got a bigger hand than the diva who sang it at the Lyric did. (Let's just say she didn't exactly give Yvonne anything to worry about.) *But why didn't I notice that Andy wasn't clapping before I nailed the "Could I Leave You?" encore????*

---

www.augiehwong.com
PRIVATE CHAT

AndyWexler: Do you *always* have to do that?

AugieHwong: Do what?

AndyWexler: Augie, you're a *guy*. Once in a while you need to remind people before they forget.

AugieHwong: But I do! I play soccer and I'm on the swim team and—

AndyWexler: And you tell people that in your last life you were the Andrews Sisters. All I'm saying is that sometimes it gets a little intimidating. Just a little.

I don't remember the rest of what he said. And I probably wouldn't want to anyway.

Augie

Alejandra

Dear Jacqueline,

In 1951, everyone knew you as Black Jack Bouvier's radiant daughter. You'd gone to all of the best schools, you'd studied with the most gifted professors at the Sorbonne, and you were as dainty and delicate as a porcelain Southern belle who hadn't heard of the Civil War yet. Then Charlie Bartlett introduced you to a young senator named John F. Kennedy, who wasn't exactly paparazzi bait yet. In fact, he was so minor league when he first winked at you, I'm surprised you didn't make him wait in the lobby. And yet something clearly happened to transform the fluttery Ms. Bouvier into a national legend, because twelve years later the *London Evening Standard* wrote: "Jacqueline Kennedy has given the American people from this day on one thing they have always lacked—majesty." That difference could only have been Jack.

Suddenly I find myself following in your footsteps, and frankly (no offense), who needs it?? In September, I owned academic honors from the most respected academies in Washington, D.C., and Mexico City, I'd made friends with some of the most well-known people in the world, and I had the answers to just about any question put to me. Now I'm writing letters to Mary Poppins and trying to build a baseball diamond in a wasteland. And I don't even know *why*!!

It was his Christmas present that did me in. If I'd thought the "sway-ah" had compromised my resistance to its limits, I was in for an even ruder shock—and opening Augie's gift first only set me up for it. Underneath the wrapping, I found a silver-framed 1948 photograph of Patricia Morison singing "So in Love With You Am I" in the original Broadway production of *Kiss Me, Kate*, along with an inscription that read: "This is just the beginning. Merry Christmas. I love you. Augie." So I was already weepy when I discovered that his brother had managed to track down an out-of-print hardcover rarity that's escaped me for two years: *The Burden and The Glory: The Speeches and Hopes of John F. Kennedy*. Beneath the black and gold cover, he'd written on the flyleaf: "For Alé. Let us never negotiate out of fear. But let us never fear to negotiate. Love, Anthony." Know what got me? It wasn't the quote from the inaugural address, and it certainly wasn't the "Love" (boys apply that word just as liberally to lizards and auto parts). It was the "Anthony." He *hates* being called Anthony—which is precisely why I began using it in the first place. I thought it would chase him away, but I was wrong. Who knew it was such a strong and honorable name after all?!

From: AlePerez@earthworks.net
To: TCKeller@earthworks.net

I just got a letter from Fred Hoyt at Manzanar. "Dear Ms. Perez and Mr. Keller: Thank you so much for your interest in the Manzanar National Historic Site. We are most grateful for your proposal to restore the camp's baseball diamond, and we will consider the various possibilities. Meanwhile, if you and your young friends would like to think about organizing a baseball game to celebrate the Park's official opening in April 2004 (at a nearby ball field off the premises, of course), we might even make it part of our festivities! Very truly yours, Fred Hoyt; cc: United States Senate (individually)." I think we've won.

From: TCKeller@earthworks.net
To: AlePerez@earthworks.net

Oh no we haven't. "Young friends" is the tipoff. Translation: "Dear Ms. Perez and Mr. Keller: No way are we going to restore your baseball diamond, but we need to keep you ginks occupied until April so you won't have time to write any more pissy letters to senators." Trust me. There won't be a baseball game either. This whole thing is a ruse. Now it's time to step up the pressure. If you're not doing anything on Thursday after rehearsal, I can explain things a lot better over hangaburs and fries.

From: AlePerez@earthworks.net
To: TCKeller@earthworks.net

How did you become such a cynic?

From: TCKeller@earthworks.net
To: AlePerez@earthworks.net

It's part of the Red Sox gene. Hey, have you heard from my brother? He dropped off my scope two days ago.

From: AlePerez@earthworks.net
To: TCKeller@earthworks.net

I was going to ask you the same thing.

I couldn't find much time to visit with friends in Mexico City over Christmas because my calendar didn't have any more room on it. If I wasn't on my cell with Anthony, I was sitting in front of our television set with a workbook in my lap and a DVD entitled *American Sign Language for All* spinning in its tray. (I'm sorry—I simply *cannot* allow him to know more things than I do.) You're lucky that Jack didn't have any deaf adversaries in his life, because nothing in *American Sign Language for All* would have prepared you for the basic niceties like "How are you enjoying the Politburo, Mrs. Khrushchev?"

Things I Hoped to Learn

"A spoonful of sugar helps the medicine go down."

"It's a jolly holiday with Mary."

"Wipe the hot chocolate off your face."

"Anthony said no, and that means no."

"Use the red crayon for that."

Things I Learned

"I'd like a room on the second floor."

"Where is the post office?"

"Do you serve luncheon here?"

"I'm allergic to cats."

"The toilet is not working properly."

If I hadn't discovered ASL Online, I'd have been up a creek.

Mamita had met Anthony and Hucky briefly when she picked me up at The Word Shop Café for a dental appointment, and (like anyone else they smile at) she was absolutely enchanted. So she spent most of December 28 helping me download assorted signing dictionaries from the Internet, and on the 29th we tracked down a subtitled copy of *Mary Poppins* ("*Por qué está flotando ese hombre en el techo, Señorita Poppins?*") in order to translate as much of it as possible with our fingers. I now have a mother who's learning American Sign Language in Spanish.

"*Let us never negotiate out of fear. But let us never fear to negotiate. Love, Anthony.*"

I think I'm losing my mind.

Fondly,

Alejandra

P.S. Speaking of Mamita, she and Papa attended Parents' Night at school. I was deathly afraid that they were going to find out about my secret life as an errant ingénue, and I had good reason: Mrs. Fitzpatrick couldn't wait to blab to them about *Kiss Me, Kate*. Fortunately, Papa and Mamita know as much about musical comedy as Augie knows about Max Schmeling and Joe Louis, so when Papa pressed me for more details in the limo on the way home, I assured him that *Kiss Me, Kate* was nothing more than a kids' version of *The Taming of the Shrew*. (Papa approves of both Shakespeare and serious drama—though I never actually said that *Kate* was either, Your Honor.) I don't know how long I can keep this up. What if they want to come to a performance??

INSTANT MESSENGER

TCKeller: You really think they'd *care*?

AlePerez: Of course they'd care! One of these days they're going to find out that the closest their daughter is ever going to get to an ambassadorship is playing Sally Adams in *Call Me Madam*.

TCKeller: Who said they wanted you to be an ambassador?

AlePerez: You're *so* lame. It's understood!

TCKeller: And you're *so* like back in pre-school if that's the best you can read parents. Did you see how puffed up your father got when Mr. Landey told him about your science grades? What do foot-pounds have to do with Eurodollars?? He's *dying* for you to find another career.

AlePerez: That's idiotic. Papa and Mamita are two of the most respected dignitaries in any hemisphere—

TCKeller: Right. And how many major countries have you insulted personally?

AlePerez: Is Finland a major country?

TCKeller: Yes.

AlePerez: Eleven.

TCKeller: You *see*? They're scared to death of you. You could sabotage the whole empire. If you actually told them you wanted to work at the U.N. this summer, they'd probably have a stroke.

AlePerez: Then why did Mamita bring up an internship at the French Embassy?

TCKeller: So you could run perfume errands for the ambassador's wife and fall in love with her ginky son. Which

by the way is going to happen over my
dead body.

AlePerez: Do you mean *any* of this?

TCKeller: Actually, no. But your ears look
like they're about to blow off the side of
your head. Get a grip. You belong in a
spotlight. We'll deal with the other stuff
when it happens. Parents *always* cave in
sooner or later.

UNITED STATES SECRET SERVICE
WASHINGTON, D.C.

CLINT LOCKHART
AGENT

This kid's got your number and he uses it well.

Princess, you're rehearsing for your first performance as a star at the same time you're going head to head with the U.S. government over somebody else's civil rights and asking a fictitious nanny to help a six-year-old boy believe in himself. This from the kid who wouldn't listen to *The Little Engine That Could* because she refused to accept that locomotives had vocal cords. What do you think all those trips to the library were for?? To teach you how to do what you're doing right now, that's what.

So whether you realize it or not, your last handful of "I can't," "I won't," and "I shouldn't" excuses just went out the window. Enjoy it. I know *I* will.

xoxo,
Clint

Dear Jacqueline,

I was in no mood to be crossed during rehearsals this afternoon, especially since nobody's learned the second act yet except for the songs, and we open on Valentine's weekend for a three-performance run. That's only five weeks from now! How on earth am I supposed to pull it all together by then??

"Get up there on the stage," ordered Anthony from his customary seat in the front row. "You'll have it down cold in *half* that time."

"*Yeah,*" signed Hucky from his customary seat by Anthony's right elbow. "*There's no business like show business.*" (Augie taught him that in Vermont. Anthony and I both agreed that if Hucky begins quoting Bette Davis next, we're not allowing Augie within fifty feet of him. Ever.)

REHEARSAL NOTES

1.   We began with my first scene. Fred Graham is a theatre director, and Lilli Vanessi is a star. Even though they're divorced, they've agreed to play Katharine and Petruchio in this production of *Shrew*—and you can tell right off the bat that there's still some attraction there. For reasons of her own in choosing our Fred, Mrs. Packer cast Keith Marshall, a good-looking tenth grader who hasn't brushed his teeth since the Clinton administration. In fact, you can always tell when he's entered behind you because the aroma precedes him every time he breathes. (Unless my costume is equipped with an oxygen mask, the kissing scenes are going to be toxic.) This afternoon, his bouquet-of-lunch was still so pungent, I didn't even bother to face him while we were performing "Wunderbar." Instead, I deliberately sang it out front to Hucky—who grinned bashfully

and waved to me. Since he clearly knows nothing about Method Acting or the Fourth Wall, I waved back.

2.   Mrs. Packer had to take a telephone call in the faculty lounge, so the rest of us moved out into the auditorium to watch Augie run through "Too Darn Hot." It's the only song in the show that's ready for opening night, but we all get such a kick out of it that there's at least one command performance at every rehearsal. When Augie stomps his feet and sings, "But I'd be a flop with my baby tonight, 'cause it's too darn hot" and then winks at Andy, it's too darn cute. But today there was no stomp and definitely no wink. As a matter of fact, they didn't make eye contact once. Something is radically wrong.

3.   I used my downtime to explain the story of *Kiss Me, Kate* to Hucky, which was clearly going to be a challenge. The signs that Mamita and I downloaded from the Internet had certainly covered basic English, but I wasn't sure how well they embraced Cole Porter lyrics.

"Now, the scene you just saw," I began, pointing to the stage.

"Was about you and T.C.," he concluded, nodding like he already knew.

"What??"

"She pretends she doesn't like him and he pretends he doesn't care." I had no handy rebuttal to that particular allegation and wouldn't have been able to come up with one if I'd been given a week's notice. So I countered with the only safe reply I could think of.

"The toilet is not working properly."

4.   Mrs. Packer called places for my final number, which still hadn't been staged yet. This was the battle I'd been dreading since

the day I'd been cast as Lilli—so while the chorus assumed their positions behind me, I knelt down on the edge of the stage and whispered nervously to my director, who was taking notes on a yellow pad in an aisle seat.

"Mrs. Packer?"

"Yes, Alejandra?"

"Uh—I'm sorry, but I just can't sing a song called 'I Am Ashamed That Women Are So Simple.' I have a NOW card." From the back of the stage, I heard the always-reliable Lee fanning the flame toward a brushfire.

"Hear, hear," she mumbled. Mrs. Packer put down her script patiently as though she'd been through this argument before.

"Alé, I understand your concern, but it's an important part of the scene."

"Yes, but—"

"Honey, we can't work around it." She shrugged and signaled Mr. Disharoon to cue the number. By now, the other kids had gotten wind of what was going on, and rehearsals promptly stopped dead in their tracks for the next twenty minutes as entire armies formed on both sides of the Continental Divide. Predictably, all of the girls stood behind me and Lee as their leaders, while most of the boys backed up the dentally challenged Keith as theirs.

"But Kate's right. Men are more complicated."

"Hellooo? What universe spawned *you*?"

"Aw, chill out. It's not like she sings 'I Am Ashamed That Women Are So *Stupid*.'"

"Don't go there. I'm warning you." This last rebuke came unexpectedly from Mrs. Packard, who realized she'd inadvertently taken sides in a gender war. What else could she do??

5.   Once the offending number had been eliminated, we wrapped up rehearsal with a walk-through of "So in Love With You Am I." This is one routine I know so well, I could perform it under a general anesthetic. But halfway through the second verse, I happened to glance toward the back of the house and noticed an out-of-place yet familiar curly head nodding in time to the Cole Porter rhythm. *Carlos?? What's he doing here?* My brother's unexpected presence so threw me that I went up on my lyrics for the one and only time in my life. Even Mrs. Packer was startled.

"Uh, Alejandra?" she cued, looking up from her script. "It's 'in love with my joy delirious.'"

"I know." I blushed. "Excuse me for just a moment." While an oblivious Mr. Disharoon continued to play the melody line, I made my way up the aisle and accosted my brother like I'd just discovered what "fratricide" meant.

"You can't just show up without warning me," I hissed, leaning down to him in the last row. "You're not even supposed to *be* here!" In reply, Carlos turned on one of those easy grins that have made him a regular fixture on several of our larger continents.

"Hey," he admonished defensively, "if I'm going to go to bat for you, I need to know that you've got the right stuff." Then he glanced up at the stage and turned back to me. If it were anybody else, I'd almost think he was awed. "Sis," he whispered, "you're *really good!*"

Now I know why Hucky believes in chalk pavements pictures. Right now, I'm ready to believe just about *any*thing.

> Fondly,
> Alejandra

INSTANT MESSENGER

AugieHwong: "Mrs. Packer, I just can't sing a song called 'I Am Ashamed That Women Are So Simple.'" In front of my eyes you turned into Helen Lawson. "Get rid of the ballad!" "Fire Neely O'Hara!" "Set up a couple bottles of the grape!" Oh God, you were HEAVEN!

AlePerez: What happened with you and Andy? And why haven't you told us?

AugieHwong: It's over, that's all. He doesn't get me. Big deal. Slow curtain. The End.

AlePerez: Are you okay?

AugieHwong: I still love him, if that's what you mean. But Dad says it fades after a while. The weird thing is that I'm not sure I want it to.

Don't worry. "Good times and bum times, I've seen them all and, my dear, I'm still here."

The Globe

EMAIL FROM   *LISA WEI HWONG*

Dear Alé,

You're an angel. I've been trying to do something about "I Am Ashamed That Women Are So Simple" ever since I first heard it twenty-two years ago and assumed it was a practical joke.

If you're keeping a list, the next horror to be eliminated is that ghastly monkey's paw from *Fiorello!* "I'll Marry the Very Next Man." With lyrics like "Who cares how frequently he strikes me?" and "I'll fetch his slippers with my arm in a sling," even Jack the Ripper would have been embarrassed.

Wei

INSTANT MESSENGER

AlePerez: Did you find anything out?

TCKeller: He just says it's over. I hate it when he puts on his game face with me. What does he think I'm *here* for??

AlePerez: Who broke it off—Augie or Andy?

TCKeller: Augie did. What's up with *that*?? When my brother commits to something, he's like a puppy who won't let go of his favorite sock.

AlePerez: I know. And it spills over. Remember his UPI bulletin the week after Thanksgiving, when they'd held hands for the third time? At 12:34 in the morning he e-mailed me a Barbra Streisand song called "If You Were the Only Boy in the World" and promised it would "lull me to sleep faster than five milligrams of Xanax on an empty stomach."

TCKeller: Why couldn't you sleep?

AlePerez: I was having trouble making up my mind about something.

TCKeller: Did it help?

AlePerez: No.

TCKeller: Oh.

Alé, would it be okay with you if we could rewind to the first day and just be friends? Without all of my secret plans to make you fall for me? Because I figured out over Christmas that I need to know we can always count on each other no matter what. Okay?

AlePerez: Did somebody actually talk you into *trying* that old routine??

TCKeller: Uh, yeah. Pop did. He said I'd know when the moment was right.

AlePerez: He was also born in 1952. Things have changed since then. And you both deserve a time-out.

Dear Jacqueline,

Another plot between father and son. "Would it be okay with you if we could rewind to the first day and just be friends?" Honestly. At least the "um" possessed a peculiar sort of subtlety. Even a blockhead like Helena wouldn't have fallen for *this* one. Do men really think we're all idiots?? But if we're not, why did Anthony suddenly get cuter?

Dinner was supposed to have been about our baseball diamond, but that only took ten minutes. In fact, the hangaburs hadn't even made it to the table yet.

MANZANAR BATTLE PLAN—PHASE 2

1. Find out who the leaders of the Japanese American

community are and let them know what we're trying to do. (Anthony has 4 names already.)

2. Get ahold of a lawyer named Dale Minami in San Francisco who got them their civil rights back in 1983. (Anthony has his address but Alé writes better, so she's in charge.)

3. Start tracking down the old guys who used to play for the San Fernando Aces. (Maybe the Hall of Fame can help us.)

4. Make sure that everything we mail out is CC'd to the Senate and to Fred Hoyt. (Especially to Fred Hoyt.)

5. It's time to bring in the heavy artillery and call Aunt Ruth. Since she's usually willing to start any House of Representatives committee that pisses off the president, she'll be our secret weapon when we need her. (Anthony and Alé should both talk to her.)

At his insistence, we met at the Brookline Café so we could sit in the Bobby Kennedy booth. Of course, the waiter had no idea which of the two seats the tantrum-throwing attorney general had actually occupied—but we figured it was probably the one by the window, so that's where I made Anthony sit. He was welcome to any karma that still lingered, though personally I'd have gotten rid of it all with Lysol. Wouldn't it be funny if everyone who sat there became whiny and self-centered?

It turns out that the Brookline Café—despite a menu that spells "spinach" with a t—holds a place of honor in the Keller family, since it's where Anthony's father took his mother on their first unofficial date together. Anthony is always so hesitant when he speaks of her that when he awkwardly showed me the picture he's begun carrying in his wallet, I was momentarily startled—though I could see instantly who gave him his blue eyes. She reminded me of a young Emma Thompson, only lovelier. Evidently, Ted and Nikki met at Fenway Park on an October afternoon in 1978 when an annual fluke put the Red Sox one game away from the American League playoffs, as though they actually deserved to be there.

"Pop's scalper on Kenmore Square charged him $215 for Infield Grandstand Section 20, Seat 103," confided Anthony, "and Mama's scalper on Yawkey Way only charged her $125 for Infield Grandstand Section 20, Seat 104. She never let him forget it." (I liked her already.)

They didn't say much to each other for the first few innings—she brought him a beer and he brought her a hot dog on two separate trips to the concession stand, and that pretty much maxed out the conversation. But as soon as the Red Sox had gone up 2–0, they both began to panic at the same moment—and by the time Bucky F. Dent had come to bat in the seventh inning for the Yankees, with Chris Chambliss and Roy White on base, "Mama and Pop were squeezing each other's hands like two *Titanic* survivors who were getting ready to jump off the stern together."

After the Yankees had won it all by the predictable score of 5–4, Ted and Nikki remained in their seats for another stunned half hour without uttering a sound. (Come to think of it, if I'd just spent $340 on two tickets worth $13.80, I'd have taken my time too.) Then they introduced themselves to each other, and "Pop invited Mama to have dinner with him in Bobby Kennedy's booth. Mama was sitting where you are." (I have no information on how she felt about your ratty brother-in-law.)

Ted was a college baseball player with a B.A. from Boston University who wanted to build houses, and Nikki was a Newburyport native with a master's degree in American history from Brandeis. Boy, did she make him sweat. They didn't agree on movies, wine, or books, she wouldn't let him give her flowers, and she never seemed to be at home when he called. (According to Anthony, "She was actually sitting by the answering machine listening, but he didn't find that out until their second anniversary.") Finally he couldn't take it anymore.

"Nikki, this is Ted. These are my terms. I'll learn to like cabernet, I'll give *To Kill a Mockingbird* one more shot, and I won't send roses. But on Saturday night I'm taking you to see *The Buddy Holly Story* in Cambridge and after that we're going out to dinner. You can pick where. So if you've already made other plans, break 'em. And meet me at the theatre at 7:15 because I'm not going to call you again."

She got there at 7:10. And at 11:30, he kissed her for the first time on the corner of Church Street and Mass Ave.

INSTANT MESSENGER

AlePerez: Oh, my God. It's the most romantic story I ever heard.

AugieHwong: Yeah, Pop knew what he was doing. Did Tick tell you about the star his mom named "Anthony"?

AlePerez: The one over Plum Island or the one over Maine?

AugieHwong: Hold it. *I* never knew there was a second one in Maine! Double-crossed again! First Andy, now this. Excuse me while I go shoot myself.

AlePerez: What happened with Andy?

AugieHwong: Gender confusion issues. He didn't exactly appreciate my Yvonne DeCarlo. That's all I'm saying. I wish I lived in a movie like *Meet Me in St. Louis.* He'd show up at the Christmas dance in his tux, tell me how sorry he was, and we'd get a duet that Frank Sinatra and Ella Fitzgerald would sing together at the Oscars.

Anthony was born on February 16, 1989, and even though his mother had been hoping it would happen two days earlier, she still called him "my Valentine baby" for the rest of her life. She helped him figure out Santa Claus's secret identity (he was really Mr. Zentz at the drugstore), she taught him how to find lost purple balloons ("Watch the sky and remember how much you love it, and it'll come back to you"), and he even got a letter in the mailbox from the Tooth Fairy, thanking him for the cookie he'd left with his molar.

Then, when he was four, his goldfish Cleo died, and he cried for two nights in a row—not because of Cleo, but because he was afraid that one day his mother was going to die too. So she sat up with him until he finally fell asleep, holding his hand and repeating over and over, "I'm not going *any*where, and I'll be here as long as you need me." That was a month before she found the lump in her breast.

Anthony knew his mother was sick, but when you're that young there's no real difference between chicken pox and cancer. Just before she started chemotherapy, she was teaching him how to ride a bicycle by himself. First she'd walk along the sidewalk with him— holding the handlebars so he wouldn't wobble—and once he'd gotten the hang of it, she'd let go. But somehow he always managed to topple over into the grass. So when he raced into her hospital room three weeks later and jumped onto her bed, the front-page headline was, "Mama! I made it to the end of the street without falling off once!" Nikki immediately broke into a huge smile and wrapped her arms around him tightly.

"Now, *that's* good news," she said, kissing the top of his head. "Do you know how proud I am?" And that was the last time he ever saw her. She died the following morning, and all Anthony could remember was "I'll be here as long as you need me."

"I was only six," he mumbled quietly, finishing off his french fries, "so I thought that since I'd told her I could ride a bicycle by myself, maybe she didn't think I needed her anymore. That's why I always figured it was my fault. I should have kept my mouth shut."

There was nothing for me to say. Even if I'd been able to.

INSTANT MESSENGER

AlePerez: Augie, please tell me he didn't put himself through all of that.

AugieHwong: Yeah, he did. He never told anybody but me, and I couldn't talk him out of it. I *so* should have tipped off Pop. And he wouldn't ride a bike again until we were ten.

During the walk home, Anthony was back to making plans for our baseball diamond, but I didn't hear very much of it. *No wonder he's tracking down Mary Poppins for a six-year-old boy. I could never have survived losing my mother. How can there still be room in his heart for Buck Weaver and Manzanar and Hucky and Augie and me too??*

Jacqueline, whether or not I ever give the American people majesty, I'm going to fall in love with Anthony Keller anyway. As soon as he learns that all I want him to be is Anthony. Without the ploys and gimmicks.

Why is it so hard to keep them real?

> Fondly,
> Alejandra

Julie Andrews

Dear Hucky:

I recently heard about you on England's side of the Atlantic Ocean. Is it true that you can finger-spell supercalifragilisticexpialidocious and you're only six? Even *I* can't do that. You must have had a very special teacher.

Popping in and out of chalk pavement pictures takes a lot of practice, so be patient. You may not be able to master it until you're at least ten. (One trick I learned is to begin by closing your eyes and imagining candy apples and steam calliopes. That always helps.)

Please promise me that you'll continue to do well in school, because the penguins won't let just anyone dance with them. Bert had to have good grades first, and they'll expect the same from Hucky Harper.

Hugs to you.

My loveliest of wishes,
Julie Andrews

---

www.augiehwong.com
PRIVATE CHAT

AugieHwong: No wonder she won an Academy Award. She really *is* Mary Poppins. Okay, maybe she's making all of it up, but the calliope part sounds pretty real to *me*. I may even try it to see what happens.

TCKeller: But she signed it "Julie Andrews"! Hucky never *heard* of Julie Andrews. Didn't we tell her he thinks she's a real nanny?

AlePerez: I thought it was understood.

AugieHwong: Only to us.

TCKeller: This isn't going to do any good. We can't let him find out it's just a part in a movie.

AlePerez: At least we can save it for him until he gets older. It's a lovely letter.

AugieHwong: Yeah, but what about *now*?

TCKeller: Look, it's not like Mary Poppins is the only one who can have tea parties on the ceiling, you know. Maybe it's up to us to show him the same kinds of things ourselves. That's all he needs. Like teaching him that frozen ponds are really secret entrances to the North Pole.

AugieHwong: Tick, if we're going to be flying up any chimneys to dance on rooftops, please let me know ahead of time. Because I don't want to be wearing my Versace slacks.

Dear Mama,

When I first had the Julie Andrews idea it was only because I knew it's what you would have done if you were me and I was Hucky. Except that it wouldn't have stopped with a letter. When I came home from school one day, she would have been sitting in our living room with you, drinking tea and eating cakes, and you would have said, "T.C., Mary Poppins came over to see you," like it was the most normal thing in the world. After that, she would have walked me to Emerson Garden holding my hand, and when we got there she'd have sat on the bench with a smile on her face while I knelt on the sidewalk with my colored chalk and drew a picture of merry-go-rounds and penguins and talking horses. Once I was finished, she would have stood up and said, "All right, T.C. Spit-spot! Let's get ready to take a trip." Just like we were really going to hop inside of it. But at the last minute, she'd have stared down at the Ferris wheel and said, "Oh dear. There's a thunderstorm coming just over the hill you drew. I'm terribly afraid that if we pop inside for a visit right now, we'll be washed away with everything else." Well, I wouldn't have wanted that either, so I'd have let her take me to The Word Shop Café instead—without even knowing that she was secretly Julie Andrews, who didn't really have special powers, because I'd always believe that Mary Poppins had saved my life by not letting me get erased in the rain. And while we were eating cookies at the café, all the other kids would be whispering, "Hey, look! That's T.C. Keller with Mary Poppins!" Phyllis would have been impressed too, even though she'd know the truth. ("Anthony Keller, you march yourself over to Aisle 2 and pick out a thank-you card for Julie—for Mary Poppins.") On the way home, we'd stop by a church so we could sit on the front steps and feed the birds bread crumbs (tuppence a bag), and then she'd come over to our house for dinner. You'd ask her how Bert and Uncle Albert were doing, and Pop would want to know how she could get any sleep with Admiral Boom shooting off that cannon next door. Finally it'd be bedtime and Mary Poppins would tuck me in and kiss me on the forehead. And just as I was nodding off, she'd whisper how much she loved me.

But I have all of the things you taught me on my side, so I can work a little Mary Poppins magic of my own. And I know just where I'm going to start.

I love you,
T.C.

P.S. I figure I set myself back three months with Alé by pulling the "just friends" routine. Pop says it's not his fault that nobody sent him the rule book upgrade. Meanwhile, I think I found a gray hair.

INSTANT MESSENGER

TCKeller: I'm going to get Pop to take us to Plum Island for the day. When it gets dark out, we'll sit on the beach and name a star Hucky. I'll bet Mary Poppins never did that.

AugieHwong: Which reminds me. I heard a rumor that there's a star named Anthony in Maine too. How come I never knew that, big brother?

TCKeller: Because I only remembered it in November, you hoser head! There was this lighthouse near the shore, and the guy who worked there took us up to the top at night. Mama didn't want to waste the view so she let me pick out the brightest star in the sky sort of as a backup to the first one. I think it was Venus.

AugieHwong: How could you forget something like that, you gink?? Whole *movies* have been written about less.

Tick, have you ever been ashamed of me?

TCKeller: I'll kick his ass.

AugieHwong: Whose??

TCKeller: Andy's. Is that what he said to you???

AugieHwong: No. I mean, not exactly. But wouldn't I be less of a freak if I acted like a normal guy once in a while?

TCKeller: And turn into somebody your own brother wouldn't even recognize??? I swear to God I'm going to kick his ass.

AugieHwong: You don't have to. You just answered my question.

Student/Adviser Conference

Lori Mahoney/Anthony C. Keller

LORI: Naming a star after a six-year-old can mean a lot to him. You should know.

T.C.:   Maybe. But not all by itself. Alé and Augie and I figured that if we can keep him busy with lots of different things like that, he might forget all about Mary Poppins.

LORI: It's easier than you think. What's the most magical thing in *your* life?

T.C.:   Well, this week it's lying in bed at night with my Discman and listening to "Suite: Judy Blue Eyes."

LORI: But you get the picture. Natural wonders come in so many different disguises. Like watching the tide at sunset, walking up Comm Ave when it's snowing, seeing a baby smile for the first time—

T.C.:   Sneaking down to court-side seats at a C's game.

LORI: That is *not* a natural wonder. It's a criminal act.

T.C.:   By the way, Pop's going to invite you to Plum Island with us.

LORI: I'm busy that day.

T.C.:   I didn't even tell you when we were going!

LORI: Are you inviting Alé?

T.C.:   I thought about it, but I haven't decided yet. I'm still skating on thin ice with her from listening to Pop.

LORI: Then I'll think about it too. But I won't decide yet.

T.C.:   Is this a bribe?

LORI: *You* figure it out.

Dear Mama,

When Aunt Babe came up for the weekend and saw Hucky jamming on his keyboard, she invented a new holiday on the spot—Saint Sivithius Day—and bought him a present for it. It's a big plastic electric guitar that's the same kind of yellow as the keyboard is. Augie was the one who picked it out. He says the reason the Pet Shop Boys never made it to the A-list is because they weren't color-coordinated.

Mr. Landey was right—deaf kids can rock to music as much as anybody else can. They just feel it differently. But as far as we know, the only thing Hucky ever listens to is *Mary Poppins*—which is why Alé and Nehi and I took him over to Augie's for the afternoon with a handful of our CDs. I mean, there's a whole world outside of "Jolly Holiday With Mary" that he didn't even *know* about. Yet.

WHAT HE LOVES

Crosby, Stills & Nash
Christina Aguilera
Avi Vinocur
Body Politics
'N Sync
Kid Rock
Damn Yankees

WHAT HE HATES

Backstreet Boys
Destiny's Child
Marc Anthony
Bob Dylan
Stephen Sondheim (at least we think so. He listened to 60 seconds of *Sunday in the Park With George* and then went outside to play in the mud with Nehi. Alé swears it was a value judgment.)

His hands-down favorite was Snoop Doggy, especially "Step Yo Game Up" (which turned Augie's face the same color as third base by the sixth inning). Once Hucky had listened to "Doggy Dogg World" and "Ain't No Fun if My Homies Can't Have None," we knew we were in a jet stream, so Augie halfheartedly raided Mom's red-flagged "these-people-need-to-be-run-out-of-town" DVD collection and found the *Undercova Funk* Madison Square Garden concert. For the next hour and a half—while we all sprawled across the floor—Alé and I jammed on "Snoop Bounce," Augie glowered in the corner, and it turned out to be the first video (except for you-know-what) that Hucky's wanted to sit through twice in a row. Inside of ten minutes he'd begun swaying his shoulders and lip-synching the first five words of "Up Jump the Boogie" right along with "Snoopy Dog"—which is actually kind of scary when you realize he can't *hear* any of it.

"*Can I play a concert in Madison Garden too?*" he begged while I put on his coat at the end of the day.

"When you're nine," I promised, zipping up the hood.

Before we took him back to the Children's Residence, we all went over to Brookline Music together to buy him some CDs of his own: *The Doggfather* for Hucky, and *Crosby, Stills & Nash* for Mateo. (He figured they could trade them back and forth with each other, along with their rabbits' feet, Gummi Bears, and Legos.) But I realized when we hit the sidewalk again that he didn't know anything about the sixties, and my gut told me that he ought to learn at least some of the facts if he was going to understand why CS&N rocked.

"People wore beads around their necks and bands around their heads and ugly pants with bell bottoms," I told him, holding his hand as we crossed the boulevard.

"*Why?*"

"To stop the war in Vietnam."

"*How?*"

"I don't know. Pop didn't explain that part." By the time we'd gotten to Beals Street, two things had happened: (1) He was already losing patience with the whole concept of Woodstock ("*Why wasn't there anyplace for all of those people to pee??*" "Don't blame *me!* I wasn't there!"), and (2) I noticed out of the corner of my eye that Alé was shivering, even though it was almost thirty degrees out and she was already bundled up like an Eskimo. So while Hucky and I were arguing about Porta Potties, I wrapped my arm around her to keep her warm, like it was something I was used to doing every day. And she didn't even try to stop me—probably because I was still pretending to pay all of my attention to Hucky. Nehi saw the whole thing and barked in appreciation. "*Smooth move, dude!*" I even think Alé's reconsidering the probation she put me on.

Kids and dogs are great props. Why didn't Pop ever tell me *that* before??

I love you,

T.C.

P.S. Hucky still cries during the night, but not as much as he used to. Wait until he starts falling asleep with "Suite: Judy Blue Eyes" tickling his temples through his Discman. Maybe the crying'll even stop completely. Who needs Mary Poppins?

INSTANT MESSENGER

TCKeller: I just got off the phone with Aunt Ruth. She had a couple of minutes free in between busting chops, so she called Fred Hoyt and said, "This is Ruth Mellick from the House of Representatives. Is it true that we can look forward to a baseball diamond at Manzanar? What a splendid idea." When she finally hung up, he was still saying things like "Er" and "Uh," but nothing else. I hope they sell Kaopectate up there. He sounds like he needs it already. By the way, we just passed 600 hits on our website (in only 4 weeks!) and we've got 71 names on our petition.

AlePerez: I've never met anyone who operates the way you do. I'm still not convinced that it's appealing, but it's definitely singular.

TCKeller: By the way, Pop's taking us to Plum Island on Saturday. Lori said she'd come if you do too. So my father's future is in your hands.

AlePerez: I need to think about it.

TCKeller: For real or am I still on suspension? No offense, but I don't do anxiety well.

AlePerez: You don't exactly do spontaneous well either. Don't think I didn't

> notice the premeditated arm-around-the-
> shoulder thing while we were walking
> Hucky home.
>
> **TCKeller:** You weren't supposed to see
> that!

Dear Mama,

Kiss Me, Kate is on its way to Broadway. It *has* to be. They had a run-through of the first act on Saturday morning and I never saw anything like it in my life. I know I'm not a theatre critic like Mom is, but I recognize a Tommy Award Winner when it's plopped down in front of me.

BEST SCENE #1: Lee Meyerhoff singing a song called "Tom, Dick, or Harry" when she's trying to choose between three guys. Two of them are played by Augie and Andy, who get to have a fake fistfight onstage. But from where we were sitting, it didn't look like Augie was faking *any* of it.

BEST SCENE #2: Lee getting pissed of at Bill (Augie) for always gambling, so she sings "Why Can't You Behave?" to him. Funny, I've been asking him that same question since we were six.

BEST SCENE #3: Alé reminiscing with Keith about when they used to be married, but turning in the other direction so she wouldn't smell him any more than she had to.

AWARDS: Augie for Best New Star (like this is a surprise?)

Lee for Putting Up With Augie (Medal of Honor maybe?)
Alé for *People* Magazine's Sexiest Woman Alive (at least)

We left for Plum Island right after the run-through ended—and since Pop and Lori hadn't been there, Alé and Augie sang them all of the songs in the show during the forty-five minutes it took us to drive north through Massachusetts. I signed as many of the words as I could for Hucky, but they left me in their dust back in Lynn. All I remember is that while I was trying to keep up with "We Open in Venice," I got confused between the sign for *open* and the sign for *fart*, so it came out a whole lot different than Cole Porter meant it to.

When we got to Newburyport, Pop drove us by the house you grew up in and told the story about the first time you introduced him to Grandma and Grandpa Hokenstad. ("She really had me thinking that she'd let them believe I was a gun runner for the Mob. Try meeting your future in-laws with *that* hanging over your head.") Remember the coffee shop on Green Street with the Revolutionary War lamps on the outside and the shrimp salad on the *in*side? Because it's still there. I even ordered a club sandwich and pretended you were giving me all of your bacon.

After lunch, we split up for the afternoon. Pop and Lori went for a walk along the waterfront with Hucky, Augie and Nehi took off to check out the old firehouse, and Alé and I strolled up High Street to find a shop where we could buy blue glass figurines. Okay, maybe that wasn't exactly *my* idea.

"What about here?" I asked, pointing to a window display. Alé was wearing a white zip-up coat with a hood that had piles of fluffy fur around her face, making a fuzzy frame for her frown.

"This is a snowblower store," she replied, narrowing her eyes.

"Yeah, but maybe they have snowblowers in blue glass."

"You think?" For the next three blocks of red cobblestoned sidewalks, she shot down one suggestion after another: bath and body shops, pharmacies, furniture finishers, even a Ben & Jerry's. ("Look! Blue glass Oreo cones!") But finally we stopped in front of a jewelry store that had a teensy glass puppy in the window, sitting between two Rolexes, where it actually looked like it was about to lift up its leg and pee on the left one. So naturally my mind began racing. I mean, I had fifteen dollars in my wallet and I was feeling sporty anyway.

"Let's go in," I offered, holding open the door.

That was a mistake.

Clue No. 1
The store had carpets four inches thick
and smelled like a bank.

Clue No. 2
The guy behind the counter was wearing
a suit and tie on a Saturday.

TIE GUY: May I help you with something?

ALÉ: Do you—

T.C.: My sister is looking for blue glass figurines. Do you carry any of them here?

ALÉ: I'm not his—

TIE GUY: Certainly. If you'll step over to this case, you'll notice that we have five or six of them in blue.

T.C.:   Excellent. Sis, what about the giraffe?

ALÉ: Anthony, don't call me—

T.C.:   Actually, she already has a giraffe. May we see the dolphin?

TIE GUY: Of course.

ALÉ: Anthony, you don't—

T.C.:   I love this. What do you think, sis?

ALÉ: I'm warning you not to—

T.C.:   We'll take it.

TIE GUY: A perfect choice. Cash or charge?

T.C.:   Cash, please.

TIE GUY: Of course. That'll be $375.

T.C.:   *FOR A LITTLE BLUE DOLPHIN??*

ALÉ: Thank you, big brother.

Alé thought it was a riot. So did Pop and Lori. And Augie and Hucky and Nehi and the server at Tastee-Freez and the pump guy at the Shell station. Doesn't anybody know how to keep a secret anymore??

"Tony C," warned Pop. "Never ever play games with girls in jewelry stores. You're already dealing with a stacked deck anyway." Lori jabbed him in the ribs with an elbow.

"Nice tip," she shot back. "I'll remember that." We were sitting on the beach at Plum Island after dinner at The Ocean View (Pop and I had the usual honey baked ham and cornbread, and we split a side of yams for you). The moon was bright enough to read those tiny-type yawny books like *Pride and Prejudice* by—and what you could see in the moonlight was Pop and Lori holding hands, Augie pretending he'd never heard of anybody named Andy Wexler, Hucky next to me with Nehi's head in his lap, and me and Alé sitting a mile and a half apart like the *Monitor* and the *Merrimac* with North Carolina in between them. But for now it was okay, because I had promises to keep. I wrapped my right arm around Hucky and pointed to the sparkly sky—and since this was the whole reason we'd come to Plum Island anyway, everybody was watching me. What does Augie always say? "I'm dead without my audience."

"How many stars do you think are out there?" I asked. Hucky's head instantly turned eyes-up before he wrinkled his forehead.

"A thousand and six?"

"Right! And which one's your favorite?" After hardly a second's hesitation, he pointed to the brightest twinkler he could find.

"That one." It was actually the North Star, but he definitely didn't need to know that.

"Wow!" blurted my hands. "That one doesn't even have a name yet! Why don't we call it 'Hucky'?" Hucky was a little tougher to convince than I was. What I got at first was his you're-being-spurious-again face.

"*Are you allowed to do that? What about the police?*"

"The police name stars too. It's the same as calling dibs on the Slinky before Mateo does." That seemed to do the job. Sort of. Because first we needed to agree on terms: It had to be a wishing star, it had to be named "Hucky Evan Harper and Shut-the-Door," nobody else could wish on it but him, and he wanted to color it blue. Normally his last condition would have been the deal-breaker, but all I had to imagine is what *you* would have said.

"Okay," I told him. "But you have to be in fourth grade before you can color it. That's in the rules." If he hadn't been yawning already, it might not have gotten off the ground. Instead, he just nodded, picked up Shut-the-Door, and leaned against me with his eyes half-closed.

"*Can we stay a couple of whiles so I can show Shut-the-Door our star?*" I promised that we could stay for all the whiles he wanted—but by then he was out cold. That's when I suddenly remembered the song you used to sing to me while I was falling asleep.

> *Now run along home and jump into bed.*
> *Say your prayers and cover your head.*
> *The very same thing I always do,*
> *You dream of me—and I'll dream of you.*

A long time ago I learned how to cry without making any noise so nobody would know when I was doing it (which is strictly a guy thing). But Alé must have sensed a disturbance in the Force because she automatically reached for my hand. I figured she was just feeling sorry for me, but it worked anyway.

So I *know* it was a present from you.

I love you,

T.C.

P.S. The bad news? Even though Hucky slept through the night, when I woke up at 8:15 this morning, he and Shut-the-Door and Nehi were watching *Mary Poppins* again. I noticed while I was rubbing my eyes that the two little Banks kids on the screen were singing "The Perfect Nanny," and Hucky—in his Luke Skywalker pajamas—was lost in that whole other world like he'd never been there before.

This is going to take a little time.

LAURENTS SCHOOL
BROOKLINE, MASSACHUSETTS

VIA E-MAIL

Dear Ted:

Your son is a cross between the Pied Piper and Annie Sullivan. Now I'm beginning to understand why Liz Jordan can only sputter whenever I check in with her. "Lori, until November Hucky hadn't spoken to anyone other than Mateo for fifteen months! And we have a professional counseling staff here!" Does this sound like the kid who ran us around the block in Newburyport? Have the Pod People gotten ahold of him? Or is Anthony a miracle worker?

Incidentally, don't you think Hucky would have had a better time with Augie and Nehi at the firehouse than with a pair of middle-aged farts?

Lori

KELLER CONSTRUCTION
BOSTON · GLOUCESTER · WALTHAM

ELECTRONIC TRANSMISSION

Dear Lori:

Which pair of middle-aged farts? You and the harbor-master?

There's a second way to look at your last question: "Don't you think you and I would have had a better time if we'd had a chance to be alone together for at least a few minutes?" In which case the answer is yes.

However, it's only fair to warn you that small children make their male caregivers appear both sensitive and irresistible to single women. So you might have been falling for a ruse.

Ted

Laurents School
Brookline, Massachusetts

VIA E-MAIL

Dear Ted:

Get over yourself.

And don't be too impressed with the hand-holding on the beach. You could have been just about anybody. I have a problem with vertigo.

Lori

KELLER CONSTRUCTION
BOSTON · GLOUCESTER · WALTHAM

ELECTRONIC TRANSMISSION

Dear Lori:

When you're *sitting*??

Ted

Augie

From: AndyWexler@earthworks.net
To: augie@augiehwong.com

Dear Augie,

I'm not writing this because of the cold shoulder I've gotten from some of our friends or because of the talk your brother had with me or even because of the way you almost beat the shit out of me during "Tom, Dick, and Harry" at rehearsal. The reason I'm writing this is because of an e-mail I got from Alé a couple of days ago that didn't have anything in it except an attachment that turned out to be a song called "If You Were the Only Boy in the World." Which actually sucked, but I listened to it anyway.

Spidey, ever since I heard it I haven't been able to stop remembering things I never paid attention to before. Maybe that's because I'm still figuring things out and don't have it zipped in the back pocket the way you always do. But I wish you didn't have a whole different smile that you only use on me, and I wish you hadn't invented the every-other-finger thing that always happens when we're holding hands, and I REALLY wish there was at least one other guy whose hair sticks straight up when it gets snowed on and who always makes me glad that he's with me and not with somebody else. But there isn't. And the reason is because maybe you *are* the only boy in the world. Even when you're Gypsy Rose Lee.

I'm sorry if I didn't see that before, and I'm even sorrier for hurting your feelings. That's something I can promise won't ever happen again, because I also figured out that I love you. I wish it hadn't taken me so long.

Andy

DIVA OF THE WEEK

Judy Garland

("How can I ignore the boy next door?")

Dear Jutes,

I've been through a broken heart, I've survived the grieving process, and I reclaimed the fragmented pieces of my life better than Fanny Brice did after Nicky dumped her. But then he sends me a forgive-me e-mail quoting Barbra Streisand—and instead of melting again, all I want to do is kick his ass. What's up with *that*? I'm *so* not cut out for love. The rules are too complicated. No wonder Romeo and Juliet killed themselves after one night together.

I used to think I was a pushover, but you're the one who taught me the ground rules. Remember how you stood up to John Truitt when you thought he was a bully, even though you loved him? I probably should have made you my guardian diva right from the beginning, but somehow it seemed so retro. These days gay kids are a lot more worldly. We don't get points for knowing the date of your Carnegie Hall concert (April 23, 1961), when you were born (June 10, 1922), or what you said to Betty Hutton when she replaced you in *Annie Get Your Gun* ("You goddamn son of a bitch"). And we need to rewrite some of the rules together, because *Meet Me in St. Louis* doesn't play the way it used to.

The Word Shop
BROOKLINE'S FAVORITE BOOKSTORE

E-Memo From the Desk of
Phyllis Bryant

Augie, I just watched *Meet Me in St. Louis* again. Do *not* go there yet, you understand what I'm saying? That boy needs to sweat for a while. After what he put you through, it'd serve him good and damned right if you waited for a world's fair to come to Boston before you even *thought* about kissing him.

We've got underground trolleys on the Green Line. For the time being, let him get somebody else to sing to him there. "Clang, clang, clang" my ass.

Andy came over on Sunday to check out a Patriots game from 1999 that Dad had taped but never seen. This is how my father gets through the off-season without going into withdrawal. He has a whole library of unwatched videos that go back to the '80s. At the rate of one every two weeks from February through July, he's okay until the spring of 2012. Then he needs to start worrying.

It was the first time Andy and I were going to be together since that harrowing Thursday at The Word Shop Café, and because it was supposed to begin snowing later in the afternoon, Dad lit a fire while Mom made popcorn. Normally I'd have made sure to squeeze myself into the love seat next to Andy, but he wasn't getting off *that* easy. (When Dad saw me considering an armchair next to the front door, he said, "Why don't you just sit in the chimney? I can pipe a speaker up there if you want.") Coming over to our house was always a special occasion for Andy, but this wasn't going to be one of those days.

---

www.augiehwong.com
PRIVATE CHAT

AndyWexler: It's the way your parents know we're boyfriends and we never had to tell them. And they're *happy* about it. Even after what I pulled.

AugieHwong: That's because you're already part of our family. We're easy that way. (Pregnant pause.) At least, *some* of us are.

AndyWexler: Why did you watch the game from the kitchen? And how long are you going to stay ticked at me?

AugieHwong: Why did you have to say I embarrassed you?

AndyWexler: I'd *never* say you embarrassed me. I said you intimidated me. Why did you have to stop talking to me? Why didn't you just tell me to piss off and we could have duked this out already?

AugieHwong: Okay. Piss off.

AndyWexler: You too.

SORRY! USER AUGIEHWONG HAS LOGGED OFF

SORRY! USER ANDYWEXLER HAS LOGGED OFF

USER AUGIEHWONG HAS LOGGED ON

USER ANDYWEXLER HAS LOGGED ON

AugieHwong: Another thing. If I'm in the mood to be Pat Suzuki in *Flower Drum Song* for five minutes and you even *think* of blushing, it may be the last thing you ever do.

AndyWexler: I can live with that.

AugieHwong: The same goes for Kate Hepburn in *A Lion in Winter.* "I dressed my maids as Amazons and rode bare-breasted halfway to Damascus. Louis had a seizure and I damn near died of windburn. But the troops were dazzled."

AndyWexler: I *have* lived with that.

AugieHwong: Oh. Right.

AndyWexler: Are we okay now?

AugieHwong: Dude, I don't even know what okay *is* anymore.

On the other hand, finding something new to be pathological about is what keeps me in business, and I'd been worrying ever since Sunday when I watched him and my father test each other—from the tat soi right up through Mom's orange cakes—on statistics like 1993 yardage and 1998 point spreads and players with long names that didn't have any vowels in them. *Maybe Andy was right after all. Look how much fun Dad is having. Does he wish he had a son who understood football? Sure he does, you gink. Watch the way they're challenging each other about pass protection—whatever the hell that is. Did Dad ever have a conversation like that with you? Oh yeah, right. I can practically hear it. "Hey, Dad—whose idea was Bette Davis's party dress in* All About Eve*?" "Edith Head, you dope!" No wonder he's so animated. He's finally got a kid he can talk to on his own terms. I'm like SO useless!!*

I made it through the rest of the week on the snake-pit side of gloomy, wondering whether or not they let gay kids in the Peace Corps. (*"Why do you want to join, son?" "Because I embarrass my father, sir. I don't know what a down is." "Then why the hell would we want you either??"*) By Saturday night I was about as well put together as Shirley MacLaine at the end of *The Children's Hour*, lying in my bed and staring at the walls like one of those cable ads for Paxil. Of course, it helps to have a dad who can read you like a book, even if it gets a little irritating once in a while. A guy's got to have *some* secrets.

"Aug," he asked, tucking me in. "Are you okay?"

"I'm fine." I shrugged, so obviously not fine. *Why are you wasting your time with me? Your son wouldn't know a lateral pass if he was sitting on one.*

"You sure nothing's the matter?" he repeated. The sigh that shook my whole body was actually a little much—even for me.

"I'm positive." That was when he knew it was time to sit down on the edge of my bed and think for a really long minute. Which is what he did. And suddenly his eyes arched up like he had it all figured out, so he kind of half smiled and leaned in to kiss me good night.

"Don't worry," he promised confidently, reaching for the lamp on my night table to switch it off. "Boyfriends and girlfriends fight all the time. It's part of being in love."

"That's not it," I blurted. Dad's hand froze in midair and the lamp stayed on.

"Oh. Uh, well—" He sat up straight again and tried another road. "'Stage fright is normal when you've got a big part'?"

"Nope." Well, by now he knew he was really stuck between a rock and a hard place. Usually he gets it on the first whack, and once in a while it takes two. But this was a whole other solar system. So he stood up and began pacing back and forth in front of my *All About Eve* action figures. The way his eyes were lowered and his forehead was concentrating, you could tell that he was replaying everything that had happened since just before I started acting weird. Meanwhile, I was getting sleepy. Being neurotic takes a lot of hard work. I really needed him to wrap up his performance so I wouldn't zonk out in the middle of my finale. Then on the third lap he stopped dead in his tracks and frowned.

"Oh, no," he mumbled, more to himself than to me. He sat back down in a hurry and ran his hand across the top of my hair. "Augie, listen to me. If I'd had a kid who liked football, we'd have driven Mom crazy eight years ago. I got *exactly* who I wanted."

"Even if— Even if I never heard of a play-action pass before?" I stammered.

"You dopey rock-head. That's what son-in-laws are for! Now, is there anything *else* that's not bothering you?"

"No," I admitted sort of sheepishly. "That was all." When he switched off the lamp and kissed me good night for real, I turned over on my side—just the way Hucky does with Shut-the-Door—so he wouldn't see how relieved I was.

"I love you, Dad."

"I love you too."

So just before Andy showed up a week later to watch the Pats and the Colts with us, Mom and Dad decided they were going to teach me the basics once and for all—but in a language I understood.

hang time	Kate Fothergill holding a high C for sixteen bars of "I Got Rhythm"
fumble	Joan Crawford trying to sing
turnover	what happened to anyone who upstaged Ethel Merman
option play	whether or not to take a ninth curtain call

offending team	what the Sharks thought the Jets were in *West Side Story*
end zone	where the chorus stands during the finale
dropback	what Katharine Hepburn did after Cary Grant pushed her face in *The Philadelphia Story*
handoff	Jane Powell taking over the lead in *Royal Wedding* when June Allyson got pregnant

Why didn't someone tell me that football was such a no-brainer?! The Colts went for the extra curtain call but then Crawford sang for them and Marvin Harrison got in the way of the Merm. Friesz's kick held the high C for six seconds and forty-three yards, Ellison was waiting on the chorus line, and the Pats won 21–17.

> **www.augiehwong.com**
> **PRIVATE CHAT**

AndyWexler: I'm so proud of you!!

AugieHwong: "Please don't play governess with me, Karen. I haven't your unyielding good taste."

AndyWexler: *All About Eve*?

AugieHwong: How did you know *that*?

AndyWexler: You're not the only one who's been studying. Am I off the hook yet?

AugieHwong: You're pretty close.

AndyWexler: Did anybody ever tell you that loving you is hard work?

AugieHwong: NOW you're off the hook.

But I still owe him a kick in the ass. Just like you owed Mickey Rooney a couple of your own. Any ideas?

Love,

Augie

STUDY HALL
(Sssshhhhh!!!!)

Lee,

After yesterday's rehearsal, it's clear that once *Kiss Me, Kate* opens, I'm going to be typecast as a guy for the rest of my life. What a savage irony in a savage world. No one will ever remember my Countess Aurelia or Mrs. Miniver.   *—Augie*

Augie,

They wouldn't anyway.   *—Lee*

Lee,

You're *so* not helping. I need a favor. Sort of a swan song to my former life. Literally. I want to sing "Always True to You in My Fashion." —*Augie*

Augie,

That's not a favor, it's an annexation. No. —*Lee*

Lee,

Don't be a gink. It'd just be for one rehearsal and we still have ten of them left. And I'll be dressed like me, not Bianca, in case that was the next item on your "Forget It" list. Besides, this isn't just about "Mr. Thorn once cornered corn and that ain't hay" (even though I hate you every time you get to deliver that line and I don't). This is about randomly picking another boy to sing it to. —*Augie*

Augie,

Randomly=Andy? —*Lee*

Lee,

Yes, but ssshhh. After what he put me through, he's got it coming. In public and in front of an audience. It's going to be my first declaration of love, and he's the only one who's going to know it.

—*Augie*

Augie,

A bag of *concrete* would know it.

—*Lee*

INSTANT MESSENGER

TCKeller: Assuming he doesn't kill you, that's actually one of the few ideas you ever had that wasn't at least 60 percent crackpot. If I could sing, I might even use it on Alé.

I can't believe you thought Dad would rather have had a football kid than you. Where have you been hiding out your whole life??

AugieHwong: Down in the Depths on the 90th Floor. (Cole Porter wrote that one too.)

TCKeller: It's a good thing you told him that you were afraid he wanted a different brand of son—because if you hadn't, I would have.

AugieHwong: When *did* you tell him?

TCKeller: About 4 hours before you watched him figure it out for himself. I knew you wanted me to. When you made

me promise to keep it a secret, you said it
in your "Betray me" voice.

AugieHwong: I didn't think you'd make
me wait 6 days, you rock-head!! What time
do you want me to pick up Hucky?

TCKeller: 1:00. I usually keep him out
until 4:00 and then take him back to the
Residence. Warning: He's going to invent
30 minutes of excuses to make you stay,
so factor that in. Pop says I can't go
outside until Monday. The cough is better,
but he thinks I'm still contagious. By the
way—except for holding my hand on
Plum Island for unrelated reasons, Alé's
not letting me get away with *anything*
anymore. Even a casual-looking arm-
around-the-shoulder thing triggers a
military alert. Is she really going to give me
a second chance after the "just friends"
scam or did I screw it up beyond repair?

AugieHwong: You want an argument or
an answer?

TCKeller: Groan. That's what I was afraid
of. I'm going to have to pull this off as an
honest man. Without any subterfuge. How
do I do *that*?

AugieHwong: Now you want an
argument.

TCKeller: Hey, is "rock-head" new?
Because I like it.

AugieHwong: Actually, I think it's retro. But I like it too.

Dear Jutes,

While Hucky and I were working our way through Chicken McNuggets at McDonald's, I tried to put together a responsible itinerary that might get past a six-year-old. I should have known better. It sounded like a battle plan for a divorced dad when he was stuck with his kid for the day.

"Want to see *Spy Kids 3-D?*"

"*No.*"

"Want to go bowling?"

"*Why?*"

"Children's Museum?"

"*You're kidding, right?*" Then suddenly it hit me just as I dropped a french fry into my Coke. Oh, duh. Like Tick and I had never been in his shoes before. What *did* happen to my brain?

"Okay," I said, fishing through the ice for the drowning fry. "I have an idea. But wipe the ketchup off your face first."

"*I like it this way. Wipe your own off.*"

"And eat two more bites of your hangabur or we're not going *any*where."

HUCKY AND AUGIE
Schedule

Pirates: We bought eye patches at the 99¢ shop, said "Aye, matey" a lot, and ordered Phyllis to walk the plank. She chased us into the café with a saber disguised as *Angela's Ashes.*

Aliens: We came from the planet Twylo and we hatched out of walnuts. (Hucky thought the whole concept was idiotic, so this one didn't last long.)

Cops: Between lunch and cookies we arrested Clifford the Big Red Dog, Maisy the Rat, Elmer the Patchwork Elephant, and Dad. (He went quietly to jail without putting up a fight. He was no match for Hucky.)

Dino Hunters: We were trapped inside Jurassic Park after the last helicopter had taken off. So we had a picnic lunch with Barney and then we shot him. But while we were deciding where to stash the body, I realized that Hucky hadn't been tugging on his hair all day. Instead, he'd been playing with one of his front teeth.

"Does it hurt?" I asked, automatically thinking "cavity."

"No. I want it to get loose. What's taking it so long?"

"You're already six. The Tooth Fairy'll be here any minute."

Hucky glared suspiciously into my eyes as though I were pulling a fast one. *"Who??"*

"The Tooth Fairy," I repeated. "Haven't you ever heard of her before?" Well, he hadn't. But I'd really opened a can of worms by asking, because when he found out I wasn't kidding, he forgot all about Barney's corpse behind the couch and began beating me up with questions.

"Who's the Tooth Fairy? What does she do? Is she wicked or nice? Where does she come from? Does she melt?"

Jutes, you're the actress. You probably could have improvised some kind of an answer without even breaking a sweat. But all I have to my credit so far is "Too Darn Hot" and a pair of blue tights. I don't know how to think on my toes yet. I stink without a script.

I need lines! What's there to tell about the Tooth Fairy?? She flies through the window, leaves cash, and peace out—she's gone. It's not like she ever had a Who's Who bio in *Playbill*. *So how was I supposed to answer him?!* But then Hucky gave me just the clue I'd been looking for.

"*Tell me about the Tooth Fairy,*" he demanded. "*All about the Tooth Fairy. Please?*"

Jackpot. "All About the Tooth Fairy." *All About Eve.*

Thank God for Bette Davis.

ALL ABOUT THE TOOTH FAIRY

By Augie, for Hucky

Once upon a time, there was a forty-year-old Tooth Fairy who was filled with fire and music. Each night (and on Wednesday and Saturday matinees), she would fly around the world to visit all of the children whose teeth had fallen out so she could leave them shiny silver dollars under their pillows. Oh, how they loved the Tooth Fairy. But the Tooth Fairy was sad because she thought she was too old to marry her prince, and that all she'd wind up with was a book full of clippings. It's a funny business, a woman's career.

One night while the Tooth Fairy was having a little party after work, her best friend came to visit her. She said, "I have a surprise, Tooth Fairy! Outside I found a young girl who wants to do good things for people—just like you do! She's gone all across the country, back and forth and back and forth, to watch you visit the little children. Oh please, Tooth Fairy, won't you let her come in and say hello?"

Well, of course the Tooth Fairy was one of the kindest fairies in the world, so she said to her friend, "The heave-ho!" (which means "Please bring her in" in fairy talk). So her friend brought in the young girl, who was so sweet and so polite and who told such an unhappy story about her gloomy life that when the Tooth Fairy found out she didn't have a home, she invited her to stay in her castle. That way she could learn everything there was to know about being a Tooth Fairy. She even gave her a new name. "Miss Worthington."

Now, what the Tooth Fairy didn't know was that Miss Worthington was secretly mean. She didn't really like the Tooth Fairy at all. She thought it was about time that Tooth Fairies were young and pretty, and it was her evil plan to become the Tooth Fairy herself. So while she pretended to be nice, she was really studying the Tooth Fairy like she was a play or a book or a set of blueprints, just waiting for the day when she could take away the Tooth Fairy's job and the Tooth Fairy's prince from her.

The good news is that the Tooth Fairy found out in time. One morning she heard footsteps on the ceiling and knew it was her Fairy Godmother Cora—who flew right in through the skylight and said, "Tooth Fairy, get rid of that girl. She is a louse." Tooth Fairy was shocked. "Miss Worthington?" she asked, hardly believing her ears. "That's what I said, bub," replied Cora (which means "yes"). So Cora turned Miss Worthington into a venomous fishwife and everyone lived happily ever after.

Altogether, I maybe knew 25 percent of the words in ASL. The rest of it I either had to finger-spell or act out in pantomime. Did *you* ever try to play a blueprint or a fishwife?? But even if I wasn't exactly on the money, I put the main points across anyway. Hucky's eyes opened wide when they were supposed to open wide, he got sad on the right cues, and he knew Miss Worthington was a little witch before I even hit that part.

"*I SO don't like her,*" he signed on our way back to the Children's Residence. "*Not even at the beginning. She lied.*"

I still had an hour to hang out, so we went upstairs to give Mateo the eye patch we'd bought for him. Right after he put it on, he stood in front of the mirror and made Captain Hook faces, and probably could have spent the rest of the day doing it—but the minute he saw Hucky's reflection turning on the VCR, he lit out of there as fast as a pair of short legs could flee. (I don't blame him. I know every word of *Mary Poppins* by heart, and the only other movie musical I ever memorized from the ground up was *Funny Girl*. And that was on purpose.) But I had other things to take my mind off the tea parties on the ceiling. While Hucky and I sat on his bed during the opening credits, I glanced around the room and noticed that the wall above his desk was covered with drawings—and most of them were of Tick, me, and Alé. All together, we outnumbered Mary Poppins 8 to 1.

"*Augie?*" asked Hucky, looking up from "Chim-Chim-Cheree." "*Can I be your brother too, like T.C. is?*"

"You already are," I told him, reaching over to pat Shut-the-Door. "Sometimes things like that happen all by themselves."

Incidentally, this morning his tooth fell out and he told the social worker to make sure the *real* Tooth Fairy got it and not the opportunistic bitch who was trying to take her place (well, that was the subtext anyway).

He's definitely ready for *Snow White and the Little Foxe*s.

Love,

Augie

INSTANT MESSENGER

AugieHwong: Before I forget, Tick's birthday is right after *Kiss Me, Kate*, and I don't want it to get lost in the shuffle. I was thinking about a surprise party and a pair of box seats to a Red Sox/Yankees home game—but I don't know any scalpers. Does Clint?

AlePerez: I'll check. But I've already picked out something on my own. There's an online registry where you can pay to name an actual star. So now there

really is one called "Anthony Keller."
They're FedExing me a photo of it with a
certificate, and I'm having both of them
matted and framed. Do you think it's too
much?

AugieHwong: I think it's so spot-on that
the only way my Red Sox tickets are
going to compete is if they let him pitch.
But that's okay because he deserves
something special—particularly from *us*. If
it wasn't for him, you wouldn't be playing
Lilli Vanessi, I wouldn't have Andy, most of
Brookline wouldn't know ASL, and Hucky
would still be crying himself to sleep.
My brother's a dreamer who doesn't like
giving up. And it's contagious.

AlePerez: Did he tell you we were holding
hands on Plum Island? It was only the
second time since I've known him that
he wasn't plotting his next move. So how
could I resist?

AugieHwong: Actually, Hucky signed me
the news while it was still breaking. Sort
of like live coverage on CNN.

Dear Jutes,

I accidentally rewrote the last half of *Meet Me in St. Louis*, and you couldn't have played it any better yourself—even if you'd thought of it first.

```
┌─────────────────────────────────────┐
│          www.augiehwong.com         │
│            PRIVATE CHAT             │
└─────────────────────────────────────┘
```

AugieHwong: I was awake last night worrying.

AndyWexler: Tell me something new, Wonderboy.

AugieHwong: No, this is serious. Valentine's Day is in two weeks. What if we buy each other the same thing by accident?

AndyWexler: So what?

AugieHwong: So maybe we should go present-shopping together. That way we can make sure we each hit different kinds of stores.

AndyWexler: I never guessed that life could be so complicated.

AugieHwong: You want to reexamine your other options before it's too late?

AndyWexler: I picked my option back in the fall when you kept falling on me during soccer practice. So it's *already* too late.

We figured out that the smartest thing to do was plan an afternoon at the Pru. They have a good 2½ million shops in the mall there, which automatically meant that (a) we'd definitely find a pair of unconflicting valentines for each other, and (b) we'd be together for at least four hours. That was actually the whole point, but you can't just come out and say, "Dude, I want to spend a day with you." According to Alé, "Never give it away up front like that."

It only took me an hour and a half to get ready, which is ten minutes off my previous pre-date-with-Andy record. I couldn't decide between the tan slacks or the taupe ones (Dad said, "Go with tan"), and it was 50–50 on the blue shirt/yellow shirt crisis too (Mom negotiated for the blue team and won), but we all agreed on Alé's brown sweater from Christmas. So while I stood in front of the Brookline Village T station waiting for him, I was confident that the cover of *GQ* was the next stop.

Then disaster. Again.

I knew as soon as I saw him crossing Washington Street that something was definitely wrong. Usually he's sort of bouncing on the balls of his feet whenever he's on his way to meet me, but today his shoulders were slumped and his head was down. I didn't even get his supernova smile when he saw me.

"Hey, Aquaboy." I grinned nervously.

"Hey," he replied, without any expression at all. "Let's hit it." He brushed right past me as we started down the steps into the station, and by the time we'd bought our tokens I was already on guard—especially after the D train pulled in and we found seats next to each other without our usual argument about who got the window. (Like there was ever anything to look at except each other.) Instead, Andy stared straight ahead at an MBTA map, and we rode all the way to Copley Square in silence. I had it narrowed down to four possibilities:

1.   He's back to the "Be a real guy" crap again—in which case I'm ready to comply by slugging him right in the mouth.

2. He figured out that he doesn't love me after all.

3. His father found out about us and hit the ceiling.

4. He's fallen for somebody else.

Once we'd come up the stairs into the bright blue sky that covered Copley Square, we still had to walk a couple of blocks to the Pru. And since he was hunched down with his hands in his pockets, I had a chance to take an inventory of his face to see if there were any clues there. But all of the possibilities tested negative, so this was something brand-new and he had exactly sixty seconds to tell me what it was or I was going to have to force it out of him. I hate being ignored. Especially in heavy traffic by the boy of my dreams.

The clock began running when we crossed the Prudential Center's glass and marble lobby and stepped into an empty elevator. As we stood wordlessly side by side, the doors slid closed—and I finally began getting a little pissed off.

"Look, Andy," I said firmly, breaking the twenty-three-minute deadlock. "I don't know what the hell your"—but that's as far as I got. Because without any warning at all, he turned suddenly, put his hands on my shoulders, yanked me close, and—eyes wide with terror—kissed me. Right there in the Prudential Center elevator. And he didn't *stop* kissing me until the "Ping!" told us we were about to have company.

I still can't imagine what the people on the second floor must have thought when the doors opened again. Sure, by then we were standing a respectable distance apart and staring straight ahead, but neither one of us was anchored to New England terra firma anymore.

"Hey! Kids! Are you getting out or what?" Actually, for the next two hours we reminded me of shock victims who'd just survived a terrible accident and who found themselves wandering through an occasional dim flash of reality—like flipping through a copy of *Grouting Made Easy* at Back Bay Books, browsing coaxial cable assemblies at Radio Shack, or carefully checking out Medeco locks at Sentry Security. Finally we drifted into a place called Copley House and Garden. I bought a flowerpot and Andy bought paint thinner. Neither one of us remembers why.

Somehow we managed to retrace our steps to the Green Line T station without ending up in Vermont instead. We still couldn't say anything to each other, but at least now it was for the same dazed reason. Our car was packed with late-afternoon shoppers and there weren't any seats left, so we found ourselves squished together by the rear door as the motorman let her go. *"Clang, clang, clang went the trolley."*

But you know what? *N*obody sings after their first kiss. They're lucky they can still keep lunch down.

Love,

Augie

KELLER CONSTRUCTION
BOSTON · GLOUCESTER · WALTHAM

ELECTRONIC TRANSMISSION

Craig:

Strategy question. Tony C's made plans with Augie to spend the *Kiss Me, Kate*/Valentine's weekend on your side of town "just in case Augie ginks out and starts getting cold feet before the curtain goes up." Since this means I'm going to have the whole house to myself for three nights, mightn't it be a valid opportunity to invite Lori over for a "romantic interlude"?

Ted

The Word Shop
BROOKLINE'S FAVORITE BOOKSTORE

E-Memo From the Desk of
Craig Hwong

Hey, Teddy.

Sure. Just like Richard Nixon's valid opportunity to invade Cambodia. Are you *whacked*? You're still at sophomore level. The only one who gets to invite Lori over for a romantic interlude is Lori. So take her out to dinner and make sure she knows you're alone for the weekend. (But do *not* be obvious about it. Her radar could have prevented World War II.) Then halfway through the decaf cappuccinos, smack your forehead when you suddenly "remember" that you forgot to feed Nehi before you left. Explain how sorry you are that you've got to cut the evening short, but promise you'll make it up to her next time. Period. She'll either invite herself over or she won't. If she doesn't, it means she wasn't ripe yet anyway. If she does, you're on your own.

Andy kissed Augie on Sunday, and now we keep misplacing our son. Half an hour ago I found him sitting in a broken armchair in the basement with a blank stare on his face. And he couldn't remember how he'd gotten there.

Craig

Alejandra

Dear Jacqueline,

With the utmost respect, please be advised that I can no longer confide in you. This hasn't been an easy decision to reach, but the facts speak for themselves:

1. You know all of the classics by heart, some of them in two languages.

2. You associate only with kings, duchesses, and the top 4 percent of the social register.

3. Your two marriages were regal but joyless.

You've been my role model since I was eight, and these are the results:

1. I've been called "cold," "stuck-up," "snotty," and "pretentious."

2. I was actually prepared to settle for a loveless career in the diplomatic corps because it was proper and expected.

3. I was so busy waiting for my own unfaithful knight, I nearly failed to recognize the prince in the gray T-shirt.

I appreciate your past companionship, and I certainly hope that we cross paths again. But not for at least ten years.

> With warm regards,
> Alejandra Perez

Dear Ms. Poppins,

I've never apologized to a fictitious character before, but having seen your biography nearly a dozen times in the past month, I hope you'll pardon my earlier judgment in 1996. Perhaps I ought to have given you more than a fifteen-minute chance—yet even at the age of seven, I simply couldn't accept umbrellas as a believable means of air travel. I was wrong. However, I *do* wish that you'd had some tricks in your carpet bag for those of us who already know how to keep our rooms neat and whose mothers aren't necessarily early-twentieth-century suffragettes. We could use a little help with some of our own problems too.

Anthony and I have already gone out together three times since Plum Island—but since he doesn't deserve to know that yet, I've been careful to keep him from finding out that they were actually dates. The first one was disguised as a visit to a merry-go-round with Hucky, who wanted to see if this was the day our horses were going to jump onto the grass—poles and all—and race each other to an imaginary finish line. The second one was a trip to Emerson Garden so that Hucky could practice closing his eyes and jumping into chalk pavement pictures (he's determined to be up to speed when you finally come to live with him). And this afternoon was a safari to the Franklin Park Zoo, where I was positive I could convince Hucky that the animals were talking to us. At least that's what I told Anthony when I cooked up the plan last night. These days, our conversations function on two levels.

- Lunch at the Brookline Café (Bobby Kennedy's booth). I had a garden salad, Anthony had a patty melt, and Hucky had the grilled cheese. Anthony and I reached for our Cokes at the same time, so naturally our hands bumped together. "Ooops," he said apologetically.

SUBTEXT:

ANTHONY: *Do I really have a chance here?*

ALEJANDRA: *Yes. But not until you retire your collection of charades.*

- Green Line to Red Line to #16 bus at Andrew Station. Hucky insisted on sitting in every empty seat at least once between stops—so Anthony grinned and said to me, "This is a forty-five-minute trip. At the rate he's going, he'll be worn out before we get there."

SUBTEXT:

ANTHONY: How come you picked such an out-of-the-way place?

ALEJANDRA: To spend as much time with you as possible, you nitwit. Do you really think I'm going to tell you that yet?

- The zoo. Because the temperature hasn't reached twenty-seven degrees all week, we shared the park with a family from Taunton and a vomiting tiger. The remaining animals were smart enough to stay inside. While Hucky ran ahead so he wouldn't miss the Bengal's next retch, Anthony put one of my hands into his pocket—careful to keep it businesslike. "The last thing you need is frostbite," he warned, his breath glazing to ice right in front of us.

SUBTEXT:

ANTHONY: Sorry. It may have lacked creativity, but it's the best I could do on the fly.

ALEJANDRA: It was an honest move. Do you hear me complaining?

(I should also note that he and Hucky were dressed in identical Red Sox ski jackets, wool Red Sox caps, and blue Red Sox gloves/mittens. They were absolutely irresistible together. I'm surprised Anthony hasn't discovered what effective props small children make.)

After following a frozen footpath and passing one empty cage after another, we finally encountered a rumpled llama named Molly, who was standing alone in her pen and who appeared to be alarmingly self-medicated. Though I have nothing but praise for all of nature's generous wonders, llamas aren't exactly the sharpest tools in the shed—and Molly seemed to be denser than most.

"What's that?" asked Hucky as he hid behind Anthony's legs and tugged on his hair.

"It's a llama," I replied, making sure I signed it carefully so he'd know that the two "l's" were on purpose. "Don't worry—she won't hurt you." Anthony knelt down and put his hands on Hucky's shoulders.

"Listen, buddy," he began. "Her name is Molly, and she's a really good friend of Alé's. They even *talk* to each other." Hucky stared in wonder at Anthony, at Molly, at me, and then back at Anthony again. Then he began wiggling his fingers earnestly. I may not be up to speed on ASL yet, but I can most certainly read between the lines.

"Can we go back and watch the tiger puke?" he insisted. *"But all together this time?"*

TRANSLATION: What a load of crap.

It's funny how kids already know where the magic is, even if it takes the rest of us a little longer to catch up.

Fondly,
Alejandra

THE LAURENTS SCHOOL

presents

COLE PORTER'S

Kiss Me, Kate

Music and Lyrics by
COLE PORTER

Book by
SAM and BELLA SPEWACK

Starring

ALEJANDRA PEREZ   KEITH MARSHALL
AUGIE HWONG   LEE MEYERHOFF

With

ANDY WEXLER · BENJI BENNETT · NEIL REIMAN
NANCY BULL · BILLY MODINE · SAMMY SHEA
TOMMY LEE · RICARDO BARRERA

Directed by
ELINOR PACKER

FRIDAY–SUNDAY, FEBRUARY 13–15; 8:00 P.M.

INSTANT MESSENGER

AugieHwong: We're famous! We're in bookstores, we're in restaurants, and we're even in the lobby of the DuPont Chemical Building. Mr. DuPont knows who we are!

AlePerez: This has got your fingerprints all over it. What did you do—hire a press agent?

AugieHwong: Even better. I talked Mrs. Packer into printing an extra 200, and then I bet Andy, Benji, Neil, Ricardo, and Billy $5.00 apiece that I could put up more than they could. It cost me 25 bucks, but Benton & Bowles would have charged us 25 *grand* for that kind of mass saturation. We've covered the waterfront: Brookline, Brighton, Back Bay, Beacon Hill, the Fens, Allston, Cambridge—

AlePerez: Cambridge?! Augie, I need a slight-to-moderate favor. As long as we're there anyway, could we have one posted on the second-floor bulletin board in the Belfer Center for Science and International Affairs at Harvard?

AugieHwong: I see where *this* is going.

AlePerez: Then don't tell anybody.

Dear Ms. Poppins,

It's a good thing I switched my loyalties to you so recently, because Mrs. Kennedy would have been in over her head. I recall that when you put Mr. Banks in his place, you did so with a firm but gentle hand—noblesse oblige. Jacqueline would have been more tactful. And tact could never have gotten me through the past twenty-four hours.

I knew that Papa had seen the poster, because he was unusually quiet at dinner last night (squab with ginger peas and lace potatoes; *God*, how I wanted a mushroom pizza). Since our small dining room is made out of burnished walnut and has the seating capacity of Fenway Park in 1942, it seemed an appropriate setting for my Declaration of Independence. The charade had continued long enough, and the time had come for me to put my foot down. On the record.

"Alejandra," said Papa, clearing his throat. "I saw a mention of your play this morning. In Cambridge. I had no idea it was such a well-publicized event." Mamita broke into an immediate smile.

"What else could you expect, Papi?" she countered, putting her hand on top of his. "Alejandra's *in* it, after all." Next to me, Carlos froze. His instincts are swift and accurate; he can smell a political coup boiling three continents away.

"Oh, Papa, it's been such fun," I blurted unexpectedly. *Where did that come from? Get back to the script, girl.* "As a matter of fact, I seem to be doing so well, I'd like to apply to a summer stock theatre in Rhode Island as an apprentice. Experience like that'll make it *so* much easier for me to get into a performing arts college." There. Done. *Was that so improbable?* I sat back in my chair, pleased with both my delivery and my poise. Now all that remained was for the house to blow up. But I didn't really care. After four months with Anthony, Augie, and Hucky, it had become quite clear that I was a little remedial in the courage department and it was time to catch up. Especially when Mamita lowered her eyes, Papa's fork clattered to his plate, and Carlos fetched me a kick under the table that should have hobbled me for life.

"I'm sorry, Alejandra," snapped Papa, glaring. "That's simply unacceptable. There's an embassy position waiting for you in July, and we've all known for years that you'll be majoring in government at Harvard. What were you *thinking*?"

That's when I remembered you and Mr. Banks. He was fully prepared to fire you after he found out his kids had been dancing with cartoons—but by the time you got through with him, he'd have followed you to Indiana if you'd given the order. All it took from you was respect, dignity, holding your ground, and not forgetting how much you loved those children. (It also helped that you had professional screenwriters giving you the lines. I didn't, so I managed the best I could.)

ALEJANDRA
(Rising)

Papa, I'm ashamed that you think women are so simple. We can make decisions for ourselves too, you know. I'm not a child or a baby anymore, so I'm allowed to speak my mind. And if you don't wish to hear it, just tell me so and I'll go into another room—but I'll speak it anyway. I want this for myself as much as I've never wanted the diplomatic corps, and I'm going to get it—even if I have to do it alone. Excuse me.

(I'd love to take even partial author credit, but it was a mix of *Kiss Me, Kate*, *The Taming of the Shrew*, and a song lyric from some '60s musical I'd never heard of until Augie discovered it in December.)

When I'd reached my room at the top of the stairs and shut the door behind me, my heart was pounding—and not because I was afraid. *So that's what it feels like to stand up for yourself! What have I been missing out on??* The buzz lasted for the rest of the evening (sleep finally came at 3:30 a.m.), and at breakfast this morning, nobody spoke at all—except for Carlos's glowering eyes, which kept repeating silently, "You've lost your last marble and you can't have any of mine." But this was a victory all by itself. Except for a halfhearted "Alejandra, we have a few things to discuss" from Papa, at least no one was attempting to talk me out of it.

INSTANT MESSENGER

AugieHwong: You rock, girl. I AM *SO* PROUD OF YOU!!

Our first tech rehearsal passed in a blur. All I remember is that the sets were glimmering and my costume made me look like a turnip. (I'm assured by Mrs. Packer that it'll be replaced by the time we open on Friday. I certainly hope so. I don't play vegetables well.) The freshman band has a tuba player who belongs on sedatives, but otherwise they managed to keep up with us—and the afternoon's highlight came unexpectedly during a first act break when Mrs. Packer gave us fifteen minutes off so she could refocus the lights. This is usually when Augie performs "Too Darn Hot" for us, but Lee had warned me that there was an unscheduled change in the program.

"Watch this," she whispered as we slid into our seats in the third row. I was sandwiched in between Lee and Anthony, as Augie wrapped up a hasty conference from the stage with Mr. Disharoon and the band. When musical matters had been settled, he turned to face the audience.

"For this number," he announced, "I'm going to need a volunteer. Somebody to play Bill and to feed me my cues. Any takers?" Well, since Augie is Augie, nine arms shot into the air simultaneously—so he shielded his eyes from the light, examined his applicants, and pointed to a spot in the darkened auditorium. "Andy Wexler. You're it, dude." To the best of my recollection, Andy hadn't been one of those with his arm raised.

"How do you spell 'stacked deck'?" I mumbled to Anthony.

"And like, what exactly were you expecting?" he mumbled back.

Andy climbed sheepishly onto the stage and allowed himself to be positioned on a set piece; then Augie leaned down to whisper to him. At first Andy blushed, and then he broke into an automatic grin. (As well he'd better. There were three of us poised to beat him to death if he'd responded with anything less.)

"You got it," he replied with a wink. The way they were taking such obvious delight in each other—especially after the crisis they'd survived together—you couldn't help feeling jealous that you weren't either one of them. And as soon as Augie had planted himself center stage and Mr. Disharoon had cued the song, Andy—as a disgruntled Bill—called out to his boyfriend.

"Aw, doll. Why can't you behave?" In reply, Augie scratched his head as though thoroughly perplexed and turned upstage to reply.

"How in hell can you be jealous," he sang incredulously, "when you know, baby, I'm your slave?" Then without any warning at all, he lit into a version of "Always True to You in My Fashion" that would have sent Lisa Kirk in the original cast straight back to dance class. Between his pirouettes, his jetés, and his exuberant habit of shadowboxing with some of the cleverest lyrics ever written, the rest of us already looked like has-beens.

"That little twerp is better than *I* am," hissed Lee.

"We need to keep our eyes on him," I muttered under my breath in agreement, "before he replaces *all* of us." I don't know how he managed to turn it into a boy's song, but in his royal blue tights and his baby-blue tunic, even a line like "I enjoy a tender pass by the boss of Boston, Mass" landed with a reverberating crack on the guys' side of the slate. Mrs. Packer was positively stupefied. ("Should I have considered non-traditional casting??") I'm sure it's no coincidence that two other boys in the ninth grade have been courageous enough to come out since Thanksgiving, because when you've got a pioneer like Augie Hwong blazing the trail, what's there to be afraid of??

INSTANT MESSENGER

AugieHwong: Do you think I overdid it?

AlePerez: Honey, if he won't marry you
after that, he doesn't deserve you.

We had just enough rehearsal time left for a tech run-through of
"So in Love With You Am I" before we broke for the afternoon—and
since I'd never had a chance to sing it in my rose-gelled spotlight
before, I gave it everything I had. (The only notable difference in my
delivery was that I performed the entire song to Anthony without
bothering to pretend otherwise. Theoretically, this constituted a
breach of Lee's and my rule about not flirting with boys—but neither
of us had taken into account the prospect of a boy who'd have me
talking to a llama.) To be entirely frank, I've done so much better in
the past, it was with some measure of embarrassment that my fade-
out on the tag—"so in love with you, my love, am I"—resulted in an
impromptu standing ovation by the entire company.

"I'm mortified," I muttered to Lee as we made our way to our
dressing room. "I didn't deserve that."

"Then check *this* out," she replied laconically, pointing to the back
of the house. To my absolute horror, seated in the back row were
my brother and my parents. Carlos was wearing a suitably smug
grin, Mamita was beaming, and a thoroughly subdued Papa was
numbly fielding staccato-like questions from Mrs. Packer and Mr.
Disharoon, one of which clearly contained the phrase "promising
career." However, as optimistic as developments appeared from the
safe distance of twenty rows away, it was only my brother's "thumbs-
up" that prevented a cardiovascular seizure on the spot and assured
me that I'd at least won the first round. Which is as much as I could
have reasonably hoped for. After all, even *you* had to wear down the

Banks family by degrees before you could teach Jane and Michael all they needed to learn about their hearts.

"*Mr. Banks, on second thoughts, I believe a trial period would be wise. I'll give you one week. I'll know by then.*"

Mary Poppins, if Hucky ever outgrows you, you're welcome to come live with *me*.

Fondly,

Alejandra

UNITED STATES SECRET SERVICE
WASHINGTON, D.C.

CLINT LOCKHART
AGENT

Dear Princess:

I'm enclosing Augie's birthday present to Anthony: Two field box seats at Fenway Park, Aisle 44, Row D, Seats 101–102 (four rows behind the plate) for the September 26 home game versus the Yanks. On the house. The Red Sox owed the CIA a favor. You don't want to know why.

xoxo,
Clint

Alé,

Was I not supposed to notice the hand-holding with T.C.?

—*Lee*

Lee,

You were allowed. It's an open secret.　　—*Alé*

Alé,

Not anymore. Everyone's talking.　　—*Lee*

Lee,

How did "everyone" find out?　　—*Alé*

Alé,

I told Kathy Fine. Now it's on the UPI ticker.

—*Lee*

House of Representatives

WASHINGTON, D.C.

THOMAS J. HIRASAWA
STATE OF CALIFORNIA

Dear Ms. Perez and Mr. Keller:

Rep. Ruth Mellick passed along your press release to my office, and I was most impressed that two high school freshmen care so deeply about an injustice that occurred so long ago.

As a third-generation *Sansei*, I had grandparents in both the Manzanar and Heart Mountain internment camps—my grandfather, in fact, pitched for the Manzanar Gophers—so I'd be most willing to assist your efforts in any way that I can in order to restore the baseball diamond at Manzanar. Please feel free to contact me at your convenience.

Very truly yours
Thos. J. Hirasawa
D-California

INSTANT MESSENGER

TCKeller: Now THAT'S progress. I *told* you we could count on Aunt Ruth.

AlePerez: You think it means a congressional committee?

TCKeller: At least. See what you started?

AlePerez: See what you finished? Where do you want to eat?

TCKeller: Well, *Love Actually* is playing all over, but the seats are always better at the Cineplex in Harvard Square. Meanwhile, I've been thinking about the rigatoni at Uno Chicago Pizza on JFK Street (an address that ought to appeal to you). Trust me on this?

AlePerez: I'll trust you on this.

Dear Ms. Poppins,

It finally happened—and without any tricks. Maybe it's because we've shared more in four weeks than we ever did during the semester we wasted flirting like children (God, did I *really* endorse that idiotic National Recovery Act just to get under his skin?)—but the way we spontaneously locked eyes across a geography classroom last Friday made it clear that you don't plan falling in love the way you plan a formal dinner for twelve. And don't ask me what an archipelago is, because it could never matter again.

Your movie doesn't tell us whether or not you ever had a boyfriend, though it certainly seems obvious that you've got some pretty tender feelings for Bert. (Watching you cover them up with a reserved chuckle is positively darling—especially when he's trying to dance like a penguin for your benefit.) So it's just possible that I may be turning into more of an authority than you are in this arena. For instance:

1.   <u>Boys Are Thorough</u>. It took Anthony three days to ask me out on our first no-other-excuses-to-cover-it-up date. First he had to conduct the appropriate research, for which he used Augie and Lee to run interference. "Find out whether she likes comedies, dramas, or those ginky art movies with titles like *Green Plant Facing Southwest*." "How does she feel about Hugh Grant?" (I used to find him adorable—until I met Anthony.) "Does she have a problem with Italian food?" Once he'd collected all of the pertinent data, it was time to be spontaneous.

INSTANT MESSENGER

TCKeller: Hey, I still haven't seen *Love Actually* yet, and it's not going to be around much longer. Want to go? I might have a free night this week before you get tied up with *Kiss Me, Kate*.

---

2.   <u>Boys Are Predictable</u>. *"The seats are always better at the Cineplex in Harvard Square."* The seats at the Cineplex in Harvard Square are indistinguishable from the seats at the Copper Creek Cinema in Des Moines, Iowa, or—for that matter—from the seats

at the Coolidge Corner Theatre right here in Brookline. Harvard Square is also a twenty-five-minute ride on the T, assuming that the changeover to the Red Line at Park Street isn't held up because the tracks have frozen again. What the Cineplex in Harvard Square actually has going for it is that it's located on Church Street, just off of Mass Ave—the same corner where Anthony's parents kissed for the first time 25 years ago. So it hardly required a degree in sociology to figure out where the evening was supposed to lead. Did he really think I wouldn't pick up on it??

3.   Boys Are All Talk. For somebody who first introduced himself to me by means of a form letter, the prospect of our first kiss evidently had him terrified. Despite the fact that Uno Chicago Pizza has a four-star Zagat rating, he didn't even touch his rigatoni—and his dinner conversation was so fractured, I gave up trying to follow his train of thought. Among the things he chattered about were the invention of ball bearings, Johnny Peacock's batting average in 1938, and why the Netherlands is two-thirds under water.

"Is anything wrong?" I asked as he paid the cashier and dropped his wallet on the floor.

"I'm—I'm fine," he stammered, following a quarter across the checkered tile. "I sway-ah."

By the time the previews were over, his forehead was covered with sweat and he'd actually started to shake. I got him to calm down a little by feeding him Life Savers—but even so, if you'd asked him what the film was about, you'd have been just as likely to get the plot of *The Magnificent Seven*.

4.   Boys Are Precious. At 9:15, we walked silently up Church Street to Mass Ave. He'd forgotten to put on his wool cap, so I had

a chance to add "red ears" to the list of things I already loved. (I slotted it in between "soft brown hair" and "eyebrows fretted with worry." This is a catalog that's updated regularly.) But he was still shivering, and it wasn't the cold. *Go easy on yourself, Anthony. We're going to survive this!* When we finally reached the inevitable corner, I would have done anything to let him off the hook. But it was already too late.

"Alé," he mumbled quietly, as the light changed from amber to red. I turned to face him, thoroughly prepared to take charge myself, but the moment I saw the dimple in his chin (#6 on my list), my knees began to tremble. *What's happening to me??* Without any spoken preliminaries, he let me brush the bangs out of his eyes first—and then he leaned in and kissed me. It was just that simple. So simple, in fact, that I burst into tears.

"Are you okay?" he asked gently, touching his forehead to mine in genuine concern. "It wasn't *that* bad, was it?"

"I'm fine," I wailed. "I sway-ah." Then he kissed me again, and I really *was* fine.

One word of advice, Mary Poppins: Give Bert a chance.

> Fondly,
> Alejandra

Subject: URGENT!!!
From: AlePerez@earthworks.net
To: augie@augiehwong.com

I'm attaching an article in today's *Globe*. If we work it right, it's going to be Anthony's birthday present to Anthony.

We've got just 72 hours to map out a plan, and you're the brains in this department. So drop everything, including *Kiss Me, Kate*. This takes priority.

The Globe

THEATRE

ANDREWS AND GOULET
TOGETHER AGAIN

Julie Andrews and Robert Goulet will be co-hosting this year's *Broadway Cares/Equity Fights AIDS* benefit at the Shubert Theatre in New York this Sunday evening, February 15—heading an all-star cast of Broadway and Hollywood luminaries and marking the first time these two musical legends will have appeared together publicly since their Guenevere-Lancelot onstage romance in 1960's *Camelot.*

Broadway Cares/Equity Fights AIDS is a not-for-profit corporation that has been funding AIDS research through New York's theatre community since 1992.

AugieHwong: This is going to be a Mame Dennis cakewalk. I know the layout of the Shubert Theatre like the back of my hand. Once you get past the stage doorman, there's a couple of steps that lead down to this big room under the stage, right off the orchestra pit. Lots of corners to hide in during the show, but look like you belong there anyway in case anyone notices you. Then—

TCKeller: Wait. What about the "once you get past the stage doorman" part?

AlePerez: Yeah, you kind of glossed over that, didn't you?

AugieHwong: That's because it's a no-brainer! He'll

be on the lookout for gatecrashers, so kids won't even register on his scope. All you have to do is tell him that you're Blake Edwards's nephews Kevin and Seth, and that your aunt forgot to leave your tickets at the box office.

TCKeller: Who's Blake Edwards?

AugieHwong: Her husband, you gink!

AlePerez: Does he even *have* nephews?

AugieHwong: How should *I* know?? And trust me—if I don't know, the doorman's not going to know either. Just ask him if he can go get Aunt Julie for you. He can't, because he's not allowed to leave his post. So he'll wave you in and tell you where her dressing room is. (If it looks like he's getting suspicious, just have Hucky pretend to cry. Even the bottom-lip thing should push it over the top.) But do *not* bother her before the show. Hide out until it's over, when she'll have time to be Mary Poppins for him.

TCKeller: This is the worst idea you ever had.

AugieHwong: Come up with a better one. I dare you. Pop already thinks you're staying over for the whole *Kiss Me, Kate* weekend—Friday, Saturday, and Sunday. Mom and Dad thought "weekend" just meant Friday and Saturday. So without lying to anybody, we wound up with a Sunday when nobody expects to see you. It's a gift from God.

AlePerez: I got the train tickets. It's part of my birthday present. You leave from Back Bay on the Sunday afternoon Acela at 2:15 and come back on a 12:15 A.M. train that gets in at 5:30 in the morning.

AugieHwong: Which is when the Brookline Café opens, so you can hang there with Hucky until it's time to take him back to the Residence at 8:00. Then just meet us at school.

TCKeller: This is never going to work.

AugieHwong: Tick, *you're* the one who believes in magic. So prove it.

Dear Mama,

Now I know how it was so easy for Lucy to talk Ethel into capers like stealing John Wayne's footprints. When you plan it out ahead of time, somehow it all makes sense. It's only when it's all over that you get to find out whether you're a crackpot or not.

A couple of things I know for sure.

1. I could never lie to Pop. But Augie's right. When we made our plans for this weekend, Pop and I both figured I'd be staying at Augie's on Sunday too. So everything is still honest, isn't it? I mean, my itinerary just changed, that's all. Not telling him about it doesn't count as lying.

2. Pop lets me fly on the shuttle by myself to visit Aunt Babe and Aunt Ruth in Washington, as long as I have my cell phone so he can check up on me. So two ginky train rides between New York and Back Bay Station (which is practically down the street from us anyway) shouldn't be a big stretch, should it? Once we get there, we can take a cab to the theatre and another one back to the train afterwards. It's not like we'd be walking the streets—and it isn't much different than spending a whole Saturday at the Pru. Maybe even safer too.

3. I trust Augie with everything, and he trusts me back the same way. He and Mom and Dad were at a party backstage at the same theatre for the Tommy Awards a couple of years ago, so if Augie says it's do-able, then it is. He'd *never* let me get into trouble. Come to think of it, he's always the one who keeps me *out* of it.

4. Telling Pop won't work. Even if he came to New York with us, he wouldn't go along with pretending that we were Kevin and Seth Edwards who had a famous Aunt Julie. Which is the only way we're ever going to get inside to meet her. Hucky and I can pull this off by ourselves, but Pop wouldn't be able to.

5. Hucky needs this, Mama. He doesn't look out the window for Mary Poppins as much as he used to, but that could also mean he's giving up on her. And I can't let him stop believing in things when he's only six.

I love you,

T.C.

P.S. Remember back in the fall when Lori got on my case about $x + y$, and Pop said that algebra was supposed to help me solve problems? What's up with *that*?

$$x + y = ?$$

(Hucky needs Mary Poppins) + (Mary Poppins is in New York)

$$=$$

(Take Hucky to New York if Pop will let you)

or

(Take Hucky to New York even when Pop says no)

or

(Take Hucky to New York without asking first)

or

(Ask an adult to handle it)

STUDENT/ADVISER CONFERENCE
Lori Mahoney/Anthony C. Keller

T.C.:   I have an urgent question about algebra.

LORI: Then you should probably ask Mrs. Fitzpatrick.

T.C.:   This is different. She's not dating my father.

LORI: Anthony, I'm not actually "dating" him.

T.C.:   Are you going places together and having dinner together and showing up in Vermont by accident?

LORI: Well, yes, but—

T.C.:   Then I have an urgent question about algebra.

LORI: Go ahead.

T.C.:   What happens when you add x plus y but there are a couple of different answers?

LORI: That's impossible. *X* has a specific value and so has *y*. They can only add up one way. Unless there's a third variable you're not telling me about.

T.C.:   No, there should only be two. And that's what I needed to find out.

(Hucky needs Mary Poppins) + (Mary Poppins is in New York)

=

(Take Hucky to New York without third variables)

Dear Mama:

I could never be a bank robber or a hit man, because they can go to sleep the night before their crimes and not wake up once. All *I'm* doing is kidnapping a six-year-old for fifteen hours to take him to New York for a play date with Mary Poppins—and I had to use a night-light for the first time since I was seven. Is this fair?

INSTANT MESSENGER

AugieHwong: Tick, keep your cell phone charged and don't forget to take the extra battery. Except for 8:00-9:15 and 9:30-10:15 (when I have my audience to consider), I'm here. Don't worry, this *will* work. Nobody in the world could pull this off but my big brother.

INSTANT MESSENGER

AlePerez: Anthony, once we put you and Hucky on the train, it's in your hands. And if you even *think* of getting cold feet, just remember that I'll know it. And you *so* don't want to go there.

The only thing that kept my imagination from winding up on a three-state All-Points Bulletin was *Kiss Me, Kate*. Opening night was Friday, and we had the whole third row reserved just for us: Me and Hucky, Pop and Lori, Mom and Dad and Grandma Lily, Phyllis and her kids (Darius even flew in from Cornell for this), Carlos, and Alé's parents. I wound up missing the overture because there was an emergency backstage that Mrs. Packer needed my help with.

"Are you almost finished?" I asked Augie, who was still kneeling on the floor with his head in the toilet.

"I think I'm—" he began. But then he heaved again and the rest of dinner came up.

"Maybe you shouldn't have eaten until afterwards," I suggested, sitting him up against the wall and wiping the puke off his chin with a wet paper towel. "Isn't that why you say they have all of those late-night places like the Stork Club and the Cub Room?"

"The Cub Room," he repeated weakly. "Where the elite meet." Then he groaned. "Tick, Ethel Merman ate steak and potatoes two hours before she opened in *Annie Get Your Gun*. All *I* had was a fish burger and a Pop-Tart. I'm *such* a loser!" So I kicked his ass into the wings and hung around in case they needed me to shove him onstage too. Sometimes you just have to bite the bullet and practice tough love. Even if it hurts.

Of course he stopped the show. We all knew that "Too Darn Hot" was going to knock them flat, but Mrs. Packer hadn't planned on an encore. So when the whole audience stood up clapping and wouldn't sit down again, nobody knew what to do. Except Augie. He just nodded to Mr. Disharoon like they had it planned all along (it turns out they did—Augie *always* knows what sells), and then they started the whole number over from the top. This time it was Hucky who led the cheers—he got up onto his seat with both of his fists raised, and everybody else took their cue from him.

Alé wasn't exactly a surprise either. She got three curtain calls of her own, and at the beginning of the fourth one somebody handed her a dozen roses over the footlights. She had no idea who they were from (until she read the card later: "Now we've *both* been tempered by a hard and bitter peace. Love, JFK and Anthony"), so she decided to cry instead—which was the perfect thing to do, because the noise only got louder. By the time the curtain went down and the lights in the auditorium went up again, her father was *so* not happy. But when you've got a couple dozen people congratulating you on your kid, what can you *say*?

Suddenly it was 2:15 on Sunday, and as far as Hucky knew, we were just going on another special trip—but this one in jackets and ties. I couldn't exactly tell him where or why, in case we wound up on a police blotter instead of inside a chalk pavement picture with Mary Poppins. Who needed to break his heart??

I didn't realize that he'd never been on a train before, so when the shiny white Acela glided (glid?) into Back Bay Station, he couldn't figure out how to wrap his mind around it. *Is all that for us??* Not that you could tell what he was thinking unless you knew him as well as we do. With his ski jacket and wool cap and the muffler covering his face, all you could see was eyes. Meanwhile, Alé and Augie were giving us last-minute instructions as the doors slid open in front of us.

"Remember. You're Kevin and Seth Edwards. Keep saying it to yourself on the way down to New York. Don't let them catch you in a trap."

"Which one of us is Seth?"

"Does it *matter*?"

"Anthony, just think 'Buck Weaver' instead of 'Julie Andrews.' That always works for you."

"Hucky, make sure you listen to Tick and do everything he tells you to."

"*Okay! Okay!*" he replied impatiently, pulling on my hand. "*Come on! I want to see the train!*"

We found two seats in the Club Coach and waved to Augie and Alé as the train began to move. *Bye! We're going on an adventure!* But as soon as they slipped out of our view and got replaced by an empty platform and the rail yard, the smile fell off my face and the bottom of my stomach felt like it had just dropped onto the outbound tracks. Whenever Augie is with me, I never have to worry about being brave. Now he was back *there*. Why couldn't he have come with us?? Then I remembered Pop's favorite words from *Apollo 13*. "Failure is not an option." (Actually, we use it for other things too. "Onions are not an option." "Diarrhea is not an option." "Cavities are not an option.") So I decided that at least for a day, fear was not an option either.

"*What's that?*" asked Hucky. By now he was sitting up on his knees and staring frowny-faced over the back of his tall blue seat at the snack bar, trying to figure out what it was doing there. *Food? On a train? What a concept!*

"It's a little restaurant," I told him, pulling off his jacket and muffler. "For when we get hungry. Sit."

"*I'm hungry right now! Who's that?*"

"The conductor. He's taking our tickets."

"*Will he give them back?*"

"No."

"*That stinks.*" I couldn't get him to unfold his arms or take off his mad face for a good five minutes.

After lunch—potato chips, cupcakes, and cranberry juice—I opened up a map that Alé had given me so I could show Hucky where we were. There was a red circle around Boston at the top and another one around New York at the bottom, and every time we got to a new station, I'd tell Hucky what to circle next. This turned out to be a game that Augie would say "has a short shelf life." Hucky was excited by New Haven, bored by Stamford, and yawning by Bridgeport. Besides, he was having too much fun pressing his face against the window and finding out firsthand how big the world really was. The only time I had to call a peace out was twenty minutes before we got to New York when we passed Yankee Stadium—the House That Bucky F. Dent Thought He Built. So I pulled down the shade. Hucky was way too young to have to see something like that.

Once the Acela had hissed to a stop and we'd hit the platform, he was a little spooked by Penn Station—and I don't blame him. With all of the passengers pushing their way through the waiting room to get back home after the weekend, he looked a lot littler than he really is, and he held my hand a lot tighter than he ever had before.

"Why does everybody move so fast and look so mad?" he wondered, staring up at me nervously.

"They're all just late," I signed back to him. "Like the rabbit in *Alice in Wonderland.* They're not really mean, even if they act like it." But after we hit the sidewalk he turned into Regular Hucky again, staring up at the buildings on both sides of Eighth Avenue like we were in a long tunnel above the ground.

"New York is tall!" he decided as I buckled us into a cab on Thirty-fifth Street. Since we were still a little early, I told the driver that Hucky had never been to New York before, so he turned off the meter and drove us around Times Square on our way to the Shubert Theatre. (Actually, this didn't happen until I signed "Don't play with your seat belt" to Hucky and he saw us in the rearview mirror. When people find out Hucky's deaf, they like to give us things for free.) Hucky was so dazzled by the view of the colored lights from Forty-seventh Street, he could only manage to ask me two questions: (1) *"Doesn't it look like Christmas?"* and (2) *"Why is that man peeing on the street?"* So I told him (1) "Yes," and (2) "Because that's the way they do it in New York. But you have to have a license first." I had to lie through my teeth about the last part because I'd already jumped ahead to what he was planning when we got out of the cab.

The driver dropped us off in "Shubert Alley," which is actually almost a street, and as soon as I saw the 2,000 people in tuxedoes and the photographers and the television cameras, my stomach did

another somersault. *I feel just like Augie did with his head in the toilet.*
Dude, this is so not going to fly. To Hucky, it was just another chapter
in our Sunday—*"Look, T.C.! Men dressed like the penguins!"*—but
that only reminded me how much was riding on this. So I grabbed
his hand and thought about Buck Weaver and purple balloons.

"Spit-spot," I said confidently, like we weren't about to wind up
on an episode of *Law & Order.*

The outside walls of the Shubert Theatre are painted gold, and
right in the middle is a door with a sign that says "Stage Entrance." By
the time we'd crisscrossed the crowd and found ourselves standing
in front of it, my heart was thumping faster than it did on the night
I kissed Alé. *Right, you gink! And that worked out, didn't it? It's an*
omen. So just to make sure I had all of our bases covered, I crouched
down in front of Hucky and gave him one last instruction.

"Okay," I began, trying not to let him see I was sweating bullets.
"When we go inside that door, there's a man I'm going to talk to.
Now, if I squeeze your hand three times—like this—I want you to
pretend you're crying, okay?" Hucky was all over it. He's a bigger
ham than Augie is. (Almost.)

"Okay." He grinned. *"But how come?"*

"It's a game. You'll see." Then I stood up and yanked open the
gold door before I had any more chances to chicken out or barf.
Whatever was going to happen was going to happen right now.

Inside, it looked just like Augie said it would. There was a ragged
old guy in a beat-up cubicle on one side of this little entryway,
who wore the same kind of "you've got exactly five seconds or else"
attitude that Mrs. Fitzpatrick wears whenever she can't get us to
stop talking after recess. In the background, you could see all of

these actors running around in different costumes and bumping into each other and using the F word like it was a contest, and you could tell from Hucky's face that he couldn't figure out *what* was going on. *Cowboys and baseball players?! What's up with <u>that</u>?* In the meantime, the doorman didn't seem too happy to see us.

"Whadja want?" he snapped, like he was accusing us of shoplifting or something.

"Um, I'm Kevin Edwards," I mumbled, positive that my red face was going to give us away, "and this is my little brother, uh—" *Seth, you gink!!* "Seth. My aunt forgot to leave our tickets at the box office and now she's back here somewheres." *Where did "somewheres" come from??* The doorman gave us the kind of squint you usually get in a police lineup.

"Who's your aunt?" he grumbled.

"Julie Andrews," I blurted, praying that the FBI wouldn't come out of the closet with a warrant. This wasn't turning out to be the cakewalk that Augie had promised. Because he just kept glaring.

"Your aunt, huh?" he repeated.

"Yes, sir. Could you maybe get her for us?" And while I was asking, I was also squeezing Hucky's hand three times. Half a second later, he began to sob. *They really should have cast him in* Kiss Me, Kate. *He learned his cues faster than Alé did.* So I crouched down in front of him again and made a big deal out of wiping the tears off his little blond face and signing, "It's okay, buddy. We'll find her." That was all it took. When I stood up again, the doorman had already moved on to other things in his head.

"Look, kid," he muttered, "I can't leave here just to find your aunt." Then he jerked his thumb behind him. "Go down those steps, cross to the other side, and turn right when you get to the hall." After that, he answered a telephone.

I don't remember if I even said thank you, because I was numb. *It <u>worked</u>?? HOLY CRAP, IT WORKED!* I grabbed Hucky's hand before anybody could find out what posers we were and dragged him down the steps into Augie's "big room under the stage, right off the orchestra pit" that I already knew was going to be there. There was a long table with food on it for the actors and some chairs pushed up against the back wall—so I took over the seat in the corner where we wouldn't get in anybody's way, plopped Hucky onto the chair next to me, and breathed for the first time in an hour and a half. *Houston, all systems are go. Except one.*

"Dude," I signed to Hucky, "you can stop crying now."

"*Why? It's fun!*"

"Because we won."

The next two and a half hours would have been my brother's idea of what heaven looks like, but I could barely keep my eyes open. Before each production number in the show, the chorus rehearsed their dance steps one last time in our orchestra room, whispering the words so the audience upstairs wouldn't hear them, while Hucky and I ate smoked salmon off the table and watched. The only thing that kept me awake was seeing how many of the routines I could recognize from all of the ginky musicals that Augie and Mom drag me to—and I actually wound up batting .800. I nailed *Oklahoma!* (Mom hated it), *Sweet Charity* (Mom tolerated it), *West Side Story* (Mom loved it), and *South Pacific* (Mom *really* hated it). I only missed out on the one where everybody was wearing pajamas (but Mom would have hated that too—trust me).

Hucky discovered *other* things to keep him awake. Somehow the chorus girls all decided that he was just about the cutest thing they'd ever seen on two small feet—especially when they found out he was deaf. So they kept coming over to pat his head and hold his hand and feed him carrot cake and tell him what a sweetheart he was. Meanwhile, Hucky had all of these bosoms in his face, and he didn't know which one to look at first. (I hope he remembers every one of them when he's fifteen, because it'll never happen to him again. I'm an authority. They all ignored me like I had a rash.) And the best part? Nobody even wondered what we were doing there. I guess they probably figured we belonged to somebody famous.

"CURTAIN CALLS, PLEASE." The voice came over the speakers in our orchestra room and everybody ran upstairs at the same time like in a Raid commercial. My heart jumped a little all over again when I remembered what we still had to do, but I also knew we'd come too far to lose in the ninth. Even the Sox could have held on to a lead like ours. So I stood up and pretended I was Carlton Fisk.

"Pick up your jacket, buddy," I said to Hucky, who was still annoyed that all of his breasts had left. "Time to move."

"*Where are we going?*" he asked, sliding off his chair.

"Surprise for you."

"*For me? What is it?*"

"What do you want more than anything in the world?"

"*Marbles?*" From the theatre above us I could hear the applause and the "bravos" and all the rest of that junk, and just a few seconds later people began flooding off the stage and filling up our room on their way to places like the Stork Club and the Cub Room. So I grabbed Hucky's hand and steered us through the tuxedoes, toward the hallway where the doorman had told us Aunt Julie would be. And all of a sudden, in between people's shoulders and necks, I saw her. Wearing a dark blue dress with glittery beads. Talking to a short man with a bald head and three other women. And I couldn't help stopping in my tracks. *OH MY GOD. THAT'S MARY POPPINS!* Hucky was too short for the view (which was a good thing because I would have needed oxygen to start him breathing again), but I had to blink twice just to make sure she was real. I mean, I wasn't expecting her to be wearing old-fashioned clothes with black clumpy boots and a hat with a flower sticking out of it, but who'd have thought she was still going to look the same anyway??

By the time we'd worked our way through the crunch to where she'd been standing, she wasn't there anymore—but I didn't panic because I still had the doorman's directions in my head. "Turn right." Which is just what we did. We found ourselves in a short empty hallway (painted the kind of yellow that looked like a baby threw up after he ate strained bananas), where we spotted a closed door to our right with a taped-up sign on it that said **MISS ANDREWS**. *Dude! Grand slam!!* But while I was raising my hand to knock, there was a voice behind us.

"Hey. You kids. Get away from there!" I turned around and saw a security guard ten feet away and closing in on us fast. Hucky hid behind my right leg, scared to death and I don't blame him. This guy reminded me of the Hancock Tower, but blue and with feet. We backed up into the corner until we were trapped under a glass case with a hose and an axe in it—and just as he reached for my arm, the door opened and Mary Poppins stepped into the hall with a big question mark on her face. I was so grateful to see her up close, I knew right away how those two little Banks kids must have felt when they noticed her floating down into Cherry Tree Lane. The movie wasn't lying. All of the things they asked for in the nanny song were still there. "Kind." "Witty." "Sweet." "Pretty." And it didn't take her long to get a handle on the situation.

"Is there some difficulty?" she asked the cop politely, planting herself between him and us on purpose. (I mean, it's not exactly as if it looked like a fair fight.) As soon as Hucky recognized her, he forgot all about the trouble we were in and clapped both hands over his mouth. Meanwhile, I knew I had just one shot before we both got hauled off to the clink, so I'd better make it a good one.

"Ms. Andrews," I blurted, coming out from under the fire extinguisher while Hucky followed me cautiously, "my name is Anthony Keller and this is Hucky Harper. You sent him a letter, but we forgot to tell you that he thinks you *are* Mary Poppins, and he doesn't understand why you haven't come to live with him yet." Mama, remember how she sized up Jane and Michael Banks with her eyes when she first met them? Because that's exactly what she did to me and Hucky.

"I see," she said, looking me up and down. And then "Hmmmm" when she got to Hucky. I didn't know if she was doing it for show or not, but with her finger tapping on her chin just like in the movie, I got the feeling she was going to take her magic tape measure out of her pocket next. And the whole time, you could tell from her expression that she remembered writing Hucky directions about how to hop into chalk pavement pictures and giving him her loveliest of wishes. So after a second, she turned to the policeman.

"Thank you, officer," she said firmly, like he was Mr. Banks. "I know these children." *Home free!* The cop wasn't exactly happy about it, but he probably figured she could have sent him flying across West Forty-fourth Street just by waving her hand, so he grumbled his way back down the hall and left us alone. By then, Mary Poppins had turned all of her attention to Blake Edwards's youngest nephew, Seth, who still couldn't believe he wasn't dreaming the whole thing—especially when she knelt down in front of him and signed, "You must be Hucky." Mama, you had to see the eyes-wide look on his face. *It's HER! It's really HER!!* All he could manage to do was not fall over on his six-year-old butt.

"I think we need to have a little talk, don't you?" she asked, putting her hands on his shivering shoulders. Hucky nodded. It was the only time since that first day at Amory Park that I'd ever seen him speechless. (He's kind of like Augie that way.) And when she stood up to take his hand, he turned to me in shock. *Is this really happening??* You'd think he would have learned by now not to keep his nanny waiting.

"Spit-spot," she signed sternly, tugging on his arm. As she led him into her dressing room, he glanced over his shoulder at me with his bottom jaw still hanging open. So I signed a fast warning right back at him.

"Close your mouth, Hucky. We are not a codfish." Then they were gone.

Nine seconds later my phone rang. I didn't even have to check Caller ID to find out who it was. My brother and I invented synchronicity when we were six.

AUGIE: Any news there?

ME: The Eagle has landed. He's in her dressing room.

AUGIE: Holy crap! I didn't really think it was going to *work*!

ME: Then what did you send us down here for??

AUGIE: To see if I was wrong. What's she saying to him?

ME: I don't know. Maybe she's making things fly around the room. I'm out in this baby-puke hallway. You should have come with me. They have all of these women with big hair who you'd probably recognize.

AUGIE: Like who?

ME: Well, there's a check-in sheet on this bulletin board that says Elaine Stritch—

AUGIE: Oh, my God.

ME: —Maggie Smith—

AUGIE: Oh, my God.

ME: —Judi Dench—

AUGIE: Oh, my God. What about Liza?

ME: Well, "Liza Minnelli" is listed, but I don't know what
             she looks like.

LIZA: She's standing right behind you.

When I glanced over my shoulder, I recognized her right away.
She was the "Maybe This Time" one. I had to watch her sing that
damn song the whole year I was ten, before Augie got tired of her
and moved on to her mother. Right now she was wearing a black
dress and a black coat with fur, and she didn't seem too pissed off
that I wouldn't have known her from Clint Eastwood.

"Who's on the phone?" she asked, poofing up her big black hair
and smiling at me like I was maybe her best friend or her agent.

"My brother Augie," I said. "Look, do you think you could talk to
him for a second? He knew your birthday by heart when we were seven,
but he's not really weird." She didn't say anything back, but instead
took the cell phone out of my hand and put it up to her green earring.

"Augie? It's Liza."

Pause.

"March 12, 1946. It was a natural childbirth." I couldn't believe
he was actually *testing* her to see if she was real! (Yes, I could. He's
Augie.) I guess she convinced him, because she stayed on the phone
for another twenty seconds discussing her parents, her Oscar, and
her next concert at Radio City. If her date hadn't shown up to yank
her away, they might have used up all of my unlimited air time.

"Bye, Augie," she said in a rush. "Lenny's here." She flipped my
phone shut and handed it back to me—but before she left, she took
a program out of her purse, opened to the title page, and kissed it so

that there were lipstick lips. Then she wrote, "For Augie. *Loved* our talk. Forever, Liza." And after she handed it to me, Lenny dragged her toward the exit.

For the first time in almost twenty-four hours I had a couple of minutes to myself, and I was wiped. So I sat down on a gray stool, put my head into my hands, and tried to piece together exactly how I'd wound up in a vomit-colored hallway backstage at a Broadway theater 200 miles from home without stopping to ask any questions first. But the way it turned out, I wasn't the only one doing the wondering—because right around then my phone rang again. This time it wasn't my brother.

POP: Tony C? I just called Augie's to check in with Mom and Dad—but they haven't seen you since this morning, and Augie wouldn't talk. I want to know exactly where you are.

ME: Um—the, uh, Shubert Theatre. In—um—New York. On Forty-fourth Street.

POP: Is Hucky with you?

ME: Yes. He's in Julie Andrews's dressing room.

POP: He's *what*?

ME: That's why we're here. Augie and Alé and I got her to send him a letter, but it wasn't good enough. We needed her to be Mary Poppins for him. So that's who she's being in her dressing room.

POP: We'll talk about that later. Right now I want you to listen to me very carefully. I'm calling a car company and sending a limo over there. You're not to leave until you see one that says "Keller" in the window. Are you listening?

ME: Yes.

POP: The driver's going to have instructions to take you to Penn Station, put you and Hucky on the train, and then call me after you've left. I'll be waiting for you at Back Bay.

ME: Okay. Pop, how pissed off are you?

POP: Is he *really* talking to Julie Andrews?

ME: Yes.

POP: Then not as pissed off as you think.

I hung up the phone feeling like crap. Hucky was ten feet away from me, getting all of his wishes granted at once, and meanwhile I'd really let down my father. How could both of these things happen at the same time? *X and y have specific values, and they only add up one way.* But before I could figure out any answers, the puke-yellow door opened again. This time it was Hucky leading Julie Andrews, and not the other way around. His eyes were sparkling, and it didn't take a spoonful of sugar to see that hers might have been too.

"I think we've just about got that straightened out," she said to me in her let's-clean-up-our-room voice. "I explained to Hucky that I can only come to stay with children who've been left alone. But since he has *you*, he doesn't need me after all." For a minute I thought she'd gotten me mixed up with somebody else. *Me? Up there with Mary Poppins? ME??* And just to make sure I knew she hadn't, she narrowed her forehead the same way she did when Uncle Albert was floating on the ceiling and spoke quietly so that I'd know it was just her and me. "Do we understand each other, Anthony? I don't expect you to let him down." By then I would have said yes to just about anything she asked. I mean, the last thing I needed was to piss off Mary Poppins. But this was a no-brainer anyway.

"Don't worry," I swore on my honor. "That'll never happen." She knelt in front of Hucky one more time and brushed his favorite piece of hair out of his face.

"I want you to write to me," she signed. "And I promise to write back. All right?" Hucky nodded, not taking his eyes off of hers. "And always remember that if you ever *do* need me, I'm here." I guess that was all he really wanted to find out, because he suddenly wrapped his arms around her neck and pressed his whole face against her cheek. And when she hugged him back, I had to turn away.

How was I supposed to know that *I* needed her too?

The rest of our adventure was wrapped up by Pop. The Keller limousine showed up in Shubert Alley just like he said it would, but there were so many movie stars looking for limos of their own that we wound up dropping off somebody named Vanessa Redgrave at the Ritz Carlton on our way to Penn Station. Hucky sat through it all in a daze, holding my hand and staring straight ahead into whatever world Julie Andrews had opened up for him. Meanwhile,

I had the driver to deal with. His name was Tim, he'd been a Yankees fan since he was four, and Bucky F. Dent was one of his idols. I was ready to get out of the car at Forty-first Street and *walk*.

The train ride home was a lot quieter than the first one was. I bought cookies and milk for Hucky at the snack bar, but he nodded off just a couple of seconds after we'd gotten back to our seats. Who wouldn't have? He'd put in a long day. And if I'd known what was good for me, I'd have caught some Z's too—I had an algebra test in nine hours that I really needed to be awake for.

Speaking of algebra, I think I figured out the part that Lori forgot to tell me. Okay, maybe x and y *do* have specific values—but they mean different things to different people. Pop's x and y add up to taking care of me and falling in love with Lori. Alé's add up to making her own decisions and falling in love with me (we hope). Augie's add up to Katharine Hepburn and loving Andy and always being there for me. And mine add up to Mama, Pop, Augie, Alé, Hucky, Mom, Dad, Phyllis, Buck Weaver, and anyone else who finds a place inside my heart. So I was right to bring Hucky to New York after all. And Pop was also right to be pissed off at me for doing it. We just need to work out our third variables.

I don't know if that's going to help me on my algebra test, but seeing as it's been February 16 for the past fifty-two minutes, it's not a bad way to turn fifteen.

I glanced down at Hucky, who was out like a light—with his head on my chest and my arm wrapped around him. And for the very first time I saw something I'd never seen before while he was sleeping. A smile.

I love you,

T.C.

LAURENTS SCHOOL
BROOKLINE, MASSACHUSETTS

VIA E-MAIL

Dear Ted:

Before you come to any hasty decisions, remember what the venerable W. S. Gilbert wrote in *The Mikado.* "Let the punishment fit the crime."

Your son makes dreams come true for others. And not just ordinary dreams either. Hucky met Mary Poppins, and now she's a part of his life. I still don't know for certain whether I'm merely awed or green with envy. If that had happened to me when *I* was six, I might have turned out with a few screws tighter than they are now. At the very least, I wouldn't have been idiot enough to date that treasonous quisling Wes Kibel in high school, and I may even have been more cavalier in my dealings with the noxious concept of purloined court-side seats.

Since there's a slim chance that I might have a future say in the care and feeding of Anthony, I'm recommending leniency. I know he shattered a few dozen rules in order to pull off the improbable—but so did Rosa Parks. In other words, if you give him a hard time, I'll break your neck.

Lori

KELLER CONSTRUCTION
BOSTON · GLOUCESTER · WALTHAM

ELECTRONIC TRANSMISSION

Dear Lori:

I hated *The Mikado*. *H.M.S. Pinafore* was more up my alley. I saw it in tenth grade, and our Buttercup was *hot*.

Don't worry. Tony C may have scared the shit out of me, but if I had to balance that against how proud I am (and, not incidentally, how proud his mother would have been), there's no contest. So he'll be grounded for four weeks, but without loss of Internet or cell phone privileges. This is like sending a condemned man to San Quentin but taking all the bars off first.

By the way, I prefer you with your screws loose. But if you can find out where Wes is living these days, I'll stop over there myself and rough him up for you.

Ted

Practically
Seniors

Augie

English Assignment
Augie Hwong, 11th Grade
Ms. LaFontaine's Class

MY MOST EXCELLENT YEAR
Conclusion

DIVA OF THE WEEK

Alejandra Perez
("I've got a lot of livin' to do")

After _Kiss Me, Kate_, everybody knew that Alé was going places, but no one was prepared for her professional debut as Kim McAfee in *Bye Bye Birdie* at the Lyric Stage. God, when she changed into a floppy sweater and baseball cap while she sang "How Lovely to Be a Woman," you could practically feel the paint melting off the walls. The *Herald* called her "the find of the year," and she was nominated for Best Supporting Actress in a Musical by the *Boston Phoenix*.

INSTANT MESSENGER

AugieHwong: When are you going to teach me the moves?

AlePerez: You're *not* understudying me. So please stay away from the auditions. They may just cast you. And I can't afford the competition.

Actually, I've come to terms with the fact that the parts I was born to play are forever out of reach (especially Roxie Hart). That's why I've decided to become a director/choreographer instead. We rule, we rock, and we also get to perform all of the roles first while we're teaching them to our actors. Last year I directed a frosh/soph production of *Follies*, and no one who was at rehearsal will ever forget the way my "Story of Lucy and Jessie" turned Alexis Smith into a dim memory from a fading past.

And speaking of *Follies*, Mom may not write a theatre column anymore, but that doesn't mean she's retired her poison pen. She recently contributed a commentary to the op-ed page blasting Stephen Sondheim for his stubborn refusal to allow anyone to cast a same-sex couple in *Company*. "And this is supposed to be a musical about contemporary relationships??" (She never found out what his sentiments were after she called him "the Roy Cohn of composers," but I'm pretty sure they weren't "thank you.") She also wrote a feature article on the three of us and Hucky, and now every stage doorman in New York has to deal with gate-crashing bogus relatives. Carol Channing's son even got arrested, and all he was trying to do was pick up his mom and take her home.

Andy and I stayed boyfriends until last spring, and then we decided we were too young for a serious commitment. So even though we knew we'd be friends forever, we broke up for our own good. It lasted twenty-five minutes.

> **www.augiehwong.com**
> **PRIVATE CHAT**

AndyWexler: Spidey, what's a "wild oat" anyway?

AugieHwong: I don't know. I think it's just a figure of speech.

AndyWexler: Then why are we supposed to sow them?

AugieHwong: Nobody explained that part to me. Just because, that's why. By the way, I still smile when you call me "Spidey." It reminds me of the old days.

AndyWexler: When—this morning?!

He finally told his parents, who weren't exactly surprised. As a general rule, when your son's had a boyfriend for almost two years, it usually means he's gay. They've come over for dinner a couple of times now, which means we have *three* people glued to the couch whenever the Patriots are on ESPN: Dad, Andy, and Andy's mom. Mr. Wexler is probably the only pilot American Airlines employs who doesn't have much use for football. His game is lacrosse, which he taught me during sophomore year. I'm a wing. And the uniforms are like *SO* hot.

Mateo was adopted by a deaf couple in Back Bay (she's a teacher, he's an author), but he and Hucky stayed best friends through all of the changes. And right after they'd both turned seven, Tick and I taught them the games they most needed to know: secret agents, astronauts, Galaxy Fighters, and brothers. "Brothers" seems to be their favorite—at 8½, they're still playing it. Incidentally, when I got really proficient at ASL, I made Hucky sit still long enough for *All About Eve* while I signed it for him. He gave up in disgust halfway through it.

"What a ripoff!" he fumed. *"They stole the whole ginky thing from the Tooth Fairy story! How do these people get* <u>*away*</u> *with that??"*

INSTANT MESSENGER

TCKeller: I just checked out Brandeis online. They've got a theatre department for you and a poli sci department for me. What do you think?

AugieHwong: Andy's going to be at B.U. and Alé's going to be at Emerson. Brandeis is too far.

TCKeller: According to Yahoo, it's 7.8 miles. What did you want, dude—walking distance??

AugieHwong: Yes.

I figured out something in ninth grade that I should have known at six, when I chose a brother who could teach me how to be Augie Hwong. Up until then, I was definitely the wrong actor for the part (Lea Salonga would have been *so* much more appropriate), but we worked with what we had. And after Tick brought Hucky into our lives and I watched what happened, I figured out that it's not just the people we love, but the people we let love us *back* who show us how high we can really soar.

From: HuckyKeller@earthworks.net
To: augie@augiehwong.com

Boston University is okay, but only if you don't have to live there. You can still come home at night, can't you? Because I'm not old enough to know right from wrong yet without brothers to show me. Even when they go to college. I could get in a lot of trouble by myself, you know.

Pop and T.C. gave me a time out because I microwaved my Disk Man to dry it off from falling in the sink and getting soaping wet. How was I suppose to know it would make all the lights go out?

So I'm changing my name to Hucky Hwong again. Just until the weekend. It was Nehi's idea and I like it.

Last fall, Alé was one of the three leads up at Merrimack Rep in Stephen Sondheim's *Merrily We Roll Along* (sorry, Mom), and for some weird reason I found myself crying when she sang "Old Friends"—ironically, one of only eight happy songs that Sondheim ever wrote. It made me remember conning her into the talent show, rehearsing *Kiss Me, Kate* with her, sitting over Mass Pike with Tick and getting each other through puberty, Christmas shopping with Aunt Babe, Dad's heart-to-hearts with me about Andy, my boyfriend's first kiss (and not recovering from it for three weeks), Hucky on skis, and the way Julie Andrews came through for us. So if I have to end on a quote—and baby, Augie Hwong *always* ends on a quote—I'm sticking with Sondheim.

"Here's to us.
Who's like us?
Damn few."

Alejandra

English Assignment
Alejandra Perez, 11th Grade
Ms. LaFontaine's Class

MY MOST EXCELLENT YEAR
Conclusion

After putting up with my leading man's stagnant breath for three consecutive nights in *Kiss Me, Kate*, I was somewhat surprised to discover that his mother was a talent agent. (Let's just say that I knew for sure she wasn't a dental hygienist.) She offered to represent me after *Kate* closed, and twelve weeks later I had my Equity card. But *Bye Bye Birdie* turned out to be a stroll in the park compared to what Augie and Hucky put me through first.

INSTANT MESSENGER

AlePerez: The audition's not 'til Tuesday. I'm going to sing "One Boy."

AugieHwong: Oh, you are so *not* going to sing "One Boy." Every Kim in 19 languages sings "One Boy." Directors *hang* themselves when they hear "One Boy." Do you want the part or don't you?

AlePerez: I dare you to do this to me again.

AugieHwong: There's a rehearsal space above Dad's tae kwon do studio. We can use it whenever nobody's there. You're going to sing "Two Ladies in the Shade of the Banana Tree" and I'm choreographing it. We only have four days, so don't make any other plans until I say so.

AlePerez: I detest you.

Augie showed me the steps, I did them, and Hucky said they needed work. So we started all over again. They made a deadly team. I had no idea why I was hanging my career on the artistic sensibilities of a six-year-old, except that he happened to be right. I performed "Two Ladies in the Shade of the Banana Tree" at the audition. The other eleven Kims performed "One Boy." I got the part.

Since then I've been pretty lucky to stay employed between

semesters at school. After *Birdie*, there was *Carnival, The Sound of Music, The Fantasticks* (does *any*one know what this show is about??), *Li'l Abner, Gypsy*, and *Merrily We Roll Along*. Mamita was the first member of my family to convert. She began keeping a scrapbook of all my clippings and even has them cross-referenced on an Excel spreadsheet. And Carlos loves hanging outside the theatre so he can say, "That's my baby sister" to whoever will listen. "Whoever" is generally tall, raven-haired, anywhere from twenty-four to twenty-eight, buxom, and usually connected to international affairs. My brother has turned opportunism into both a social and political science.

Papa held out for as long as he could, but he knew I was going to be a pain in the ass until he caved in, so he didn't have much of a choice.

"I should have had another son," he grumbled.

"But Papa," I reminded him, "he'd still have been a chorus boy. It's in our blood." That usually ended the argument. It also dawned on him that I might be turned into an asset—as a face already familiar to some of the local dignitaries who attended the theatre regularly.

"Señor Perez, I saw your daughter onstage. You must be *so* proud of her."

"Indeed I am, Mme. Ambassador." Suddenly, I was actually enjoying diplomatic receptions after all—but in a black, backless floor-length gown with a rhinestone bracelet that Anthony and Hucky had given me when I was fifteen. I functioned far better as an ingénue than as an ambassador's daughter. At least nobody had to hide me in the cloakroom anymore. And if Korea wanted to behave like a brat, let it. I'd learned how to keep my mouth shut. Besides, this is what we have a U.N. for.

Not that I've given up on politics completely. Lee Meyerhoff became the first junior to win the presidency of the Student Council, though she possesses one Achilles' Heel that's going to get in her way: She likes to tell the truth. So she made certain I was elected Madame Vice President right along with her. Now whenever she paints herself into a corner, I distract the masses with an impromptu demonstration or a protest. It doesn't really matter what it's about. Believe me, when pushed, I can still make an issue out of just about anything—even if it's mayonnaise.

Tom Hirasawa (D-Calif.) and Ruth Mellick (Anthony's aunt-Mass.) have been chairing the Congressional Committee on the Restoration of the Baseball Diamond at the Manzanar National Historic Site since the summer of 2004, and Anthony and I were asked to serve on the advisory board. After conducting an eighteen-month archaeological study (for a *baseball diamond*??), the Committee proposed a formal bill that ought to be going to the floor some time this session. Fred Hoyt retired as assistant superintendent of the Manzanar Site because he'd developed an ulcer. Anthony and I sent him a get-well card and flowers. I hope he didn't think it was sarcasm.

From: HuckyKeller@earthworks.net
To: AlePerez@earthworks.net

I have an idea. Maybe you could come to my school with me and tell them that it's dangerous to make kids eat cream chip beef on toast at lunch. They do it every Tuesday. Yesterday Jack

Eller threw up onto his plate and it looked the exact same as it did before he ate it. Isn't that against the law?

Mateo says that when you get famous they'll make you move to Hollywood and wear sunglasses and punch out people who take your picture. He's wrong, right? Because why would you want to do that? *I* wouldn't. Like you can't be famous right here? So tell them no. Please?

I picked Emerson College because (a) its performing arts school is one of the best in the nation; (b) it's on Boylston Street; and (c) Anthony's grown way too handsome to be left unchaperoned in full-semester increments.

INSTANT MESSENGER

TCKeller: If you *have* to do *Bye Bye Birdie* again, could you at least wear baggy jeans? I hated the way guys were looking at you last time.

AlePerez: Hello? You're the one who's going into politics. Who was a bigger romantic security risk—Ann-Margret or Bill Clinton?

TCKeller: Say something to make me feel secure.

AlePerez: I'm always true to you, darling, in my fashion.

TCKeller: Yeah, well, that didn't exactly work.

In spite of what I'd brought myself up to believe, it turns out that I didn't know everything after all. But what I was missing is what I picked up when I was fourteen—through Augie's trust and Anthony's heart.

And the "um" *definitely* had something to do with it.

English Assignment
T.C. Keller, 11th Grade
Ms. LaFontaine's Class

MY MOST EXCELLENT YEAR
Conclusion

I was only grounded for four weeks, and after that Pop asked Mrs. Jordan at the Deaf Institute if she could send us papers to fill out so we could adopt Hucky ourselves. (It was bound to happen sooner or later anyway. Even Nehi knew that.) He slept in my room for the first couple of months and then Pop and I cleared out the guest bedroom and made it Hucky H.Q. We even put in an extra bed, an extra chest of drawers, and an extra bulletin board for Mateo's sleepovers. After all, we have traditions to pass down to the next generation. (Speaking of traditions, Hucky's the only Keller male not named for a Red Sock—at least so far. A month after he moved in with us, Aunt Helen called from Portland and said, "Thank God. Now maybe Bobo will let me name our next one Jeremiah.") Phyllis is his godmother, Augie's his godfather, and Nehi's his guardian. No kid ever had better backup.

He's pulling all A's in school except for one B in social studies, but big brother Augie's taking care of that by volunteering to be his tutor. They've already been through the Revolutionary War (disguised as a movie called *The Women*), and Hucky turned an eighty-four into a ninety-two on his first test after that. He's also kept up with his drawing, which somewhere along the line went from "cute" to "yikes!" I think he's going to be a graphic artist when he grows up, Alé thinks he's going to be an illustrator, and Pop hopes he'll be an architect. ("He can design the houses and then I'll build them.") He even tried out for T-ball a year ago and made the squad in the first-round draft. Now he's his team's ace at second base. But he insists that I call him Stuffy McInnis whenever I'm in the Amory Park bleachers watching him play. So maybe he'll end up with a Red Sox name after all.

Hucky still hears from Julie Andrews at least once a month, and he always sends her his newest drawings, his report cards, and pictures of him in his uniform. But right after we met her, he saw *The Sound of Music* and figured out that she was an actress and not a nanny—so she began signing her letters "Love, Julie" instead of "Love, Mary Poppins." It didn't make any difference to Hucky, though. A spoonful of sugar is a spoonful of sugar.

INSTANT MESSENGER

AugieHwong: Why don't we go to Emerson with Alé?

TCKeller: Because that's a song and dance college, you gink! Who's going to take me seriously with a degree in Ethel Merman??

AugieHwong: Tick, do you realize what a name you could make for yourself as the first president who ever *sang* his inaugural address? Maybe it sounds a little out there, but you won't know until you've tried. It's worth thinking about.

TCKeller: No. It isn't.

A couple of things made me decide on a career in politics: (1) Alé and I are already on a congressional committee (and we weren't even *trying*), (2) Major League Baseball finally got pressured into convening a panel to decide whether or not Buck Weaver should be reinstated, so Pop and I are looking for candidates for our next crusade, and (3) once you find yourself saying "Let the word go forth from this day on to friend and foe alike" in a blue suit in front of an auditorium filled with people, it kind of gets in your blood. Besides, Aunt Ruth is the front-runner to replace Ted Kennedy as the Democratic senator from Massachusetts when he retires, which means her seat in the House would be wide open. We might as well keep it in the family, like Grandma Lily's china.

Pop and Lori have been "together-together" for two years. (This differs from *regular* together because now when they have dinner, Lori calls it a date and not a coincidence.) I hope they wait until Augie and I are in college before they actually get married. I mean, I can definitely picture her as my mother, but seeing my adviser in a bathrobe is still a concept I haven't been able to wrap my mind around. Even if she *does* drag Pop down to the empty fifty-yard-line seats during halftime.

The Red Sox won the World Series in 2004, and Bucky F. Dent can kiss my Boston ass. Pop and Hucky and I were in the grandstand for Game 2, even though tickets were going for as much as $2,000 apiece. We didn't have to worry about that because Clint Lockhart was made head of the Secret Service last year. It always helps to love somebody who has friends in high places.

INSTANT MESSENGER

AlePerez: Do you have any interest in meeting the president of Brazil?

TCKeller: None. Why?

AlePerez: There's an embassy party for Papa in Washington that he wants me to attend. But I won't go without you.

TCKeller: Any chance we could duck out early and walk around the Jefferson Memorial holding hands?

AlePerez: Don't we always?

Even though I didn't notice it while it was happening, I got reminded in ninth grade of a few things I guess I should have known all along:

1.   A first kiss after five months means more than a first kiss after five minutes.

2.   Always remember what it was like to be six.

3.   Never, ever stop believing in magic, no matter how old you get. Because if you keep looking long enough and don't give up, sooner or later you're going to find Mary Poppins. And if you're *really* lucky, maybe even a purple balloon.

Thanks, Mama. I love you.